TWICE CURSED

J. C. JACKSON

SHADOW PHOENIX PUBLISHING

Twice Cursed

J.C. Jackson

Copyright © 2018 J.C. Jackson

Published by Shadow Phoenix Publishing LLC

ISBN-13: 978-1-7322835-0-3, 978-1-7322835-4-1

Cover designed by J. Caleb Design

 Created with Vellum

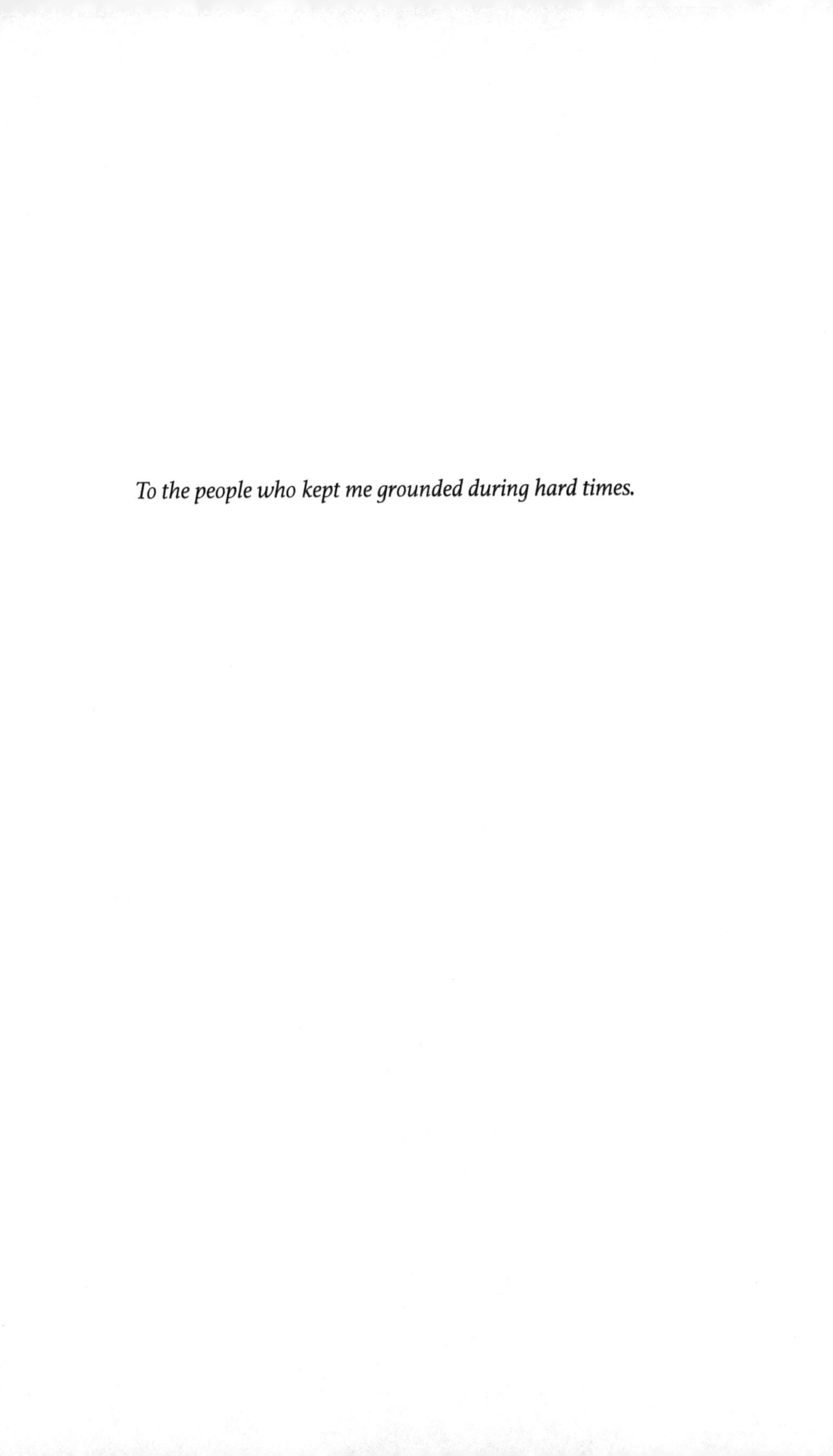

To the people who kept me grounded during hard times.

1

LATE. I never ran late. Silver would never let me live this down. My partner found childish pleasure in things to tease me about.

I hurried down the hall trying not to outright run. That would draw attention. Reaching our shared office, I stopped myself from bouncing on the balls of my feet while I held my hand on the scanner. I still did not understand the need for such heavy security on our door.

Hearing the cheerful acceptance beep and the door unlock, I rushed inside and stopped short. Silver's absence mentally tripped me. Good for me, I hoped.

Sliding out of my long black coat at a more sedate pace, I cursed myself for having lost track of time at my adopted parents' house this morning. I left Great Tree far later than I planned and the unpredictable autumn weather through the mountains made the normally easy two hour drive a little more treacherous and longer.

One of these days I would get clearance to teleport back and forth. It would certainly save on time. Though that begged the question of whether I could manage to teleport the distance. With the little I had done, I never went far.

I stopped and took a deep breath to remove the extraneous thoughts - time to get to work. Plopping down in my seat as my computer booted up, I glanced over at Silver's empty desk. Maybe he took an early lunch. It still seemed out of place. I could check the schedule.

No, I needed to get work done. I was unable to get much done this past weekend working from my tablet. It kept crashing on me in most of the programs I needed. About all I could do was keep up with my messages and most of those I read on my phone.

Thinking on what I wanted to do, I got up and started turning on the other systems in the room. I went to wake up the table in the center of the room before moving onto the large wall screen. While I thought this set-up excessive, it made parsing information much easier.

And quiet moments like this where I could work alone had become rare.

At least I could spread out the information I managed to flag over the weekend. It bothered me that I had not yet found any discernible pattern of movements from the main group Brown and his followers were part of. Even a solid name for them would be nice. I refused to use any of the "creative" ones Silver came up with.

I worried they employed diversionary tactics since it seemed every tidbit of information had been either some minor, isolated incident or a false report. And what little information I could find about the Ancient Gods, I could not understand why anyone would follow such tyrants, but I also had a hard time putting faith into any of the Gods predominantly worshiped.

Why was there such a focus in the group to find and control Atlantis? The desire for access to whatever Atlantian knowledge existed I was able to grasp, but what would they do with it?

The bigger question right now was what would they do to gain that information? Brown had killed so many in Ocean's Edge and I doubted he was anywhere near close to the final goal.

Tapping on the table, I pulled up what I had saved and slid the files across toward the wall screen. They exploded out into a neat grid.

I started shuffling the files around, looking for a pattern. I sorted articles, reports, and other information, trying to group similar things together. I scowled at the screen when I realized some of the information I flagged had not saved. That meant I would have to sift through it again. For now I figured I could work with what was in front of me.

I brushed my long bangs out of my face, failing to tuck them behind my ear. I was still not used to the new hairstyle.

I needed music. I retreated to my desk to grab my earpieces and phone. I popped the wireless earpieces in and set my phone down on the edge of the table once I started the music.

As time moved, I kept shifting the files around, trying to get a better picture, but finding dead ends. I still missed something - one piece to link these pieces together to start seeing the picture.

I jumped as one of the pieces was pulled out of my ear. "Thought I lost you there for a minute," Silver said, dropping it so it dangled down around my neck by the cord connecting both sides, making it pull awkwardly.

I glared up at him, pulling the other piece out. "You could have just said something."

"I did, Ketayl, you were in your own little world again." Silver stepped around me and held me by the shoulders at arm's length. "I almost didn't recognize you when I walked in."

I stepped back, bumping into the table. I looked down at myself. The fitted dark blue top was long-sleeved, but came off my shoulders. My jeans and light boots were common for me at this time of year. While I had gotten long, side-swept bangs cut, I kept the rest of my hair the same length, tying it with a hair elastic close to the end. "Oh, I wanted to try something different. Does it look bad? I can go change if you think it's inappropriate." I bit my lower lip. I had not thought about if the changes would make him uneasy.

"Uh, no. You look great," Silver said sounding unsure of himself. "Besides, you're the boss - you make the rules."

I gave him a look of annoyance and stepped around him to look back at the screen. "I'm not the boss." I wished he would give up on the notion. I may be listed as the team lead, but I kept telling him we were equal.

Damn, he broke my concentration.

A weight suddenly landed on my head. I moved out from under him, mentally cursing his height, and ran my hands over my hair to smooth it out. This would not be the first time he decided to try and get my perspective by putting his chin on my head.

Perhaps I needed a different approach. Maybe instead of looking for the group as a whole, I should focus on trying to find an individual. Namely, someone showing signs of delving into necromancy.

Those were the most dangerous members of the group as far as I could tell.

I tilted my head, thinking back on some other cases I had dealt with over the last few months. It felt like there might be a pattern between those and the information before me.

Moving to the side of the table, I started pulling up the lab files. I helped Sparky with a few cases since he started working in the lab which coincided with some of the reports. They might have a thread of commonality between them.

"You've got something?" Silver moved to the other side of the table as I started sending files up to the wall screen.

"Maybe?" There had been a few werewolf cases over the past several months, but I could not remember the details.

"Care to share?"

Once I started seeing a picture, I would. Silver could be distracting and I needed to focus.

As soon as I sent the last file up to the wall screen, I moved them around, finding similar files and sent the others away. I started reorganizing the information in front of me so I could make the correlation between them all. The reports were vague at best, but the news articles held more. Granted, whatever was put out by the media needed to be reviewed with caution. Some of the articles got a bit overzealous.

"Werewolves?" Silver asked, stepping in front of the table and leaning back against it. He flicked his hand to move one of the files and it immediately went back to where it had been. He made a face of frustration and simply moved over to it. I smirked at his fumble - someday he might get the hang of the controls for the wall screen.

"Look," I said, pointing at the case files and then the news articles. "The unexplained deaths of newly turned and unregistered werewolves are taking place fairly close to each other. That's quite a few unknowns in a concentrated area. This feels deliberate."

Silver leaned forward to look at the files I placed eye-level for me. "Weren't you helping Sparky with these?"

"Just to give him access to the RIG database. The werewolves wouldn't release the bodies for examination, so we're left with little information - they only wanted us to identify them. There's been a half dozen deaths in the last several months."

I pulled up a map to get a better visual of where they were taking place. Dots started appearing as I tapped the locations on the case files. They were concentrated in the northern part of Human Territory along the coast.

I double-tapped the map to zoom it in more. They looked to be concentrated between Hilldale and Ghost Forest.

Silver frowned and crossed his arms. "Okay, I know nothing about werewolves. What is the RIG database?"

Sometimes I forgot I needed to explain things. "Registered Immortal Genetic database. All werewolves and vampires are required by law to submit to it. It's only used in criminal cases either where someone has been bitten or in this case where we're hoping to identify the remains. They carry their altered genetic code as well as markers of the person who turned them."

"Immortal?"

"Because there's no known lifespan of either of the races. Usually they only live a couple hundred years due to infighting, I think. A few a century or so longer, but the Director is the only exception I know of off-hand."

"Oh. You said they carried two sets of genetic... something." I could hear that I barely kept Silver following along my train of thought. I knew little of the "immortal" races myself. I would have to find someone more familiar in the area if I pursued this.

"Neither one could be identified. The person's normal genetic code is changed when they turn and whoever is doing it isn't in the database either, but we know it's the same person doing the turning." I bit my lower lip, thinking on it further. "I'm not sure if we could try to recreate the person's original genetic code from the samples. It was never requested and I didn't have the time to pursue the idea then."

Silver stroked the small patch of hair on his chin. "If it's the same individual doing the turning, then we've got a rogue creating his own pack."

"You're right." I had not thought that far on the subject.

I looked at the map. It looked far too targeted. I went back to the table and started a search for werewolf pack boundaries. I could only hope someone thought to post information like that online. They would want people to know which pack was in an area if they needed to contact someone, right?

No luck. I stood back, folded my arms over my chest, and stared back at the wall screen. Then I glanced over at Silver, hoping he had an idea.

He toyed with the end of his braid, flicking the tail back and forth while looking over the information on the wall screen. "I love it when you pull out something like this, but I never know how you do it."

I shrugged. "This is all hypothetical. There could be no connection between the turnings and deaths. It's all been the same werewolf turning, but without seeing the bodies, it's impossible to tell the cause of death. I could be on a dead end again. It could be totally unrelated to the group we're looking for."

"No, I think you're onto something," Silver said as I heard the door unlock and open.

"Onto what?" Lockonis asked as she strode in. "Ooh, I like the new look, Ket." She patted me on the shoulder as she passed and looked at the wall screen. I rubbed the shoulder she touched, trying to get rid of the feeling.

Silver tried to explain, "The unexplained werewolf deaths." He opened his mouth to say more and gave up.

"Huh," Lockonis commented. "This is something." She turned to see what I had been doing at the table. "Werewolf pack boundaries? We usually have to request the information from the Alpha Prime. But I can save you a headache - these cases are all inside of the Alpha Prime's territory."

I pursed my lips. The Alpha Prime sat on the Terran Council. This could simply be targeting him over political issues.

Lockonis turned back to us grinning. "Anywho, I actually came up here to tell you two I need to push your training session this afternoon up by an hour. I'm bringing in someone to help. In the meantime, I'll contact the Ghost Forest branch and see if Stoney can give me more information on the werewolf deaths."

I nodded and watched Lockonis wave as she let herself out. I had forgotten about the training session this afternoon. I really was not in the mood to be picking myself up off the floor repeatedly. Silver kept trying to teach me how to fight, but I simply was not good at putting the movements into application.

"Don't look like that. You're getting better and your shoulder doesn't seem to be giving you problems," Silver said.

I rolled my eyes. Silver tried, he truly did, but there was no changing the fact I was not built for what he tried to teach me.

And I was actually more concerned now that my shoulder was free of the purple athletic tape Mogan seemed so fond of. Silver had gotten anxious about increasing the intensity.

"Lunch?" Silver asked.

I stopped and looked at the clock on the wall near the door. "Yeah, probably a good idea if we're being moved up an hour."

Silver smiled softly and I still could not figure out why. He did it every so often and I had not yet discerned the pattern of what caused it. He patted me on the head as he walked by. I swatted at his hand. *Child.*

2

WITH THE TIME change also came a change of venue. I only ever came down here when Lockonis wanted to do arcane combat training. It was the only one built to be able to handle explosive forces.

I watched Silver warm up on the other side of the large testing bay. He went through a series of swings and thrusts with his sword. His shield arm moving to block imaginary foes. The set looked out of place against the gray and white short-sleeve shirt and lightweight pants.

He wore just his normal exercise clothes like I did, but he had never brought his sword and shield into any of our training sessions before - it had always been just hand-to-hand combat. And at least the floor in that training room was padded - hitting the hard floor here was going to hurt.

Lockonis stood to the side, talking to a familiar dark-haired Human man. I had worked with Kevin several times once I realized I needed to step up my physical training earlier this year. His method of fighting I found easier, but I still struggled with it and ultimately gave up when I became too busy to keep a strict schedule.

She nodded in my direction every so often. I took a deep breath and tried to calm myself. I sat down on the cool cement floor and fidgeted with the laces of my shoes. This needed to be over so I could go back to what I had been working on.

Plus it was chilly in here - I wore the purple tank top and black calf-length pants my sister had bought me. I still did not know why she chose pants with purple lightning down the sides, but it had entertained her greatly.

The two conducting the training session went over and spoke with Silver. He appeared upset about something at first, but then nodded and listened to what they were telling him.

Why keep us separate? Normally they briefed us at the same time if someone else conducted the training session.

Lockonis jogged over to me and squatted to be closer to my level. "Sorry about that. We're trying something different to see how to adjust your training. I want you to use all of your abilities. Within reason of course."

I bit my lower lip and looked over to where Silver stood.

"You'll be fine as long as you use what you're comfortable with. It's just so we can see where to direct the two of you, so your time is more effective."

Rubbing the bare part of my lower legs, I asked, "Did you hear anything about the werewolves?" I had to distract myself before I over-thought what I was about to go through.

Lockonis paused. "Oh, Stoney is contacting the Beta. She's the one who came to us in the first place requesting help in identifying the unregistered werewolves. The Alpha Prime is too proud to ask, but for as dominant as his Beta is, she's a lot more reasonable to deal with."

"Oh." I was going to need a crash course in werewolf culture. Provided this went anywhere, of course.

"C'mon. It's your chance to lay Silver out on the floor. Let's see what you've got," Lockonis said as she stood up. She held her hand out to me.

I thanked her but stood up on my own. How was I supposed to fight someone not only armed, but well trained in those arms?

Silver strode forward confident and ready for this. I hesitated as he spun the sword around at his side. This was ridiculous. I bit my lower lip and glanced over to Lockonis who took up a spot next to Kevin. She stood with her arms folded, face betraying nothing.

In that brief moment Silver attacked. I avoided the downward slice of his sword, but stepped in the way of his shield. I let the hit to my ribs throw me away from him and rolled along the floor. I knew I would not be out of his range for long.

As I got to one knee Silver was already quickly closing the gap and I had just enough time to roll out of the way again.

"Fight back, Ket. Don't just avoid," Lockonis called.

Easy for her to say.

Silver stopped his attack and walked toward the other two. "This isn't fair."

Lockonis waved him to go back to what he had been doing. "When Ket finally gets her head where it needs to be, you'll be meaning that for you." She looked past him to me. I had just managed to get myself back up. "I meant what I said earlier."

I nodded, scared. I needed to focus, but I feared I might hurt Silver.

His shield arm went back. I cast my shield spell just in time to deflect and slid back a few feet from the force of the throw. I cast a wind spell immediately after, knocking him backward and his shield in the direction of the targets on the far wall.

"Better, Ket."

Silver stood back up grinning. I began to think he had gone mad. He would find this fun. He clenched his fist and flexed his left arm, his shield reappearing. I had hoped I would be down to just having to deal with the sword.

When he attacked with a downward swing again, I stepped along his sword arm this time, kicking out at the back of his knee. He went down long enough for me to get some distance.

"You're still avoiding, Ket. I know you've got more than that."

Lockonis could come out here and show me what she meant. Going on the offensive like I had against the slave traders would be far too dangerous in a training exercise.

I did not catch the movement in time and got knocked back by Silver's shield. That thing hurt - I did not think my ribs could take another hit. I made it to my knees and found the tip of his sword at my throat. Air escaped my attempts to take it in as I stared down the blade.

Fear kept me frozen and my eyes locked on the blade. I swallowed hard and prayed to whoever would listen that this was simply a nightmare.

About the time I started getting lightheaded, I felt large, rough hands pulling me back. Silver knelt down in my line of vision.

It broke the trance I found myself in. His sword clattered to the cement floor. What just happened?

He brushed my bangs out of my face. "I'm so sorry. I should have held back more."

"No, I think that was what we needed to see." I had not expected Vince's voice. When I looked over, his attention was on Lockonis.

Lockonis walked toward us, her gaze first on where Silver's sword lay and then to me. "Fairly certain, but I want Ket's input when she's ready."

"What?" It came out as a whisper. What just happened?

Silver stood and I heard a low growl - his fists clenched tightly at his sides. "I told you this was a bad idea!"

Kevin spoke softly. "Did you not trust your ability to keep your partner safe during this test?"

"No, I knew *I* could keep her safe," Silver answered firmly, "But I didn't need to scare her half to death."

"Unfortunately, it was likely the only way we were going to force out her other ability," Vince said calmly.

What other ability? My mouth was too dry to ask the question.

Lockonis squatted down in front of me and held out a bottle of water. "Think you can analyze something for me?"

I took the water, still shaking, and nodded. It would give me something else to focus on. I quickly downed close to half the bottle.

She pointed at where Silver's sword lay. "I'm guessing you didn't notice, but Silver couldn't pull his sword away from you. What do you see arcane-wise?"

I scanned at the area and then myself. "There's no remnant. Nothing."

"Anything divine?" Lockonis asked, looking up at Silver.

Silver glared down at her for a moment before doing his own evaluation. "No."

Vince asked, "Sounds like the theory holds."

Lockonis sat down on the floor with me. "Remember the end of your fight with the slave traders?"

I nodded. I remembered, even though I wanted to forget the whole ordeal.

"Your encounter with the captain was the same. Ket, did you know you had telekinetic abilities?"

I tilted my head to the side. There was no way - there had never been any evidence to support the existence of the phenomenon that I had heard of. "There must be another explanation for what happened."

"Her eyes did do the color-changing thing as if she was using her power at a high level," Silver noted, his words still sharp, but he had toned down. He stood over us with his arms crossed over his chest, his weapons away.

"I'm thinking in a way they're both one and the same, but manifest differently," Lockonis said. "We can work more on this later. Take a break for a few and we'll get to the actual training session."

I laid back on the cool floor, not caring who was present, and put the closed cold bottle of water across my eyes. Today was not going the way I hoped. *First running late and now this. And my ribs hurt. At least I might have a lead on something.*

Someone tugged at my hand. "Come on," Silver said softly.

I let him drag me to my feet and lead me to a bench on the other side of the large bay. He muttered apologies the entire way, but I paid his words little attention. I bit my lower lip while I attempted to wrap my head around what just happened.

"I still think this was stupid," Silver grumbled, glaring in the direction of the three talking on the other side of the bay. "The only reason I agreed is I knew I could keep you safe. I didn't want to chance them choosing someone else if I refused."

I would have been more concerned about me accidentally hurting him or worse. I rubbed my ribs which continued to ache from taking a couple of hits from his shield. The tenderness of the area told me bruises were likely already forming.

"Show me," Silver said. His attention now on me.

I wrapped my arms around myself. "It's nothing serious."

Silver gave me an exasperated sigh before moving my hands, lifting my shirt. I shifted out of his reach and nearly off the end of the bench. His grip on the hem was probably the only thing keeping me from falling.

"Humor me?" he asked once I stabilized myself.

I sighed and sat still. I reminded myself this was nothing he had not already seen. Fighting him while he was in overprotective big brother mode was a waste of energy.

He knelt down in front of me and lifted my shirt gently, but only high enough to see the damage. "Gods forgive me," Silver muttered. "Ketayl, you really need to tell me when you're hurt this badly."

Glancing down at where he tenderly touched, I winced when he pressed a little too hard in the large dark area. The bruise showed up faster than I expected. "It looks worse than it feels."

"I honestly didn't think I hit you this hard. I am so sorry." Silver spread the fingers on his right hand before gently touching the injured area.

The only thing I could do was sit still while his healing spell worked. I gave up months ago trying to get him to stop using his power on me. Even I could admit I would probably still be wearing the stupid sling if he had not insisted on pushing along healing my shoulder.

"Why did you mostly just avoid? It's much more fun when you fight back," Silver said once he finished and gave me a lopsided grin.

I looked away. "You should know that answer by now."

"Ketayl, I'm tougher than I look. And if nothing else, I can heal myself."

"Your partner has a point," Kevin said. When had he come over here? "The worst you did was knock him off his feet. But at least you remembered the first thing I taught you: get out of the way."

I sat quietly, looking down at my feet. That was a lesson I learned long before I took any training from Kevin.

"Come with me. Let's see if we can boost your confidence a little before trying this again," Kevin said.

Fine. I still thought this whole training session a waste - I would never be good in a fight. My time would be better spent trying to come up with other leads.

"Vince and Lockonis have given me access to the information on the Dark Ops mission you took part in. I've analyzed the videos of both that fight and the one from your first field assignment. Plus we've also had a chance to work a little before now so I've got a fairly decent idea of where to go with you." Kevin knelt next to a bag and pulled out a metal cylinder and a wooden staff. He handed me the cylinder.

What was I supposed to do with this?

"There's a button. You have to press it down fairly far to get it to release. Just make sure you're clear of the ends before you push it. Trust me, it hurts if you don't pay attention to where you're pointing it."

I held the cylinder away from my body as Kevin instructed before pressing the button. He was right - I needed to push over halfway through the cylinder before the ends released and now I held a metal staff. The way it had been built the pieces expanded to keep it smooth and the same circumference throughout.

And it was far lighter than I thought it would be. A flash of a memory of another Elven woman holding a staff went through my mind. No, I could not be distracted by the past right now. Odd it happened now and not in any previous class with Kevin.

"Okay, we'll go through a few drills slowly, so you remember how to use it," Kevin said.

As he walked me through, the pace picked up and the pattern became like a dance.

"Good. Now we'll use this as sort of an equalizer. I still want you to use all your abilities. Find the mix that works for you, but don't try to overpower him. Your strength in this training session is in your agility. You'd be better knocking him off balance. Use his strength and momentum against him."

I nodded. I still thought this was a bad idea. I looked over to see Silver talking to Lockonis - his back was to us.

"Let's go see if they're ready," Kevin said as he waved me along.

I pushed the button again and shrank the staff. I was curious about the technology which went into creating this weapon. Far more curious than finding out if I was capable of wielding it.

Lockonis caught sight of us and signaled to Silver to turn around. "Ready to try this again?" she called.

I held the cylinder behind my back, shifting my weight from one foot to the other, still as nervous and unsure of myself as before. I glanced around. Where had Vince gone?

Kevin stood next to me. He said quietly, "Just take it easy. You'll find what works for you."

Silver had his sword and shield out and once again appearing far more confident in his abilities. He came forward at more of a jog than a full-on charge this time, again with a downward swing. Now I knew he was trying to get me to see a pattern.

And lure me into an opening. I dodged along the side of his sword arm and his elbow started coming back. I turned the cylinder so one end pointed at his back and pressed the button.

Silver stumbled several feet before turning around with wide eyes and an open mouth. As soon as he saw the staff in my hand, a broad grin graced his face. "Now we're talking."

Once I directed his next attack away from me, I slid my hands along the staff and hit Silver across his back. We continued using roughly the same pattern for a while, his speed picking up each time. The parries and attacks also became more complex as Silver added his shield into the mix. Occasionally I found an opening to sweep a leg out and knock him over giving me a chance to get some breathing room.

Silver appeared to be enjoying himself immensely. I would not be able to keep this up for too much longer - I was drenched in sweat and breathing hard. Was it time for a break yet?

With Silver a distance away, I took the chance to glance up at the time. We should be done soon. In doing so, I almost missed his movement and held the staff up in front of me with both hands, casting my shield spell in time to deflect. I did not want to take another hit from that.

"That's it, Ket!" Lockonis called. "Start adding in your other abilities."

Silver charged at me before she finished. I managed to parry the attack, but sent a low-level electricity spell along the staff, which traveled up his sword, zapping him. He grunted and knelt on the floor.

I worried I had hurt him.

Silver's frame shook and then I heard his laughter as he got back up. Not exactly the reaction I expected. My partner was crazy.

Stepping back away from him slowly, I did not know what would come next.

He rubbed the shoulder of his sword arm. "Didn't see that coming."

"Okay, enough," Lockonis called as she started walking toward us with Kevin following. "Take a break and we'll start working on cooperative tactics."

She turned to Kevin and started discussing something, so I began making my way over to where I left my water bottle. A hand hit my upper back hard enough to make me stumble for a few steps.

"Sorry about that," Silver said as he grabbed my arm to steady me. "I guess I'm still caught up in the moment. We should do this more often."

"I'll pass," I said flatly and moved away from him. How was it no one understood how easy it would be for me to seriously hurt someone?

A hand on my shoulder stopped me. "Ketayl, what is it? You were doing great. Still mostly reactionary, but it'll take time for you to get fully accustomed to using a weapon. And you didn't hurt me if that's what you're worried about."

I took a drink from my water bottle to give me a moment to organize my thoughts. "I can't guarantee I won't."

A towel appeared in my vision. I took it and wiped down my face and neck. I wanted a shower in the worst way.

Silver sat down on the bench and said, "Which is exactly why we need to practice more. The more confident you get, the better you'll be at controlling a battle. I'm guessing you didn't realize I kept trying to get you to move in a certain direction or take specific actions. Though you surprised me a few times."

I sighed and took a seat next to him. I doubted myself and thus doubted the people who had confidence in me. How were we supposed to work as a team if I could not trust myself enough to believe what others saw in me - especially from people with far more experience? I set one end of the staff on the floor and leaned my head against it.

"So you worked with Kevin before?" Silver asked after a couple of minutes.

I sat up and looked over to where he and Lockonis were still talking. "Yeah. I participated in some of his classes while you were training."

Silver glanced at the weapon. "You used a staff in those?"

"Not often. He teaches mostly hand-to-hand, but it's defensive. Grapples, pressure points, joint locks - things like that. Unfortunately I'm no good with that stuff." I had been hoping to find something I could work with.

Silver let out a short hum. I chanced a glance and he appeared to be deep in thought, flipping the tail of his braid back and forth. After a few moments he said, "Makes a little more sense now, but I still don't have a full picture."

I tilted my head in hopes I could make sense of his cryptic response. "What?"

He turned to me in surprise as if he had not expected my question. "When you were fighting those slave traders. It looked like you couldn't decide on how you wanted to fight. The only consistency was toward the end, but I don't know what was going through your mind then. You haven't exactly wanted to talk about it."

I was about to retort that I still did not want to discuss those events, but stopped. Silver only wanted to help piece together what happened. Analyze it. I could appreciate the effort.

Taking a deep breath, I summed it up for him. "I was running on instinct at that point."

Silver made another noise I could not place. I shrank the staff and put it on the bench between us, leaning my head back against the cool wall and closing my eyes. I wanted to get back to my werewolf theory, not talk about the past.

A few moments later I heard the staff extend and looked down to where I had put it, but saw Silver decided to take interest. He had a look of awe on his face. He spun it between his long fingers a couple of times before stopping and holding it in the center on two fingers. "This is incredibly well balanced. A little thin for my hands, but you looked like you were comfortable with it."

It was not something I considered at the time, but I guessed it worked. I shrugged in response.

Silver stood up and started mimicking some of the drills I had worked on with Kevin. "You already showed you could combine at least some of your arcane abilities with this. How far do you think you could take that concept?"

I leaned forward on my knees and watched the staff as Silver worked with it. It took him a minute, but he got the hang of using it. Watching the fluid movements, he would be able to wield it far better than I could.

"I'm not sure. I never thought about combining my power with a weapon like this before. I've toyed with the idea with firearms, but either it was underpowered or, well, I don't think Darius has forgiven me for melting that one yet."

"Something new to explore then," Silver said grinning. He shrank the staff back down before handing it to me.

"Break's over. Let's go!" Lockonis called. I should have known her moving it up an hour really meant she just wanted to extend the training session. What about the other work I needed to get done?

3

I STRETCHED as I debated the open dresser drawer before me. I was still sore from yesterday's extended training session. Thankfully I was only scheduled for desk work the whole day.

Rummaging through my shirts, I could not decide. I glanced back at the small suitcase I had not yet unpacked in my haste to get to work yesterday. There were some new clothes I bought when Mother dragged me out shopping with her this past weekend. I made the mistake of mentioning to her that I had been contemplating about trying something different.

The idea originally started while spending time with Father when I was forced to take time off after the events in Mystic Port this past summer. Father had invited Silver to stay at the family house and Kitteren had not yet taken the temporary transfer meaning both could pester me. One afternoon I hid in his workshop in an attempt to find some peace away from them and Mother.

Father had been working on refitting an older motorcycle. I spent part of the day helping him. He pointed out I should try to find things I liked, not what I thought people expected of me - things beyond work and the arcane. It might take a little trial and error, but to find my own path. Especially since I was unable to play my violin at the time.

Normally I would have spent time with Father this past visit, but every autumn he worked as a guide for inexperienced and visiting hunters.

I shook my head to clear the extraneous thoughts. I pulled one of the new shirts out of the bag and got ready for the day. I assumed Silver had not noticed I was late yesterday and I certainly did not want to be late today. Besides, he would be looking for me at breakfast.

With any luck, Lockonis would have some news for me. If not, I could at least start looking for other similar patterns.

Once I made my way to the dining hall, I hesitated just inside the door for a few moments, glancing around for Silver. There were not many people here at this hour and he usually chose the same spot if he got here before I did, but I never knew when he felt like he wanted to mix things up.

I sighed and went up to the counter. It had become rare for me to beat him here. I learned fairly quickly I could not just skip breakfast and start working. He would find me and pester me to go eat until I caved.

Roland smiled at me and put a tray up on the counter already prepared. "Almost didn't recognize you. Lookin' good."

I had a feeling I would be getting a lot of similar statements. I forced a smile and thanked him, taking my food. I made my way over to our usual table and pulled my tablet out of the small bag I carried. At least I could start making my way through my messages in peace. It would likely crash again if I attempted much else. Eventually I would have to bring it to the cyber team for repair, but I cringed at the thought of having to explain that I had no idea what I did to cause the issues.

Half my plate was gone and I leaned my head against my hand, fork hanging loosely in my fingers while I scrolled through a fairly lengthy message from Personnel about getting Winter Solstice time-off requests in early this year. The holiday was still over two months off. How far ahead did I need to be thinking about it?

I remained undecided if I wanted to take time-off for it or not. Kitteren would be back from her temporary transfer by then, but despite the fact Silver had an open invitation from my adopted parents to stay at the house, I still did not feel right leaving him alone on holidays. And it was incredibly awkward having him around the house, though likely I was alone in that opinion.

At least he and Kitteren had stopped fighting.

"Hey, boss - almost didn't recognize you," a chipper male voice said. I looked up from what I was reading to see Sparky taking a seat at the table. I wish people would stop calling me their boss. "Metal boy not around?"

I rolled my eyes at the nickname the Halfling gave Silver. The two of them had a weird friendship. Glancing at the time I commented, "He's usually not this late. Don't usually see you here this early either."

"Eh, couldn't sleep much. Got notice of another werewolf case last night. I'm going to need some help," he said the last part with hesitation. I still did not understand why he fluctuated between being comfortable and uneasy around me.

"RIG access?" I asked, absently stabbing a piece of fruit while still trying to get through my messages.

"No, actually they managed to get my access rushed. They're letting us investigate this one, but there's rumor of arcane stuff."

Now he had my full attention. "Divine also by chance?"

Sparky shrugged, his mouth full. "Haven't gotten anything in yet. I don't have an ETA either."

Even if this did not pan out as something with a necromancer, at least I would get my curiosity satisfied. I bit the tip of my thumb for a moment - there was nothing either of us could do while we waited. "Keep me updated. I should be able to spend more time in the lab for a while."

It still felt odd not being down there as much, but after telling off one of the branch lab techs when they started trying to push Sparky around, the workload leveled off and he handled it on his own. With the exception of anything arcane or divine of course.

Breakfast ended without Silver ever showing. This was highly unusual for him. En route to the office, I checked our schedule on my tablet, but it was clear. Might he have something only on his schedule? Something he forgot to mark on our shared calendar? He usually forgot to update it when he had a change.

Then my tablet went black and restarted itself. Great, the problems with it were getting worse.

NOON ROLLED AROUND and Silver was still missing. Sparky had not sent me an update on the ETA for the evidence coming in either. I thought Lockonis might contact me with more information, but it had simply been quiet.

I rapped my fingers rhythmically on my desk. When had I started needing to have people around?

Shaking my head, I picked up my phone and scrolled through to find Silver's number, but before I started typing up a message, the door beeped and unlocked.

Lockonis strolled in. "Oh, good, I caught you before you went to lunch. Where's your other half?"

I put my phone down and shrugged. "I haven't seen him today."

Lockonis stared at me blankly for a moment before she snapped her fingers. "Oh, that's right. He was going to meet with Kevin early and then had an appointment with the armory."

"Armory?" This was the first I heard of it. And why was he meeting with Kevin?

"Yeah, we want to get him into something a little more modernized, so he won't stand out with that full plate armor of his. Plus, it's completely inefficient to put on in a hurry. Might as well get you two geared up before you go out into the field again." Lockonis came around to see what I had been working on. "Anything new?"

I thought she came here for a reason. "No. I'm waiting to hear from the lab on the incoming case."

"About that..." Lockonis said, rocking back on her heels. "I put a conference call on your schedule for this afternoon. Just wanted to make sure you saw it. Stoney has some news regarding the werewolf cases, but he didn't say much in his message."

I quickly clicked over to my calendar to confirm it.

Lockonis glanced back at the clock by the door before she took a seat on the edge of my desk. "We've got a few minutes. I want to talk about yesterday."

Please, no. I wanted to forget about yesterday's training session. I turned and stared at the break between the two screens in front of me, my jaw clenched tightly.

"First of all, I'm sorry about what we put you through, but we all needed confirmation. You had never shown this type of ability before confronting the slave traders a few months ago and not again until we forced it." Lockonis sounded sincere, but I still did not want to talk about it.

"I still think there's a different explanation," I said quietly, resigned to the conversation. I could fight it, but then the whole thing would get dragged out. Better to get it done and over with.

Lockonis took a deep breath before continuing. "A couple of months ago I might have agreed with you, but I couldn't come up with anything and inquired with Magus Engelil. Discretely, of course. You being telekinetic is not outside the realm of possibilities. Ket, you've grown a lot stronger in a short period of time. Your scores at the EAC have been extremely high. I can only imagine what the discussion is going to sound like when they finally settle on assigning you a rank."

I still did not care about having a rank. "Why?"

"Why what?"

I cringed. I did not think I had spoken out loud. Well, I had already dug myself in this far. "Why all of this?" I waved at the room. "Why me?" Why had I been chosen over all of the other Researchers at the Arcane College? Surely there must be others with siblings in a similar situation.

Lockonis shifted back and to look at me for a few long moments. "Why not?"

I frowned and crossed my arms. I needed a better answer than that.

"Look, I knew of you to some extent before we were dragged before the Terran Council to take a liaison so it was an easy choice. Ket, you showed serious potential from the moment I picked you up. And now," she waved at me, "you're starting to move forward. I just wish it hadn't taken almost losing you a couple of times in the process to get you to start coming out of your shell."

This was really not the time for this discussion. Not with everything else going on. I filed Lockonis' statements away for later.

The door thankfully chose that moment to beep and unlock. Silver stopped when he saw both of us, his jacket half-off. "Should I come back later?"

"Nope, I think we're good for the moment," Lockonis said cheerfully and spun her legs around and bounced off the front of my desk. "Why don't you two head to lunch? Conference call here at 1400. Can't make it much later - the old man needs his beauty sleep."

It was an order spoken as a suggestion. I slowly reached forward and locked my system more out of habit than anything else. Lockonis left before I finished.

Silver took his jacket off and hung it up behind the door. "What was that about?"

I shrugged, not wanting to get into the conversation. "She came to tell me about the schedule change."

Silver tossed me a look to let me know he knew I held back. It was not the first time I had gotten it. "Seemed like more than that."

I hesitated before I said, "She wanted to talk about yesterday also." I set my jaw again thinking about it.

"Oh." Silver stood next to the door with his arms crossed. "We should get going."

I eyed Silver for a moment before standing up and following him. Normally he would press. Was he hiding something?

Lockonis was in our office when we returned. She had already pulled up the files we had been working with and arranged them around the wall screen. "Oh, good. I wanted to pull the information up in case we need it, but I can't remember how you had this set up yesterday. You two were the ones to figure it out."

"Her, actually," Silver said as he passed by me. I stared at his back. Why did he do things like that?

I approached the wall screen, taking in the current layout. "Is there any information available for the new case?"

Lockonis shook her head. "Stoney's keeping it local for the moment, but if he's got it, you know it's in the Alpha Prime's territory."

Well, at least it's something. I shifted a couple of files around so I could quickly remind myself of my previous train of thought.

When Lockonis reached forward to start the conference call, I moved behind the table to not be in the front of the group. I fussed with my hair, trying to make sure I looked presentable - video calls still made me uneasy.

An older Dwarf with white streaks through his dark gray hair and beard appeared on the screen. I had been introduced to Old Stoney at the badge ceremony for Silver and Sparky a few months ago.

"Hey, Stoney!" Lockonis said cheerfully. An Elven man stood next to him. "What do you have for us?"

"Well, I talked to the Beta yesterday. Actually, she called me shortly after I got off with you. I guess they're done running in circles trying to figure this out on their own." Stoney reported. "I can have everything priority shipped once you say the word. Talon here reported the possible arcane usage." He gestured to the Elf next to him.

"To be honest, I'm not sure. It was barely on the edge of my ability to sense," Talon said. "I'm no mage so I couldn't even begin to tell you what I picked up on if it was anything relevant."

I frowned at that - it gave me nothing to go on. I wondered if there was someone with a stronger ability to sense we could get out there.

Lockonis turned and eyed me for a moment before returning to the video call. I tilted my head, unsure what could be going through her mind. She said, "Actually, I'm thinking of sending you a few extra hands from here."

Oh no. She must have had the same thought.

"Thanks for approving the request - I could use more experienced people. Gave me the bottom of the barrel on this round and I think this is going to be past what my rookies can handle. This them?" Stoney nodded at us and then paused for a moment. "Oh Hells, Lockonis, you know how to make an old man happy. Though you're sending me another rookie as well."

I looked over at Silver who scrunched up his face in annoyance and crossed his arms over his chest defensively.

"Two actually. I'll be sending a lab tech to you as well." Lockonis must have meant she intended to send Sparky. "Ketayl will be of better use in the field. And you know I wouldn't send you just anyone, Stoney. Not with something this sensitive. Though they'll need a primer on dealing with werewolves."

"I'll forward it along. Dealing with normal packs is a little different than dealing with the Alpha Prime's pack. It's hard for even those of us who've been around them awhile to play their dominance games. As soon as you send me their travel schedule, I'll arrange a meeting with the Beta. Sasha's gotten desperate enough to ask us for help - I'm not missing the opportunity. Nickolai will be returning from the latest set of Council sessions in the next few days and his pride might get in the way if we don't get started soon. Both of them are fiercely protective of their people. While none of the victims have been members of their pack, the fact these bodies keep showing up in his territory has got to be some sort of challenge or warning to them."

"Alright then, I'll have Fletch forward you their travel plans as soon as they're made. Joint operation, Stoney - Ket and her team need full autonomy while they're there. And support from your end wouldn't hurt either."

Why me?

"Don't you worry. I think your girl and I will get along just fine." Stoney smiled and then cut the connection.

"You could've warned us you were planning to send us out," Silver said. At least he voiced what I had been thinking.

"I wasn't sure I was going to until just now. I wanted to hear what he had to say before committing to the thought. Besides, I thought you wanted to get out and do something." Lockonis smirked at him.

"I do, it's just..." Silver's eyes slid over to me.

"This isn't the first time we've sent Ket into the field on short notice. I'd think you of all people would remember that one," Lockonis pointed out. "Has Colburn set you up with new armor yet?"

Silver seemed thrown off by the question. "The jacket is ready, but not the rest."

"Okay, take what you can. Leave your TIO coats behind - the werewolves will be more comfortable if you don't roll in all official. Keeping this quiet and contained is what they'll be looking for. I'll inform Sparky and have gear bags ready for all of you by the time you're done packing. Meet me by the hangar control station in two hours." Lockonis waved us out the door.

I grabbed my bag and my coat and followed Silver without thinking about what I was doing. What was I doing?

MY MIND TRIED to make sense of everything. Why had Lockonis chosen me as lead? I had absolutely no training or qualifications for it. What was expected of me?

"Ketayl?" Silver asked. I ended up following him to the armory before I realized what I was doing.

I shook my head to clear the extraneous thoughts so I could focus on the here and now. I hurriedly pulled my coat on. "Sorry, I best go get packed."

"No, wait," Silver said, pausing before he entered, his hand still on the door. "Are you taking your staff with you?"

"Do you think I should?" I barely started working with it and Kevin insisted I keep it. I bit my lower lip unsure if I should bother.

Silver moved closer. Too close. I backed away for breathing room. "Ketayl, look at me." I did as he asked and blue eyes searched for something. "One step at a time. I'll be there with you."

I held my hands to keep from fidgeting. "I don't think I can do this." The words were out of my mouth before I could stop them.

Silver stepped back. "Yesterday's training session really threw you off, didn't it? Let's go get your staff and come back. Maybe Coburn will have something so you can carry it on you."

My hand went to my bag and I pulled it out. "I'm not sure why I packed it this morning." I held it on my open palm to him.

A raised eyebrow was the initial response I got. "Well, that saves us a trip. I'll help you pack after we finish here."

"No," I said quickly. I tried my best to keep others out of my quarters. "Thank you, but I can manage."

"I'm helping you otherwise you'll be second guessing yourself on everything," Silver said more firmly before taking the shrunken staff and heading into the armory and over to the front desk. How was I supposed to keep my quarters my private sanctuary if people just invited themselves in?

"You should go pack your own things - we don't have a lot of time."

"Exactly. I'm helping you because we don't have time for you to be second guessing every decision. Besides, it's easier to have a second set of eyes so you don't forget something. We don't know how long we'll be away."

I rolled my eyes and sighed, crossing my arms. Arguing with him when he was in overprotective big brother mode would take longer. I just could not shake the uncertainty about being selected as lead. I was second guessing even small decisions now. Perhaps he was right to insist on helping.

"Hey, you're back! Wasn't expecting you until tomorrow. Is there something you wanted to adjust?" a male Dwarf with black hair and a tightly bound beard said when he came around the corner.

"No," Silver said. "I need to borrow what's ready. We're heading out on an assignment."

"Yeah, no problem. I'll get the jacket for you. Anything else you need?" He looked back and forth between the two of us.

Silver put the shrunken staff on the counter. "Do you have anything that would work to hold this?"

"Don't tell me you're switching up your weapons. We finally got it all figured out," the Dwarf said as he took the staff, turning it over before extending and retracting it. "Though this is a fun one."

"Not me - her." Silver pointed over his shoulder at me.

The Dwarf looked at me, stroking his beard. "Hm. I don't have a holster made for it, but if you can give me an hour, I can whip something together. Hidden under the coat?"

"I think that would be best," Silver answered.

"Yeah, I can throw together a simple thigh holster then. I can make you something better when you get back," the Dwarf said, smiling. "Just leave this with me so I can get the sizing right."

"I'll pick up my jacket then also."

"Works for me." The Dwarf gave us a salute with the staff and headed back into the workshop area.

Once we were outside of the armory, I asked, "Was that really necessary? He seemed busy."

"Coburn wouldn't have agreed if he didn't have time," Silver pointed out.

I had to practically jog to keep up with Silver's long strides. "I don't know..."

Silver stopped abruptly and I almost ran into him. "Ketayl, you wanted us to be equal on this team, right?"

"Yeah..." I said unsure of where this was going. It was a conversation we had gone through a few times before now, but he never seemed to listen.

"Then trust me on matters like this, okay? I've not been helpful in trying to find leads, but this I know how to handle."

I took a deep breath. Silver was right - he had far more experience with armor and weapons than I did. "Okay."

4

Sparky bounced lightly on the balls of his feet next to his suitcase, wringing his hands. His bag was almost as big as him. He stood next to the control station for the platform to raise and lower the Shrikes from the hangar. I wondered which one of us standing here was more nervous.

I shifted uncomfortably with the holster holding the staff attached to my thigh. Silver insisted I wear it after Colburn made the final adjustments.

My partner sent me ahead to the hangar. What was taking Silver?

"Oh good, I was starting to get worried - thought maybe I misunderstood who was going," Sparky said once Silver showed up.

"Needed to get a few things," Silver said. He wore the jacket he picked up at the armory. Black covered most of the front and back, as well as coming down over his shoulders. White composed the remainder with blue trim between the two and around the edges. The stiff, heavy textured material covered from high collar to down over his hips.

He grinned down at the Halfling and I mentally groaned at what was about to happen. The two of them teased and argued with each other non-stop when in the same room if there was no one to stop them.

And I already knew I was not one who could stop them.

"Hey, Ket, you got your tablet?" Lockonis' voice came from behind me.

I turned at the question and patted at the bag at my side, opening it up to make sure the device was still in there. "Yes."

"Hand it over," she said, signaling she wanted it.

Slowly I pulled it out and gave it to her. With the way she spoke I thought she might take it away from me. I would need it for this assignment, right? I should have brought it in for repair before this, but I could make due.

"Oh geez, you really did need to get rid of this thing," Lockonis said, looking over the device.

"But..." I stopped when a different tablet was held up in front of me. Cautiously I took it.

Lockonis smiled broadly. "I've already loaded everything you use on it and the primer Stoney sent. Tonkey showed me the error reports your old one was sending from this weekend. The new one will still use the same charging cable, but I packed the one it came with in your gear bag." She stopped and looked at the men behind me. "The two of you have been issued ones also - they're in your gear bags."

I looked longingly at my old tablet in her hands. It had my school books on there. Keeping up this semester was going to be difficult with going out on assignment. The thought had not even crossed my mind until now.

"I said everything, didn't I?" Lockonis teased and pointed at the new one in my hands.

Opening the cover, I slid back and forth between the screens seeing the same setup as what I had. I opened the program containing my books and found my library. "Thank you, but..."

"Nope, not taking it back. You've been way overdue for an upgrade. I think you're going to need it." Lockonis patted me on the shoulder before walking past. "You two report directly to Ketayl. This isn't class reunion time boys - keep your heads on the assignment. From here you'll be heading to Great Tree and will be shown to your next flight. You three get to borrow the big guy's jet."

Vince had a jet? I guess it made sense where he had to travel around the world to meet with people and conduct business. What if he needed it?

Lockonis rapped her knuckles on the console a couple of times and looked over at the Human man waiting to operate the platform for the Shrike. "I guess if I have anything else I'll contact you. Get going."

The men picked up their bags and loaded into the back seat. Silver picked Sparky up and put him in while he was climbing.

Lockonis grabbed my shoulder as I passed. "One moment, Ket."

I stepped away from her and turned to see what she needed and rarely had I ever seen her sapphire blue eyes so serious. I rubbed the shoulder she had touched to try and erase the feeling.

"The gear bags are in the back. They contain what I think you'll need that the Ghost Forest branch doesn't have - and even some stuff they do. Stoney's promised full access of his facility to you. Trust in yourself and your team. You've got this. Now go figure out this puzzle."

I nodded, worried she put too much faith in me. Now I not only had the two to figure out how to lead, but Lockonis' expectations to live up to.

I hurried toward where the back sliding door remained open. There was a lack of space to sit.

"Front seat, Ketayl," Vince said as he flipped switches, getting ready to take off.

Silver took my suitcase from me and I rushed to the front, not wanting to upset the Director of the TIO. The last time I had flown with him I slept through most of it on the way back from Ocean's Edge this past summer.

As soon as I settled in the seat a headset was held out to me. I took the equipment and stared at it for a moment before putting it on. I shifted the ear pieces until they stopped uncomfortably pinning the extended points of my ears back.

I heard Sparky make a noise of excitement as the platform started to rise.

"Looks like you're going to have your hands full with those two," Vince commented softly. It would have been impossible to hear him over the sound of the engines and the chatter in the back without the headset.

My hands shook as I buckled myself in. I bit my lower lip to force down the nervousness. My bag with my tablet and other items I carried regularly sat on my lap and I debated starting to go through the information Lockonis loaded, but if our next stop was Great Tree then we would not be in the air long.

I could hear Silver and Sparky talking in the back, but the headphones and the sound of the engines whirring muffled it.

"And for future reference, Ketayl," Vince said, his voice even, "Team leads sit up front."

"Sir, I'm..." I gave up. They kept trying to force something on me I would never be. I fidgeted with my hands.

"Don't think too hard on it."

I gripped the edge of the center panel and the side of the door as the platform locked into place jarring the Shrike. The twin tilt rotors took us off into the air, rotating down once Vince cleared enough of the facility.

I tried to focus on the fall foliage to calm my nerves. I should contact Kitteren and our adopted parents soon to let them know I would be away. It was better than obsessing over what being team lead meant.

SPARKY'S SMALL form bounded up the stairs to the jet ahead of the rest of us. The pristine white aircraft was small, but still seemed far too large for just the three of us.

A small crew stood in the doorway waiting. A couple of the crew members had come down to gather bags as soon as the Shrike settled on the ground.

I followed one of the crew members and heard Vince tell Silver, "Bring her back in one piece. I'm tired of seeing her return broken."

"I intend to," Silver said firmly.

I rolled my eyes. Great, now Silver was going to be in overprotective mode. Annoying big brother was bad enough.

The Elven man ahead of me who was part of the crew turned back to speak over his shoulder. "First time flying in one of these, ma'am?"

"Yes," I said quietly - it might have been too soft to be heard over the wind and the engines.

"Then you're in for a treat." He stopped to let me get ahead of him once we entered.

It was not what I expected at all. Couches, chairs, and a table decorated the interior of the jet. A screen idling on its menu sat in an open cabinet on the back wall. There was a corridor heading further back. I bit my lower lip and looked around knowing how out of place I was here. I sensed the steward right behind me and went in, putting my bag down on the table.

I could see why Vince would want something like this - it was basically a mobile office.

Sparky had already sprawled out on the couch along the wall.

"Make yourself comfortable, ma'am. We'll be taking off as soon as everyone is settled." He then took the bag I carried and stowed it in a compartment above me along with my suitcase, which he had insisted on carrying. He smiled broadly. "And if you need anything, just ask - it's what we're here for."

I gave him a quick bow.

Silver glared at him as they passed each other. Had I missed something of his conversation with Vince?

I took a seat on the forward-facing couch at the table. I might as well take the spot where I could get some work done en route.

Once Silver took a seat across from me Sparky sat up. "Isn't this amazing? We get to fly in style." The Halfling then kicked back on the couch again.

I twisted my hands nervously in my lap and stared at the table. At least someone was excited. I still worried about too many things.

The Elven man from before came back and instructed us to buckle in and explained where things were in the plane we might need. One of the pilots would be relaying our flight times and stops to refuel through the screen at the back of the cabin.

It was going to be a long flight to get us to the Ghost Forest branch. How much could I get done in that time?

"So what's the plan?" Sparky sat across from me and looked at what I had written in a notepad.

We had been in flight for a couple of hours already, but he had spent much of it exploring the cabin. Silver appeared to have dozed off on a chair in the corner.

"You're mean. I can't read Elven."

I looked at my notes. It mattered little to me now what language I wrote in, but it had been a long-time habit in order to keep my work as much to myself at the Arcane College.

"Um... I..."

Silver sat up and looked at us. "Those are her notes," he pointed out. So much for not having to deal with him as well at the moment.

I glanced at the information on my tablet about werewolves. Much of it I thought too in-depth for what we needed, but I combed through it anyway.

Now Sparky wanted a plan of action. Silver likely did as well. But where to start? I admitted, "I don't have much information right now. I'm hoping for a schedule update when we reach our first stop to refuel."

Both men stared at me as if expecting more. I wished they would stop that.

I bit my lower lip and looked between my notes and the information currently displayed on my tablet. I pieced together what I did have into something. "I'm going to assume there will be a meeting with the Beta some point shortly after we arrive. There's also the evidence the Ghost Forest branch gathered that will need to be processed." Even I could hear the uncertainty in my voice.

I still wondered how Lockonis had the foresight to have the Ghost Forest branch hold the evidence.

I got so wrapped up in parsing out the information I read I found myself unprepared for this. They needed me to delegate out the work. Work I was used to handling on my own.

Silver came and sat down next to me. "Sounds like there's more."

I disliked being stuck between him and the wall and slid closer to the wall to get a some breathing room. I stared out the window at the fluffy sea of clouds to gather my thoughts. "I thought about going to visit a few of the more recent sites where the bodies were found, but if there was any arcane usage, the remnants would have broken down by the time we got there."

"What if they were powered by divine energy again?" Silver asked.

Mentally I kicked myself - I had not thought of that. Or had I? There must be a reason I had not bothered with the idea.

I bit my lower lip and picked up my tablet, switching to the map I created with the locations of the bodies. A few taps later and it showed the little red dots on a satellite image. Then it clicked why. "They've all been found in the heavily forested areas away from the city. Brown used his spells to affect those who were arcane and divine sensitive which was why he targeted a heavily populated area. It seems unlikely."

Sparky stood up on the bench across the table from us and looked at the map upside down. "It looks like they might have been trying to hide the bodies."

"I'm hoping there are images from the earlier finds so we can piece together how they died. Going through the primer, I don't want to take a guess until we can examine the type of damage done," I said.

"Type of damage?" Silver asked putting his arm along the back of the couch behind me and leaning over my tablet. The movement set me on edge and I stiffened up.

Picking up my notepad in an effort to combat my unease, I flipped back a couple of pages. "It could be a political message, or it could be personal. With them being newly turned werewolves, they could have picked a fight with the local fauna they couldn't win. There are too many options to consider without more information."

"That's a lot of notes for a couple of hours," Sparky commented. "I'm doubting this new one will be in RIGs."

"Run it anyway. I don't want to chance missing something," I ordered. Even if there was only a slim possibility of there being something in the database, I did not want to pass it by.

Sparky looked up at Silver and made a weird face. Their games would have to wait.

While I flipped through my notes, Silver said, "I can go over the injuries on the bodies. I should be able to give you a decent picture of what happened."

I jotted down Sparky's and Silver's tasks. "I'll comb through what's remaining and see if I can't piece something together."

"Ma'am?" The attendant stood at the end of the table. "I'm sorry to bother you, but there's a call waiting."

"Oh, um..."

He signaled the direction I needed to go to take it.

Silver slid out of the way and I followed the attendant down the hall toward the back of the plane. I glanced over at the two men watching me and then told the attendant, "Thank you." Picking up the handset, I quietly said, "Hello?"

"Just so you know, your phone will work in-flight," Lockonis teased.

I patted my pocket where I kept it turned off. "Sorry, I didn't..."

"Easy, kid. Stoney arranged for the three of you to meet with the Beta immediately after you arrive. I'd recommend making sure all of you get some rest beforehand."

I bit my lower lip. I had been hoping for more of a buffer - at least a chance to look at the evidence. According to the primer, I would have to be the one to talk. Possibly prove dominance for my group somehow, but I hoped it was an exaggeration or we would be given a pass. "I understand."

"And that's all I've got for now. The big guy will kill me if I rack up too much time on this line. Bye!" Lockonis said cheerfully.

Hearing the line go dead, I slowly put the receiver back. My hand hung on it and I thought about how little we had accomplished so far. We still had several hours ahead of us, but this pushed back getting started processing the evidence. Sparky would need more rest than myself or Silver. Both of them were going to need at least a heads up about what to expect in the meeting. Or what I could gather to expect. Perhaps I should ask Stoney to explain.

There was no mention of how formal the meeting would be. That would greatly shift what would happen. I leaned back against the wall behind me and pinched the bridge of my nose. I had to keep focused on the task at hand. I could not afford to let the Beta distract me. We did not have time for dominance games.

I started to think I had been better off without having read the primer.

"Ketayl?"

I jumped at the sound of Silver's voice.

"What is it?" Blue eyes showed concern. He had every right to be - I had no idea how to handle this. What if I failed the two with me? Or Lockonis' faith in me? What happened to me did not matter as much as those around me.

Taking a deep breath to calm myself, I pushed off the wall and shooed Silver out of the way. "We have a meeting with the Beta when we land."

Sparky asked, "Even me?"

"All three of us," I confirmed. "I'd recommend reading through the primer, but I don't know what we're walking into. Lockonis also suggested we get rest before we arrive."

"We're getting food at the first stop soon, right?" Sparky asked. Sometimes it seemed all he thought about was food.

I glanced over at the attendant who had just entered. He nodded. I relayed, "Yes."

Silver started giving Sparky a hard time about his fixation with food. I ignored their banter and collected my things off the table, opting for the corner chair Silver previously occupied.

I pulled up the primer again. The weight of the meeting would fall to me and Stoney with Lockonis classifying it as a joint operation...

Maybe I was over-thinking this. The TIO existed as a separate entity from the werewolf packs. The labeling of something in one did not necessarily translate over to the other in this instance. I put my notepad on top and flipped back and forth trying to find something definitive.

A bottle of water appeared in my vision. "Take a break," Silver said softly. "You need to step back so you can see the whole picture." He held out my headphones in his other hand.

Silver had gotten to know me too well in the past few months. I still felt like I missed something not going through the same training he and Sparky did.

Reluctantly, I took the bottle of water and opened my hand for him to drop the headphones in. As soon as my hands were full, he took my tablet and notepad away from me. "Hey!"

"Break," Silver said firmly.

I dropped the headphones in my lap and reached for the tablet. At least with the device I could work on something else.

"Geez, don't piss off the boss," Sparky commented. "On second thought, go ahead. I want to see her lay you out."

And now these two were dragging me into their childish games. I did not understand why people kept trying to portray me with abilities I did not have. Though I did knock my partner down in yesterday's training session - that had been a first.

Silver shook his head and put my stuff on the table before leaning against it. He crossed his arms and stared at me.

"If we weren't in a metal tube flying at hundreds of miles an hour, I might just. Give me back my tablet," I said and stood up, depositing the items I held on the small shelf along the wall.

I heard Sparky make a noise, but paid him little attention - I was busy trying to stare Silver down. And with only coming up to his shoulder, it would be a feat in and of itself.

A raised eyebrow from Silver was my only response.

Fine. Raising my hand to the side, I reached out with my power for the item I wanted, warping a flight spell to bring it to me. I turned on my heel and returned to my seat.

Sparky sat forward, laughing. "Did I just see what I think I saw? Big brother Blaise just got schooled."

"Oh shut up," I heard Silver snap at him.

"Enough. The two of you should have a copy of the primer on your tablets. I recommend reading through it." If they wanted orders then fine, I would give them some.

———

SILVER SAT up from where he had stretched out on the couch along the wall. "Ketayl, get some rest. We'll be arriving in a few hours."

Sparky continued his soft snoring from one of the benches by the table. The lights in the cabin had been dimmed for them to get rest. I sat in the chair in the corner still working on my tablet, my feet tucked underneath me.

Shaking my head, I said, "I will in a little while. I just need to go over the information one more time. Don't worry about me."

"You said that two hours ago." Silver tossed the blanket off of his legs and got up. "There is such a thing as over-preparing."

I rolled my eyes and went back to what I had been reading. *As of UT 2 all petitions to turn for immortal classified races were subject to government regulations...*

My tablet disappeared from my hands. A warm blanket landed over my head. Pushing the offending material away, I glared up at Silver.

He knelt down next to me, putting the tablet on the shelf. "Please, Ketayl. You're going to need to be rested for the meeting." Great, he was in overprotective big brother mode.

I rubbed the bridge of my nose. "I'm just not ready to rest yet. Soon, okay?"

Silver sighed and stood up, moving away. He lost his blanket though. I squirmed down further into the warmth before reaching for my tablet. Hands on my shoulders stopped the movement.

"Silver..." I warned. This was one of a number of habits he had gotten into when he thought I needed a break. I wished he understood I absolutely needed to know what I was doing before walking into the meeting with the Beta.

His hands moved to start releasing the tension I had not known was there. "You've got a lot on your shoulders. Just don't forget you have us to help."

I shifted uncomfortably, eying where Sparky slept. It was one thing when it was just the two of us. "I'm fine," I said firmly.

An exasperated sigh proceeded Silver saying, "You need to rest."

"I don't like being touched," I said softly, but it came out as more of a whine. It was something I would throw at him every so often, but we both knew there was no threat behind his actions or my words.

Silver snorted softly.

"I can take care of myself," I said in an attempt to get Silver to forgo this idea. I knew I should put up more of a fight. I could work through being tired.

He made the same noise again.

I yawned, my body betraying me. I started getting drowsy. Maybe if I closed my eyes for a few minutes he would leave me alone. All I wanted to do was get back to what I had been reading. I was not ready for this. And if I was unprepared, how would I guide these two?

5

A CALLOUSED hand touched my face and I feared I jumped a mile, nearly falling off the couch. How did I get here?

"Good job, metal head. Scare the boss," Sparky said.

Where? Plane. Werewolves. Case. Meeting. I blinked a few times to finish getting myself orientated. What time was it? How long had I been resting? Why had I been resting?

Silver brushed my bangs out of my face and I batted at his hand. "Sorry to wake you, but I thought you might like a chance to clean up before we land."

So much for closing my eyes for only for a few minutes. "Yeah, thanks." A day old might not be the best first impression with the Beta.

I grabbed my suitcase from the overhead compartment and went into the bathroom. It was spacious for an airplane bathroom. I put my bag on top of the closed toilet seat and dug for a fresh set of clothes I thought would be appropriate. I used my power to clean up instead of trying to take a shower - I forgot to ask how much time remained. A thin layer of dirt and oil lifted from me and went down the drain.

Once finished, I ran my hands over the fitted high neck purple shirt, taking in my reflection. The outward changes were still foreign, but I was more comfortable with them than I expected.

I redid my hair and thought I looked presentable. I picked up the last piece I needed, staring at the gold-colored metal. Only a few months ago I tried to return my badge.

Not in resignation, but because I felt undeserving of it. Silver refused to let me and now here we were. I could not let him and Sparky down, but I worried I would not be able to handle the responsibility given to me.

Taking a deep breath, I clipped the badge to my waistband. The gold stood out sharply against the purple and black I wore.

After repacking my bag I exited the bathroom and stopped short. Both men stared at me with wide eyes. "What?" I looked down at myself to see if something was wrong.

"Just don't see you all dressed up very often, boss," Sparky commented. "I think the last time was our badge ceremony."

I would have rather worn something more comfortable, but business attire seemed a safer bet.

Shaking my head, I put my suitcase away. "One of us needs to be presentable."

"She's got a point," Silver said. He pulled his suitcase down and headed for the bathroom.

"Hey! That's not fair! I'm too short!" Sparky shook a fist in his direction.

I sighed and pulled Sparky's suitcase down for him. Dressing the part was one thing, but I worried these two would cause issues on top of dealing with the werewolves. I pinched the bridge of my nose to alleviate the building tension.

"Boss?" Sparky said, his voice sounding unsure.

I looked down at the Halfling mentally preparing myself for whatever it was he needed.

The intensity in his brown eyes confused me. I had seen a range of emotions from him over the past few months, but never this.

He said, "Look, I know me and Silver get on each other's case, but we've got your back and will follow your lead."

I wished people would stop using that word. I doubted my ability to lead myself out of this.

The attendant came up to us. "Ma'am, if I might have a word?" I started getting sick of people calling me that as well.

No point in being aggravated about it. It would do me no good to be this irritated going into the meeting. I nodded and followed him toward the front of the plane.

"The pilots said we'll be landing within the hour. There will be a car waiting for you and your team."

I gave him a short bow. "Thank you. And thank you and the rest of the crew for all your help. If you can pass that along to the others?"

"Of course and it's our honor, ma'am. You're far less demanding than our normal passenger." A mischievous smile graced his face. "Is there anything I can get you or your team?"

Glancing down the hall, Silver stared in our direction with his arms crossed and a frown on his face. He wore his armored jacket with a blue collared shirt and black dress pants. Sparky must have gone to change. "I think we're good, thank you."

"Anytime. If you change your mind, just let me know."

I gave him a short bow and returned to where Silver stood. "What was that about?" he demanded.

"He was giving me an update on when we would land and that there will be a car waiting for us. I told him we didn't need anything else, but..." I bit my lower lip - I probably should have checked with both of them first. I moved my bangs out of my face. Maybe I should put my hair up in a bun?

"Looked like more than that," Silver said flatly.

I eyed him cautiously. What was going on? I had not seen him this borderline confrontational with someone for no discernible reason since he and Rathal had both been exposed to the necromancer's spell.

"I thanked him for his help and asked him to pass my gratitude along to the rest of the crew."

"You...?" Silver dropped his arms and looked at me with wide eyes. "You know, I should probably do the same." He picked up the holster with my staff off the table. "You should wear this."

"Don't you think this is a bit much?"

"Please, Ketayl? I'd rather you be armed. Just... please?"

Silver's behavior concerned me. What was he anticipating?

I sat down to strap the holster to my thigh. If I kept my coat on, it would stay hidden. Not that I would be any good with it if it came down to a fight.

How could I possibly be ready for this?

STONEY WAITED for us at the bottom of the stairs to the plane. A black truck, similar to the one I drove in Ocean's Edge, sat not far away. I shivered against the cold and wrapped my arms around my waist. Silver and Sparky insisted I leave the luggage to them and the crew, but I had grabbed my day bag anyway.

"It's good to see you again, lass," Stoney greeted with a broad smile on his face.

I bowed.

"None of that now. I told you before I owed you one and now I'm probably going to owe you again," Stoney said, signaling for me to follow him. "I know what Lockonis said about the rookies, but I want to get your input." He tossed a wary glance back at them as they came down the stairs.

I paused, biting my lower lip for a moment, unsure how to answer. "Sparks has taken over all of the lab work and I couldn't ask for a better partner than Silver." I bit my lower lip. It had sounded better in my head.

"We'll talk more later. For now we should get over to the Prime's residence." Stoney popped the back hatch of the truck so they could load the gear. Then he pointed me at the front passenger seat.

Taking a deep breath, I got into the warm truck. I waited for Stoney to get into the driver's seat before I admitted, "I read through the primer, but I'm not sure what to expect."

Stoney gave me a wide-eyed look. "Don't tell me you read the whole thing. I put most of that together to keep my rookies in line so they don't piss off our neighbors. Dealing with Sasha is going to be like dealing with anyone else. She might get a bit testy, but who wouldn't with something like this happening in their backyard?"

His comments put me a little more at ease, but not enough. I linked my fingers together to keep from fidgeting.

"And actually, a lot of it is simply things I've learned over the years of dealing with them. They realize most people aren't familiar with their culture and thus don't stand on ceremony. If another wolf was to screw it up, that's a different story." Stoney laughed. "And I don't think Zack has lived down his shame to this day."

I heard the back hatch slam shut and then the back doors open. The other two for my team quickly got in and settled.

Stoney leaned over and said quietly, "At least they know how to move. My newest ones are still tripping over themselves."

As he drove, I stared out the windows taking in the autumn scenery. The city gave way to a creepy dense forest. The white trees looked like ghosts even in the daylight with hazy light filtering through adding to the atmosphere. At least the colors on the leaves were pretty.

I had to trust Stoney spoke true about dealing with the were-wolves. He had a lot of experience with them if the primer was any indication.

The drive to the Alpha Prime's residence felt far longer than the hour the clock said it had taken to get there. A large mansion appeared from behind the dense trees. I stared openly at the sheer size of the place as we pulled into the long, curved driveway.

"I probably forgot to mention this is more than just the Prime's residence," Stoney said. The question was probably plain on my face. "It operates as a central gathering point for his pack and a home for a number of werewolves - especially the recently turned. Nikolai is actually a simple man and would not have something so grand for himself. That's my theory anyway."

Once he turned off the engine, I got out and looked up at the massive building. My adopted parents lived in an overly large estate, but this made it look like a modest home. I followed Stoney up the stairs.

Wooden double doors at least twice my height opened when we reached the top. I tried to ignore the elaborate stone, metal, and woodwork beyond to focus on the task at hand. A Human woman stood in the doorway with a clipboard. Her brown hair was pulled up in a messy bun and she appeared to be barely into adulthood. Her jeans and short-sleeved shirt made me feel overdressed.

"Lexi!" Stoney called as we crossed the large landing area and reached the doors. "Don't tell me you've been waiting."

"Heard you coming," she said tapping her ear. "Your vehicles make a distinctive sound."

How? Then it hit me she was probably a werewolf. Of all people, I should know what appeared before me was not necessarily what I should expect. I hoped my power would remain quiet during this meeting.

Lexi smiled and signaled for us to follow. "Come on, Sasha will welcome a change of pace."

It sounded like what Stoney told me earlier was true - they were just like dealing with anyone else.

We followed Lexi quietly. Stoney fell back to walk alongside me. Was this to show equal standing? But if we did not need to follow the normal protocols then...

I also felt uneasy about being in front of Silver and Sparky. I wrung my hands both out of nervousness and to warm them up. I got cold far too easily.

"Easy, lass," Stoney said softly, "Just remember what we talked about."

Lexi opened a large door and let us in. I stopped next to Stoney before the grand wooden desk containing paperwork strewn across the surface.

The Human woman behind the desk did not even look up when she said, "Lexi, I told you I wasn't taking anymore petitions today." Her wavy light brown hair appeared to have been pulled back hastily with a clip. Her age seemed similar to Lexi's, but I had a feeling she was older. The raw power she exuded felt stifling and my own became curious in response.

It had not fully occurred to me until now that I would be dealing with someone so high up in the leadership of a people. It only made this whole situation more complex.

Stoney crossed his arms grinning. "There's a problem the day I'm here to petition."

"Stones!" Sasha's head shot up from the papers she had been reading. Her eyes drifted over the rest of us. Hazel eyes lingered on me the longest and I stood as still as I could despite the strong desire to fall back with the two behind me. "If this is your help, they don't look like much."

"And it's rare you get caught off-guard," Stoney commented.

Sasha grinned broadly, bearing her teeth. Then she put her hands up defensively before sitting back. The weight of her raw power eased up. "You'd think the petitions would drop off with the way the news keeps being creative with what little we allow their journalists."

Stoney waved her off. I had to be missing something, but he acted easy around her - they must have known each other for a long time. "You wanted to meet the people coming in to help. They're going to need cooperation from the pack. They've already got mine. Worked enough with the lass here to know she's going to have the pack's best interest in mind."

"Ah, but where are my manners," Sasha said standing up. She reached her hand out to me, "Sasha Orel. Beta for the Alpha Prime's pack."

I tried not to show my hesitation in taking her hand. "Ketayl." I did not know what else to call myself anymore. Her firm grip surprised me given how delicate she appeared. Once she released my hand I forced myself not to rub it to get off the feeling of raw power. Dominance contest? If so, this one was subtle.

I remembered not to cross my arms as it would be more of a sign of insecurity. Or was it something else? I settled for putting my hands on my hips and prayed it did not come across aggressively.

Stoney stepped in. "My understanding is Ketayl wears a number of hats these days. Her team will be running the investigation and using mine for support."

Sasha kept her eyes on me. "You are certainly an interesting one, Ketayl. I look forward to seeing how your team performs."

I clenched my teeth at her statement. *Question me all you want, but not those behind me.* I felt my power push at me gently, but it still seemed more curious than anything else.

Silver took a step forward and I raised a hand to stop him. "I understand your position, ma'am, but trust I know my team."

Sasha grinned. "It's rare for me to apologize, but I am sorry for this. I fear it's been a long day and I've been needing to forcibly take control of some of my wolves. They've been spooked since the first murmurs of dead werewolves in the area and it gets worse when we find another."

The power in the room lessened further. She said her people were scared. Perhaps she was as well, but dealt with it differently.

I nodded, keeping my head high. This was how I needed to act, right? I knew I should have gone through the primer one more time. "What information do you have about the deaths?" I asked. Even Stoney remained silent.

Sasha smiled softly, bowing her head briefly before moving to pick up a box next to her desk. "These are copies of everything we have including the reports from the TIO confirming all of them as unregistered wolves. I believe your name is on them."

"Yes." It would be. Only just recently did Sparky get access to the RIG database.

Sasha picked up a business card off the corner of her desk and put it on top of the box. "Then I wish luck to you and yours. If you need anything from myself or the pack, don't hesitate to call."

I nodded and reached for the box when she moved it to my side of her desk.

A side door slammed open and a tall Human man strode in holding a mobile phone to his ear. The raw power in the room felt like it jumped tenfold from what the Beta created initially. My own pushed back in response, but again it acted the same way as with the Beta. I bit the inside of my cheek trying to hush it.

"Marcus, I was the one who recommended the current petition restrictions," he growled. "I won't sign a repeal and good damn luck getting it through the Council without it." He tapped the end button angrily and then glared at us. "What is this?"

I took my hands off the box, stepping back and putting them on my hips again. My feet managed to stay planted where they were despite desperately wanting to fall back behind everyone.

Sasha rubbed the bridge of her nose before responding. "Nikolai we talked about this already. We need to involve the TIO. Stones has promised discretion."

Nikolai came around the desk and stood in front of me. I forced myself to meet his gaze. I had gotten enough practice staring Silver down and the Alpha Prime was not as tall.

A long couple of moments passed before he asked, "These two yours, girl?" He waved at the men behind me.

"Yes." I would not break eye contact. Looking away would be a sign of submission. I think. Why did werewolf procedures and politics have to be so complicated? I knew Stoney said it would be like dealing with anyone else, but these people were scared and needed something familiar to comfort them.

At least that was how I rationalized this.

"Nikolai," Sasha said. He broke eye contact to look at her. I could breathe again with his attention elsewhere. "Don't you think that's enough? They aren't wolves. They're here to help."

He muttered something I could not understand and walked away.

Sasha gave me an apologetic smile. "Ketayl, please find whoever is doing this. We need to give our people peace of mind."

Nikolai's head whipped around when she said my name and I stiffened up under his gaze.

I nodded and bowed, taking the box. It was heavier than I anticipated. Silver moved to take it from me as soon as I turned around. If he wanted to take it, I was not about to argue. I snagged the card from the top. I turned back to Sasha, giving her another short bow and said, "Thank you for your cooperation. I'll keep you updated."

"Thank you," she said softly.

Stoney signaled the two behind me to leave and I followed.

"Ketayl," Nikolai barked as I reached the door. I turned to find him staring intently at me. "I will not accept failure."

I simply nodded, unsure of how else to respond.

Stoney waved me out the door Lexi held open and I forced myself to move. Only parting goodbyes to Lexi were spoken until we got in the car.

The Dwarf let out a long breath. "I guess it was a good thing you went through the primer so thoroughly. I'm sorry I misled you. And I certainly didn't expect Nikolai to show up. Usually he takes a few days after a set of Council sessions before coming back."

I rubbed my arms unsure if it was from the cold or having dealt with two very powerful werewolves. "It's okay. They're scared."

I heard a shaky laugh from the backseat and looked at Sparky who was white as a sheet.

"You okay?" I had not even paid attention to how they were doing. Silver sat directly behind me so I could not see him without twisting further.

"It's okay, kid. Just leave it to Ketayl to deal with them. I don't think I've ever seen someone stare down Nikolai and he's the only one I've ever seen do it to Sasha. Taking on both I thought would be impossible."

Stoney gave me more credit than I thought I deserved. Werewolves could smell certain emotions such as fear and I was sure my attempts at playing their games failed.

6

____

STONEY DROVE us to the hotel so we could check in and relax for a short period of time after the meeting. I had the box Sasha gave us brought up to the suite with everything else. I should take inventory of what Lockonis packed, but I really wanted to get started on the contents of the box.

I shakily picked up my suitcase once the men rushed off to one of the rooms in the suite. Making my way to the remaining room, I put it against the wall and sat down next to it, rubbing my arms. I did not think I could do this. I had never felt so out of my element before. I was an Arcanist. An Arcane Investigator. A lab tech. Not any sort of leader.

My power pushed at me gently as if to remind me it was still there. And it also reminded me that I was just as dangerous as the werewolves.

I pulled my knees to my chest and buried my face. What had Lockonis been thinking sending me? I shook. There had been so much oppressive raw power in that room.

An arm wrapped itself around my shoulders and calloused fingers stroked my bangs on one side back. Silver. "Please leave. I need to be alone," I managed to get out.

"Not right now," he said softly. "I think you need another perspective."

I raised my head to look at him. What did he mean?

Silver shifted. The floor was uncomfortable, but I had not noticed until now. "First of all, when the Beta looked at me, I couldn't hold her gaze for long. Second, even Old Stoney ended up focusing on you. I'm guessing for the same reason. He didn't even try to meet the Alpha Prime's gaze."

"I read the primer..." I started.

"No, I read it. You studied the primer, which helped. Old Stoney wrote it and he couldn't keep up with the dominance contest," Silver said.

I bit my lip, still worried about the impression I left. "But what if I was too aggressive?"

Silver remained silent for a moment before he said, "I think they were looking for strength - someone who would follow all the way through. And likely they appreciated that you respected their customs."

I turned away and stared at the floor. I should tell him not to touch me and leave me alone, but somehow him being here helped ground me. I thought about Nikolai's parting words and shuddered again.

"What?" Silver asked.

"The last thing the Alpha Prime said..." I hoped it meant only my neck was on the line.

Silver sighed. "We won't. It may take time, but we won't. And while I'm fairly certain Sparky was borderline ready to wet himself, both of us will stand with you."

Speaking of... "Where is he?"

"He went downstairs to try and find something to eat," Silver said, resigned.

I rolled my eyes. More than once I needed to remind Sparky not to eat in the lab, but he found comfort in food. I settled my chin on my knees and thought about where to start.

"Talk to me?"

I took a moment to organize my thoughts first. "I need to start going through the box. Once we get to the office, I'll see about getting it into the case file on our system."

"One of these days you'll stop trying to take on everything yourself," Silver said, exasperated.

I moved away from him and got up. "You don't like paperwork."

"True, but I told you I'd go over the injuries, and Sparky's here too," he pointed out.

The holster pulled against my leg oddly and I sat down on the edge of the bed to take it off. Should I change up into something more comfortable? I still needed to meet Stoney's team.

I glanced at Silver and he had changed. Granted, his normal attire relaxed little from what he wore to the meeting. How long had I sat on the floor shaking before he came in?

Everyone else allowed themselves some measure of comfort, I should probably do the same. I pointed to the door. "I want to change before getting started."

Silver gave me a mischievous grin and left without another word. He was such a child sometimes.

***

"How can tracks just appear at random?" Sparky asked. He did not lift his head from the file he currently read. His hand reached into one of the bags next to him for a snack. The sheer amount of food he could consume never added up against his size in my head.

I paused and thought about his question for a moment. "Teleport? Some other kind of transportation?"

"But teleport implies we're dealing with a mage. The wounds look physical," he pointed out. "I thought there had been rumor of arcane stuff involved."

"Doesn't mean we're not dealing with a mage," I said. I remembered some from the Arcane College liked inflicting pain as much physically as they did magically.

I would have to look at the images more closely later, but Silver would be best to analyze them. He had gone downstairs to grab us something to eat.

Each file contained detailed notes. I had to give the werewolves credit, they were thorough. What bothered me more was that there was no record in the system of the werewolf doing the turning, which meant the individual was likely outside of any pack structure completely. I thought either Nikolai or Sasha would have an idea of who, but they seemed just as baffled.

The door opened and Silver came in with bags in hand. He put them down on the side table next to me, but I had become too engrossed in the file I held to pay attention further.

Flipping through, I found a handwritten note at the end: "Unknown werewolf possibly previously rejected petition."

I sat back on the chair and contemplated the note for a moment. I wondered if there were others. It might show a pattern and Sasha would hopefully give me access to the information if needed. I mentally shuddered at the thought of having to face her or Nikolai again any time soon.

"Eat, Ketayl," Silver said sternly.

I signaled for him to wait a minute. I flipped through a few more pages. Because the turning process changes the petitioner's DNA, there was no match. Most had died as wolves though a couple were found in hybrid form. What would cause someone to think it was a rejected petition?

"Hey, don't. Can't you see she's onto something?" Sparky's voice filtered through and I looked up.

Silver's hand stopped where it had been reaching for the file I held. I glared up at him. "You really need to quit doing that. It breaks my train of thought." I folded the file closed and put it back in the box. We still needed to take the box back with us, so I tried to keep the files neat.

"What do you have?" Sparky asked.

A white box appeared on my lap. Apparently lunch.

"I'll need to check the other files, but there was a note in that one saying the person might have been a rejected petition."

"It'd give them a way of getting volunteers to be turned," Silver commented. He dug into his food.

Sparky quickly swallowed what he was chewing. "Yeah, but how is the person doing the turning not in the database? Everyone is supposed to be in RIGs."

"Not everyone follows the law," I said. "The average lifespan of a werewolf is 200 to 500 years. Longer if the original race was say Elven or Dwarven. If they were turned before the RIG database was created they could've slipped by. I think they've been collecting DNA samples for only 10 or 20 years."

"Yeah, okay. I thought they didn't have a lifespan; hence the term immortal," Sparky commented with his mouth full.

I grimaced at the sight.

Silver spoke this time while I fussed with opening my box of food. "You really need to read the primer. For werewolves, it's their minds that go and it can turn them into anything from manipulators to berserk beasts of destruction. So they're killed when they start showing signs of insanity."

I raised an eyebrow at him. *For someone who claimed to only have read it...*

Silver shrugged. He surprised me sometimes.

There was a knock at the door and Sparky bounced up. "I'll get it!"

I shook my head and let him go. I stabbed a vegetable while I pulled another file out and flipped through it with my free hand.

"Well, you certainly don't waste any time," Stoney commented. "And if you tell me you have something already then I'm retiring."

I looked up, quickly putting my fork down and the box aside. "Sorry, I didn't realize..."

He waved my apology off. "I didn't give you a time frame. Had a talk with my crew - the newest ones mainly. Just want to again remind you boys this isn't class reunion time. I've got about a dozen people all at various stages, but with the exception Talon and Joe who remain with me, they're all less than two years on the job."

I barely made three years with the TIO now.

"If you or your boys have any trouble with mine, come to me. I swear a couple of them should never have passed basic training. This right here is the difference between the top and the bottom," Stoney said. "I should let you finish up." He took a seat on the other side of the low table we were working at.

Tentatively, I picked up my food box again and continued to eat, flipping through the next file to the end to see if there was a note like the last one. I frowned at not finding one, but it did not rule out the possibility. This one had been found full wolf while the last one died in a hybrid form.

"Don't tell me you're hitting a dead end already," Stoney commented.

Swallowing quickly, I told him, "I'm not sure. There's no note like the last file, but it doesn't mean the deceased wasn't possibly another rejected petition."

"Sasha's been holding back on me." Stoney leaned forward.

As I put the file back I said, "I guess there's also the possibility they were either forced or decided to bypass the petitioning process completely. It'll be easier to sift through this when I can spread the information out."

Stoney grinned. "Don't worry, you'll have your own area to work."

"Ketayl," Silver said quietly. I looked over to him and he pointed at the food on my lap. I rolled my eyes. I had a feeling he planned to be the overprotective big brother this whole trip.

I finished my meal as quickly as possible. I needed to get this thing solved before the Alpha Prime really started breathing down my neck.

7

STONEY GAVE quick introductions when we arrived at the branch office and then signaled for us to follow. I was fairly certain I would not remember most of their names.

"Silver! I heard people from the main office were coming. Didn't imagine I'd see you again." I vaguely remembered the Human woman who approached us as being part of his and Sparky's training class.

"Here we go," Sparky muttered just loud enough for me to catch it.

"You've never responded to my messages. I'm hurt." The Human woman pouted, though her tone was teasing. She hooked her arm under his and gave me a slightly worried look. Then it clicked she was the one who came and talked to me after their badge ceremony.

"I had work to do, Campbell, and I still do," Silver said, his words clipped. He set the box down to get his arm away from her.

I picked up the box and told him, "It's okay if you want to stop and talk for a few minutes. I need to get this in the system anyway." I struggled between the weight of the box and my gear bag, but I could make it as long as I did not have to go far.

Stoney paused in hearing us stop, but I caught up as quickly as I could manage, following him around a corner and down the hallway. Silver tapped my shoulder before taking the box back.

The Dwarf opened the door to a room roughly the size of the office I shared with Silver. "We don't have the latest gadgets, but something tells me you folks will do just fine with what we've got."

A few tables were pushed together in the center and there was a desk on the other side of the room with a computer on it. A projector hung mounted to the ceiling. "Thank you."

"Don't thank me yet," Stoney said. "Keep me advised and I'll give you who I can for support as you need it."

I bowed, grateful for his offer.

Stoney laughed and left. The door remained open and I think I preferred it that way. I wondered if I could convince Lockonis to take the heavy security off our door.

"Where do we want to start?" I asked.

"Well, you said something about getting the files in the system, but I don't see how in here," Sparky commented while he walked around the room.

"I've got that covered." I forgot Sparky did not know about some of my spells. I made my way over to the computer and turned it on. Might as well get the process started. "Sparks, can you go ask Old Stoney where the evidence is? I'd like you to start getting it processed."

"I've got it," a male voice said from the doorway. "Well, most of it. There's stuff in the lab too." I looked up to find a Human man standing in the doorway with a box. He set it down on one of the tables. He walked over and reached out his hand, "My name's Mark. I was in the same training class with these two."

I took it out of courtesy. "Ketayl." I resisted the urge to rub my hand to get rid of the sensation. "Do you know if there's a chance we can use your lab?" I asked.

"Oh, absolutely. I can show Sparky down there if you want," Mark said.

"If you don't mind, Sparks?"

"You know where I want to be." Sparky grinned and walked up to Mark. "I'll take that down in the lab. Might as well keep everything together."

"Sure, no problem."

And with that they were gone.

Silver grinned. "You're more of a natural at this than you think."

I rolled my eyes and returned my attention to the computer. This one was slow compared to the ones I used at the main office which meant it would take longer to transfer the information.

Finally the login screen appeared. My fingers flew across the keyboard to get into my account. I walked away while I waited for everything to load. I opened the box again and started pulling files out, attempting to put them in some semblance of order on the tables. Should I start with the newest or oldest first?

"What do you need?" Silver asked coming up to hover over my shoulder.

The whole room and he chose there to stand. I thought about telling him I needed space, but instead said, "Do you want to start going over the images and seeing what you can piece together?"

Silver picked up a file and took a seat. "At a quick glance, the few I saw looked like animal attacks, but nothing I've seen before."

"Werewolf?" I picked up the oldest file. As good a place as any to start. Besides, I might be able to get a picture if I went chronologically to see what convinced the Beta to seek outside help.

"Possibly, but I have no point of reference for it."

"I'm sure there's something we can use to compare," I said offhand.

Silver made a noise of agreement. "I'll see what I can manage for now. There might be a pattern I can make out."

The silence in the room was only broken by beeps, key clicks, and the scratching of a pen on paper for the next hour. Silver thankfully remembered I needed to concentrate while using my spell to copy the files onto the system. I still had to pause to type in what it was for and any reference words I thought necessary.

My phone rang just as I picked up another file. I pulled it out of my pocket and answered without looking to see who was on the other end. "Ketayl."

"Ket, how could you?" Kitteren's voice came through loudly. I held the phone away from my ear, wincing. Apparently she found out I had been sent out on assignment.

I sighed. I had been so caught up in preparing I forgot to message her or our parents that I would be away. "I'm sorry. It was last minute. I got busy and forgot."

"You're in the middle of something, aren't you?" Kitteren sounded amused.

I put the file down on the desk and started preparing it to be copied. "Yes."

"Okay. Call me later? I don't care what time it is." There was concern in Kitteren's voice, but nothing I thought I needed to deal with immediately.

"Okay."

"Love ya, sis. Take care of yourself." Then she hung up. She knew I was uncomfortable with saying things like that - especially if there were others in earshot.

I put my phone down on the desk, but before I could start copying again, Silver asked, "Kitteren?"

"Yes." I needed more time to get all these files in.

"You could have taken a break and talked with her."

I stopped and looked over at my partner. "I'll call her later." Shaking my head, I needed to concentrate and get this in. I was only partway done with the files. It was taking me far longer than I initially figured.

Suddenly a hand appeared over the papers I had been looking at. I glared up at Silver. He leaned forward and said, "Apply what you told me earlier to yourself. Don't forget to give yourself time away from this for a few minutes to connect with others."

"And why didn't you stop to talk with your friend?" I knew I was becoming confrontational, but I did not need Silver questioning something as simple as a phone call.

It was rare to see annoyance on Silver's face. "I wouldn't call her that and I didn't want to. Usually you'll talk with Kitteren."

I stepped back and crossed my arms. "I'll call her later. She knew I was in the middle of something. Really."

"Okay," Silver said and backed away. "Just know I'm not going to let you ignore yourself during this."

I shook my head again and got myself back to where I needed to be mentally to finish the task. I had at least another couple of hours ahead of me. Possibly longer if the files were thicker.

"WELL, I called it. Not in RIGs," Sparky said. He strode in with paper-work in hand. "I'm hoping I can get something from the material found on the body. So did you guys get something to start copying those files?"

I sat at the computer slowly rubbing the bridge of my nose. I felt more drained than I thought I would be and it took two hours longer than I planned. I was unsure where the nauseous feeling came from. "It's done." I signaled him to bring me what he had.

"You don't look so good, boss," Sparky observed.

I took the paperwork and started flipping through the findings so far. I knew he was fast, but he would not be finished with everything. Just a blood sample and no body again, but the file with the images should be sufficient.

"The spell she uses took some out of her," Silver commented.

"Spell? Oh, wait, are you telling me you used magic to copy all of that into the system?" Sparky paused. "That is amazing. What branch would you call that? Technomancy?" He laughed at his own joke.

I rolled my eyes.

"Do you want to call it an early night, Ketayl? You didn't get as much rest on the way here as we did. I can see about getting someone to take you back to the hotel."

Silver's comments made me pause and I realized we did not have a vehicle, which could prove problematic.

I shook my head. "Maybe an early supper." I locked the computer before getting up. "I'm going to go see about arranging a vehicle for us."

Getting up and moving helped with the nausea. I stopped in the empty hallway and stretched. I had not been able to see any patterns while copying the information, but most of my attention had been on the spell and wanting to get the task done. I figured the Beta's decision came from the number of bodies and how they were turning up with increasing frequency.

The holster shifted slightly - enough to remind me the shrunken staff was there. Should I go back and grab my coat to hide it? No, I did not think anyone would care.

I was not sure why Silver insisted I wear it. I was not proficient with it yet. I would likely get myself in more trouble if I tried to use it in a fight.

Coming around the corner into the large open area Stoney's team primarily operated out of, I saw the Dwarf talking with a couple of agents. He caught sight of me and said a few more words before waving them off. "Girl, you look like you need a break."

"Something like that," I said, forcing a smile. "I forgot to ask before: is there a vehicle my team can borrow?"

He smirked and signaled for me to follow him. When we reached his office, he picked up a set of keys off his desk and handed them to me. "It's actually the one I drove when I picked the lot of you up. I've already pulled the risers. The only one who won't be able to drive it will be the Halfling."

"He'll be fine." I smiled and bowed. "We were thinking of heading out to grab an early supper before coming back at this again."

"Your crew, your call," Stoney said. "Ketayl, it's not hard to see you're new at this, but you've done good by them so far. Trust yourself to keep doing so. And trust they've got your back. You've managed loyalty and efficiency in a fresh team. I've spent years trying to teach some of these hard heads and I doubt they'll ever learn."

I bowed, uncertain how to voice a proper response to his compliment. I gripped the keys tightly and looked at Stoney's desk, unsure where to take the conversation next. A nameplate sat in the center front with "Owynn Stonebreaker" etched in the black.

Silence hung for a moment before he asked, "That one of Coburn's?"

I looked down at the staff holstered on my thigh. "I think so. I know he made the holster."

"May I?"

I reached down and pulled the shrunken staff from its pouch. I watched where both ends were before pressing the button to extend the staff. Then I handed it to Stoney.

"Now I know this is one of Coburn's," he said as he looked over the staff. "Always an eye for detail and damn creative about it." Stoney pressed the button again and handed it back to me.

I tucked it back in its holster while Stoney walked behind his desk and picked up a hammer with a large, square-ish, metal head. "He made my warhammer as well. I like to put it up on the desk when I have a disciplinary meeting. Reminds them 'Stonebreaker' isn't just because I bust their balls."

His quick story amused me and I allowed a small smile.

"Oh, before I forget." He pulled another set of keys from his desk drawer. "This is my spare set so don't you dare lose it. I've etched what doors they go to. Damned if I can keep track of them all otherwise. Figured you'd like to be able to lock up your work. The newer ones can get curious and I'd rather not have to deal with a case of something going missing from your investigation. Always looking to prove themselves."

"Thank you." My first thought was he trusted me too much, but Stoney obviously knew what we needed better than I did. I bit my lower lip, again unsure of what I was supposed to do. Apparently I needed to read a guide on being the lead of a team. If such a thing actually existed.

There was a long pause before Stoney asked, "How'd your boy make out down in the lab?"

His question gave me something else to focus on. "No hits again in RIGs for the newest one. He's still processing the rest, but he thinks he might be able to get something off of the material found."

"You folks really don't waste time."

Praise both Sparky and Silver needed to hear, but he kept directing it at me. They were just doing their jobs.

I took a deep breath and decided it would be better to ask Stoney than have to go back to the werewolves. "I need to get an update from Silver, but his initial thought is they were attacked by an animal. He's thinking possibly werewolf, but he has no point of reference."

He snorted. "That we can help with. I'll have one of mine pull files he can use. Sounds like you're well on your way. Now go gather your boys and get something to eat. It'll be ready when you get back."

I bowed and left, though I paused at the door. "Any place you would recommend?"

Stoney seemed surprised by my question. "Well, near the hotel there's a number of different places. All fairly good. My folks tend to end up at a place called the Wandering Drummer pretty often."

"I'll pass it along. Thank you again."

Stoney picked up his warhammer and pointed at the door. Grinning, I left. I should be more focused on the task at hand, but figured I was too tired to do so at the moment. Refueling would help.

I heard voices coming from the room we were set up in as I approached. A vaguely familiar female voice drifted out. "You could at least tell me how things have been if we're going to work together."

"I'd rather you let me work. You don't have the Alpha Prime breathing down your partner's neck," Silver replied sharply. Was it necessary to remind me of that? I enjoyed the moment's reprieve while talking to Stoney.

My feet stopped where I stayed out of sight of the people in the room. Should I come back?

"Holly, leave him be. The boss will be back any minute," Sparky sounded exasperated.

"Ball buster, huh?" Holly said.

Was I? Is that how they saw me?

"No," Sparky said quickly and then paused. "Ugh, just... ugh!" I imagined the Halfling throwing up his hands. It was a habit he often did when something frustrated him.

I should step in and end the conversation, but it felt wrong to interrupt them just as I should not be listening to the conversation. I wanted them to be comfortable in dealing with me. I clutched the two sets of keys to my chest, my feet frozen in place.

"Well what then? There's rumor she stared down the Alpha Prime, but it looks like a strong wind will blow her away. Come on, you guys have got to give me something," Holly whined. She was in there to find out about me?

There I found my opening and stepped in. "You could just ask," I said flatly. I strode past wide eyes and open mouths with more confidence than I had and went to the computer. I logged back in so I could find this Wandering Drummer and browse the other places near the hotel. The sound of my keystrokes echoed loudly in the room.

"I, uh, better get back to work," Holly said and left quickly.

The silence continued. After a few moments Sparky laughed, the sound shaky. I looked up to see what was wrong and he just stared at the door. Silver kept his attention on me.

"What?" I asked. Had I scared them?

"Thanks," Silver said.

I looked at him, tilting my head to try and make sense of his word. "For what?"

Sparky turned his attention back to us. "You got her to leave. I think you might have freaked her out with that."

"It wasn't my intention," I said, biting my lower lip. I could have just caused an issue.

Silver stood up and came to look over my shoulder. "Wandering Drummer?"

"Old Stoney said his people liked it. I wasn't sure what kind of food the two of you were in the mood for," I said quietly. I wondered if I overstepped my boundaries.

Silver stood up and shrugged. "Works for me. Sparky?"

"Yeah, sounds good." Sparky still seemed distracted.

Sighing, I moved my chair back. Mostly to get Silver to give me more space. "Tell me what I did." We needed to clear the air before we left.

"What?" Sparky looked from me to Silver.

Silver crossed his arms, looking down at me. "Nothing, honestly. The only reason you completely unnerved Campbell was because she shouldn't have been in here pestering us in the first place."

I rubbed my face with my hands and groaned lightly at my misstep. Not what I had been intending either. Now more rumors would spread among Stoney's team.

"Forget it," Sparky said coming over to the desk. "She deserved that one. Now let's go eat. I'm starving. My other tests in the lab should be done processing by the time we get back. I'm never going to say my equipment is slow again."

I HAD NOT PUT the truck in park before both of the men were out. My driving could not have been that bad. Hopefully they were simply that hungry. Admittedly the time difference threw me off. I made a mental note to do better about paying attention to their needs.

Sparky started bouncing in front of the menu in the window outside before I caught up. "Hey, this place sounds like the Waking Dawn in Ocean's Edge."

"At least we should know what to expect," Silver commented. His eyes were also on the menu.

I dug in my bag and pulled out my wallet to make sure I had the expense card for the team. Lockonis gave it to me shortly after I returned from Mystic Port, but I never needed to use it before now. Seeing the blue card with the TIO logo, I closed my wallet and put it away. That would have been a bad thing to have forgotten. Though I felt awkward using it even though things like this were what it was for.

As they held the doors open for me, Sparky asked, "I don't suppose you'll let me drink."

I sighed and shook my head. "Not on the clock - I didn't make the rule."

"It's pretty close to the hotel. We can come back after we're done for the evening," Silver commented. "Provided you're not intending on working all night."

"You're on your own to pay for it." I was not putting alcohol on the expense card. I did not need to end up in a meeting with auditors.

We were quickly seated in a booth. Both of them sat opposite me and for once I started to wish Silver followed his usual trend of sitting next to me when it was more than just the two of us. I picked up the menu in hopes of getting this odd feeling to stop. It was as if they considered me differently now than before. At least Silver seemed to anyway.

The two across from me chatted. I found what I wanted and put the menu down, staring out the window at the busy street. How would someone find out about rejected petitions? I began rhythmically tapping my short nails on the table.

Someone on the inside would be the easiest way, but something told me it was unlikely. They would not last long under the scrutiny of the Alpha Prime and his Beta. And surely they thought of it already. Both struck me as highly intelligent people.

"Hey, some new faces," a male voice said. I turned to see a Human man standing at the end of the table. His attire told me he was a server. "Are you ready to order?"

Once we gave our orders and he left, I watched him walk past others and greet them personally. There might be something in his greeting.

"Ketayl?" Silver asked, his voice concerned.

I blinked and then shook my head. "Sorry, just thinking."

"About what?" my partner asked.

Taking a moment to organize my thoughts, I idly started turning my glass of water. "How someone would find out about rejected petitions. This city seems small enough visitors could be picked out, though I'm not sure how much traffic they see."

"It would be easier to track who went to go visit the estate," Silver commented. "I can't imagine the hotel would be as big as it is without a decent number of visitors."

"You know," Sparky said with a piece of bread in his mouth. "This is a way-point for people traveling along the coast. One of my brothers and his friends did a road trip once and I think they came through here. 'Ghost Forest' sounds like a place to stop and check out."

It had gotten warm and I unzipped my coat, sliding it off of my shoulders, but I kept the bottom over my right leg to hide to holster. "There went that idea," I muttered.

"It's not a bad one," Silver said. "But we're still not sure if they are in fact rejected petitions."

Then there was that.

"Still, even if we assume that they are rejected petitions, how would someone find out? And if there are rejected petitioners who turned down some strange offer to bypass the government regulations, how do we find them? Someone like that would be able to point out who approached them at least," Sparky said, thankfully without food in his mouth this time.

"Do you think they would just let someone walk away?" Silver asked.

Sparky stuffed the last of his roll in his mouth. He quickly chewed and swallowed it. "I don't know. Should we expand our search for missing persons also?"

I bit my lower lip. That could be a big expansion, but one I was willing to take. "Yes. I'll start a search when we get back. It might take a while - I'll have to cover a fairly large area."

Our meal went back and forth tossing out theories.

I pulled my coat back on as the check came. Picking it up, I dug in my bag with my other hand for my wallet and stopped when the server said it had been taken care of.

I looked up at him and he tilted his head toward the bar. Nikolai sat there staring at me with a drink in hand. Silver and Sparky were too engrossed in their debate about what they wanted to come back and try later. I nodded and thanked the server.

Getting up, I handed the truck keys to Silver. "I'll be out in a few minutes."

Silver looked like he wanted to object and then decided against it. He ushered Sparky out the door. Once they were gone I got up and went over to the Alpha Prime. "Thank you, sir."

Nikolai looked up at me out of the corner of his eye. "Few are willing to respect the customs of the pack. And far fewer do I trust to help us. Most outside of this area see us only as monsters if they are not looking to become one of us. I heard your conversation. I will have Sasha compile the data you require."

"I appreciate the help, sir."

"Nikolai. Don't make me regret this," he said and returned to his drink, waving me off.

I gave a short bow and left. I had not planned on running into the Alpha Prime twice today, but at least this interaction had been far calmer.

Silver sat in the driver's seat when I reached them. "What was that about?"

"I wanted to thank the person who paid our bill," I said as evenly as I could. Even with this being a lot less formal, the short meeting left me feeling uneasy.

Sparky leaned forward. "Oh, who paid it?"

"Nikolai."

Silence hung for a few moments before Sparky spoke, "So this means?"

"He overheard our conversation. We'll be getting more information once they have it together." I paused and wrapped my arms around my waist. "We should get back."

I could feel Silver's gaze on me before he started up the truck. Him driving still unnerved me, but not nearly as much as talking with the Alpha Prime.

8

My mind went blank as I stared at the pictures taped to the wall inside of the room we had been assigned. The only thing I could tell was they had all been running when they were taken down. Each of the maps included in the files showed them entering the forest from different points west of the mansion and headed for it. *Running for a rescue? Going to attack? What?*

I crossed my arms and tried again. There must be something. Silver concluded they were torn apart by another werewolf, but little more than that. What was I missing?

"Ketayl, it's late. We should call it a night. Sparky's probably asleep in the lab at this point," Silver said.

I pinched the bridge of my nose and admitted to myself he was right. They needed rest. "Go tell him we'll be leaving."

Silver came around and stood in front of me, putting the back of his hand to my forehead. "Nope, no fever."

I moved away from him, batting at his hand. "Just go. I need to make sure you two don't overdo it."

Silver laughed as he left and I shook my head. He could be such a pain sometimes.

I stared at the pictures. *Maybe if I could get the images enlarged I would see it?* There was just so much destruction to some of the bodies, I wondered how they knew what it was. I guessed their better sense of smell granted them that information.

"Agent Ketayl?" a female voice came from the doorway.

I turned to see Holly hanging at the entrance. I waved her in. "What can I do for you?"

Her face paled when she glanced at the pictures on the wall. "I just wanted to apologize for earlier. I didn't mean to interrupt your team."

"Okay," I said and turned back to the wall. I figured that was all she needed to say. It was also not my place to reprimand her. Not that I felt the need to anyway.

I could see her fidgeting in my peripheral vision. "It's just... We're all curious, you know? Where the others have gone and how they're doing. I've heard from a few, but..."

I took a deep breath before telling her. "When I told you earlier just to ask me, I wasn't trying to scare you off."

"You weren't?" Holly asked, surprised. "I mean, I don't mean to be disrespectful, but..."

"I don't look like I could hold up in a fight," I said cutting her off. "You're not the only one. I'd prefer to finish this investigation without getting into one." I did not want to have to deal with people treating me like an invalid again.

Holly gave a short laugh. "I guess I can't blame you. Can I ask you something else?"

"Hm?" Maybe there was something about the level of destruction. I knew nothing of werewolf physiology.

"How's Silver been? He won't even give me the time of day," Holly asked quietly.

I blinked and then looked at her. "I haven't heard of any problems from him and he usually seems happy. I'm honestly not sure what you're looking for." I shrugged and gave her a half-smile in hopes she would understand how broad of a question she asked. "If you want, I can talk to him for you. I think he's just focused on the case. It's the first one we've managed to get out of the office for."

Holly smiled. "He never did like riding a desk, but he did it."

An interesting phrase, though I understood what she meant and smiled knowingly before returning my attention to the pictures. Silver hated desk work.

"I've wanted to ask something, and I apologize if I might have read it wrong, but Silver seemed to know you before he got his assignment," Holly said, stepping forward.

Well, the need for secrecy was long over. "He worked as a consultant on a case with me. The Director assigned him as my partner before he started training."

Holly crossed her arms. "Huh. I wondered what drove him. He was so focused, and I think Sparky just wanted to try and beat him out for the top slot. Those two got so competitive."

Her comment made me pause. When I spoke with Silver over video calls he acted like he always did, with his carefree and often childish behavior. I helped him study, but he never sounded concerned over his performance. "They both have their strengths and their specialties," I commented. I did not want to get more in depth than that. Mostly because I had no idea what she was looking for.

"I guess I'm still looking for mine," she said sadly. "Well, I think I'll be heading home. Goodnight."

"Goodnight," I said and watched her leave. I crossed my arms and thought about what she said for a minute. I wondered if there was a way I could help her find where her niche was. Though that conversation would probably start with the question of why she joined the TIO in the first place. It was a line I did not know if I should cross. Her continued training would be with Stoney's team, not me. It would only be to help point her in a direction, right?

No, I needed to focus on this case.

Sparky walked in a moment later with Silver at his heels. Silver gave me a weird look, but I could not guess what went through his mind.

"Let me just check and see how the search algorithm is doing and then we'll go." I went to the computer and tried not to look at the other two. Perhaps they listened in on my conversation with her as I had done to them earlier.

WHEN WE RETURNED to the hotel I told the two to keep track of each other and come back safe as they headed back out. It looked like the restaurant was still open when I drove by.

Once the door to the hotel suite closed and I was alone I took a deep breath and let it out slowly, hoping the stress of the day would go with it. I might as well clean up and get ready for bed.

With them gone, I took longer in the shower than I normally would, letting the water help wash the day's events away. The case would still be there tomorrow, and it was more important to come back with a fresh mind.

I wondered when I started becoming so lax. Perhaps almost getting thrown through a wall a few months ago knocked some sense into me.

Once I cleaned, dried, changed, and brushed my hair, I sat down on the edge of the bed and debated my next option. Silver helped me pack and insisted I bring my violin. It might help calm my mind further. I still felt a little on edge after dealing with the Alpha Prime.

My hand was on the door to the bedroom, and I considered closing it fully so no one would catch me, but I wanted to hear when they got back. Certainly they would be loud enough to be heard over my headphones. I left it barely cracked.

I pulled the case out and settled in the middle of the bed. Opening it gently, I ran my fingers over the purple and black finish of the electric violin. It had taken a while for my shoulder to heal and I had not been allowed to play until recently, but by then I had taken to simply listening to music. I bit my lower lip - I worried I had lost the ability to play.

No one else was around to hear how bad I might sound.

I went through a few practice drills and then found something simple to play. I cringed a few times as I had been off on my intonation.

Suddenly the door to the suite slammed open, causing me to jump and make a loud screech across the strings. I hoped it had only been loud for me.

Quickly putting everything aside, I got up to see what the commotion was. Silver carried a bag in one hand and Sparky tucked under his other arm.

I folded my arms and said, "I told you to look out for each other. What happened?"

"He got into a drinking contest with a werewolf," Silver said, unconcerned.

"I won," Sparky slurred. Silver set the Halfling down and he wobbled for a moment before looking at me. "Yer pretty. Still like 'em shorter though." He made his way to the room he shared with Silver.

So much for the reputation I started to build for this team. I pinched the bridge of my nose and returned to my room, shutting the door. They were back in one piece, though I figured Sparky would regret it in the morning. And if that was the case, I would not enjoy tomorrow at all.

There was a knock at my door and I rolled my eyes before opening it just enough to see out. A bag filled my vision that smelled delicious. "Come out and eat. Sparky will be fine," Silver said.

I sighed and opened the door fully. "You didn't need to bring anything back for me."

"We have to take care of each other." He smiled and held the bag away from me so I could not just take it and retreat into my room. Silver glanced past me. "Sorry we interrupted you."

"It's fine."

Silver moved away and set the bag on the short table we worked on earlier.

I gave up and followed, taking a seat. I was a little hungry though often enough I would forgo the fourth smaller meal. Part of me was curious about what he brought back.

Silver excused himself. I slowly opened the bag and the small cream colored container inside. It looked like a mixed appetizer tray. I could always read while I ate. I got up and snatched my tablet off the charger on the counter.

While I munched on a piece of chicken, I tapped through the case file, reading the notes from the most recent body found. The werewolves had done their own preliminary investigation. This was the first one to have an item associated with it - a piece of cloth. They found it underneath the body - I worried we would not be able to get anything useful off of it.

"Ketayl, don't you think that's enough for tonight?" Silver said, standing over me with his hand out. He had changed into the light-weight white pants and a white tank top he wore to bed.

I put the device next to me on the chair.

He shook his head, picking it up to plug back in. "How about something else to settle before resting?"

I raised an eyebrow at him when he snatched something out of the box and sat down. "Depends what you have in mind."

"Watch something on the screen?" Silver suggested.

I shook my head. "I prefer to read."

"Well, how about just talking?"

I crossed my arms and waited for Silver to continue.

"Have you called Kitteren?"

I cringed. "I forgot. I'll call her tomorrow. Besides she'll be curious, and I have nothing of note to tell her."

He grinned at me. "How about staring down the Alpha Prime?"

I rolled my eyes and corrected, "I did not stare down…"

"Yes, you did. I was there. He used his Beta trying to get his attention to look away," Silver argued.

I sighed in resignation. They were going to believe what they wanted to believe.

Both of us remained silent for a few minutes until Silver found something else to ask. "Out of curiosity, why do you sometimes call your sister Kitayl?"

I blinked, not expecting the question. It seemed like it had been so long since I called her by that name where others could hear. "I usually use it with her when it's just the two of us."

"Sounded fairly close to yours," Silver commented.

"If you spelled it in common, it would be," I said offhand and then hid my embarrassment behind munching on something else from the box. I hoped he dropped it there.

"Is that her real name?"

My luck…

I shook my head. "Kitteren is her real given name. I don't remember what her middle or family names are though. I'm not sure how to describe the other one."

Silver looked at me expectantly. I sighed, resigned to the conversation.

"It's kind of like a familial name or something you would use with someone you're really close to - my clan normally didn't hold a naming ceremony until a child reached their first decade. Kitteren was an exception because of her condition."

There was a long pause and I thought Silver dropped it until he asked, "You left your clan before you reached your first decade, right?"

If you counted running for our lives as leaving, then yes. I nodded in response. I grabbed another breaded cheese stick and dipped it in the red sauce. I loved these things though I would never tell anyone.

"So, is Ketayl not your real name?"

I paused, the food half in my mouth. I took my time eating it to formulate my response. "It's as real as anything else and I never went through the ceremony. Besides, it was what Kitteren remembered. Names are what other people call you."

Silver sat quietly and munched on a piece of chicken. I hoped that was the end of it. I grabbed another breaded cheese stick and dipped it. I should eat something else before he noticed a pattern.

"Do you know what your name would have been if you had gone through the ceremony?" He got curious about the strangest things.

I hesitated before answering honestly, "Most of it - I don't remember my family name." I remained silent about the other names those villagers would call me while they looked down at me like some abomination.

Silver leaned forward and grinned broadly. "Are you going to tell me?"

"No," I said quickly, the heat rising to my face.

"Why not?" It was as close to him pouting as he got. No, I did not need to give him something else to tease me over.

I sighed. "Because I'm fine with Ketayl. Can we talk about something else?"

"Please?" Blue eyes pleaded with me and I looked away.

"No," I said firmly.

"Someday?" he pleaded.

"Not if I can help it," I muttered.

Silver snorted. "You're so stubborn sometimes."

"Thank you," I said flatly. What else could I say? There was another reason for my silence on the matter, but then things would really get complicated.

Silver laughed loudly. "Okay, okay, I'll back off. For now."

Silence fell between us for a minute before I found something else to talk about. "Are you sure Sparks is going to be okay tomorrow?"

"Hm?" Silver seemed surprised by the question. "Yeah, I've seen him drink more than this and run his physical test the next morning without a problem. I think it's common with Halflings. If it comes down to it, I can help him with the hangover."

I found I really did not want to know. I bit my lower lip in worry about what the werewolves would think of us now.

"Ketayl, talk to me." Silver's voice was gentle.

I fidgeted with my hands while I organized my thoughts. "I'm just... What he did... Are they going to think us incompetent now?"

Silver shook his head. "The opposite probably. He did drink the guy under the table. His friends all seemed to think it hilarious."

I did not trust Silver's assessment so easily, but I had not been there either. Time would tell.

Another question crossed my mind. "Why do you always call me by my full name?"

Silver paused with a piece of chicken halfway to his mouth. He sat back and ignored the food for the moment. "Do you not want me to?"

I shook my head. "I usually just let people use what's comfortable for them."

"As long as it's not 'fairie' though," Silver said with a mischievous smirk on his face.

I glared at him and he laughed. After a few moments he said, "I don't know. It started as a show of respect since you told me to stop calling you 'm'lady' and it just stuck."

I guess I could see his reasoning. I reached for another breaded cheese stick and dipped it. They were better freshly cooked, but these were still good.

"You really like those, don't you?"

Dammit.

9

TRUE TO WHAT Silver said the night before, Sparky appeared fine the next morning. Actually, he looked refreshed. "Where do you want me to start today?" the Halfling asked when we arrived at the branch office.

"Finish seeing what you can pull from the fabric. I don't want to miss a chance of being able to identify who it was before they were turned," I said as we got out of the truck. Immediately I shivered and stuck my hands in my pockets. I wanted to get inside quickly.

"Oh man, don't tell me you guys are the ones I'm supposed to deliver this to," a male voice said. "Now I really lost." The Human man did not look well - he appeared scruffy and disheveled. He leaned heavily against the old car next to him, rubbing his eyes. The car's trunk was open and he had a cardboard box half-pulled out.

I looked at Silver and Sparky to see if they knew who the Human man was.

"Hey! What are you doing here? Had a great time last night," Sparky said approaching the man.

I leaned back and quietly ask Silver, "Who?"

"The werewolf Sparky had a drinking contest with," Silver said softly. I tried to suppress a shudder at his warm breath on my ear. I did not need him making me feel colder.

"Oh." The interaction appeared friendly so far.

"Ugh," the werewolf groaned. "Not so loud. How can you be standing let alone fully functioning? You ain't normal, but damn that was fun." He held his hand out and Sparky slapped it. "Since I lost to you and lost even more face with the pack, I got to come bring some files for a team here. Said to give it to..." He picked up a small piece of paper attached to the top of the box and squinted. "I can't read Lexi's scribble." He showed it to Sparky.

"Ketayl. That's our team," Sparky said, standing a little taller. He pointed back at me when he said my name.

The man eyed me for a moment before shaking his head. "I underestimated the short stuff. I ain't doing the same with your boss. I'm not sure what's in here, but I know they were working overnight to get it together. Lexi woke me up way too damn early to come deliver."

With any luck, it was the rejected petitions. I felt a little guilty they worked overnight.

"Oh, and here," he said and pulled an envelope from a pocket inside his coat and handed it to me.

I looked at the neat handwriting with my name on it. "Thank you."

The werewolf shrugged. "I don't know anything about that either. Anyway, where do you want this stuff?"

"I can take it," Silver said stepping forward and accepting the box.

"You're making this too easy for me. Anyway, later. I need more sleep or coffee before work in a few hours." The werewolf got in his car and left.

That had to be one of the oddest interactions I ever witnessed. "What was his name?" I asked.

Silver looked down at Sparky who shrugged. "I have no idea," the Halfling said, "I'm sure we'll see him again."

I shook my head and headed into the branch office. We had work to do and it was cold out here.

ONCE WE GOT in and settled, I pulled up my search from last night hoping to start cross-referencing names. There would be little reason to put the new files from the werewolves in the system. There had been half a dozen deaths and there must be dozens of files here. All by date starting from about a year prior to the first death.

I sighed and pulled the envelope out of my pocket. I supposed I should read this first before I got too ahead of myself. Sparky had headed straight for the lab when we got in and Silver decided to go see if he could get a cup of coffee, leaving me alone in the room.

The envelope betrayed nothing, so I gave up the inspection and opened it. In the same neat handwriting as on the envelope there was a note from Sasha asking me to call her when I got a chance. Seemed a little elaborate.

Shrugging off my coat, I pulled my phone and her card out of my pocket and stared at her contact information for a moment with trepidation before dialing.

It rang not fully once before the line was picked up. "Hello?" I recognized Sasha's voice.

I hesitated before I said quietly, "This is Ketayl. You wanted me to call you, ma'am?"

"No need to be formal. Sasha is fine. I take it my courier found you." She sounded more cheerful than I expected.

"Yes. Thank you for the files, we'll begin working with them immediately."

"Actually, I wanted to talk to you about those." She paused. "If you happen to find any reference to someone missing, will you let me know? We're trying to track down people on our end, but our resources are limited and we're trying to be discreet. I don't want to alert these people that they may be targeted. We're starting with the oldest ones in the range I thought would be sufficient."

Her statement caught me off-guard. I had not thought about how rejected petitioners might feel. "I'll start working through the newest ones then. I understand the need for discretion and I appreciate the assistance the pack is offering."

Sasha gave a short laugh before she said, "Not too many people impress Nikolai these days and even less both of us. I don't suppose your team has anything else?"

"Not at the moment, but I've been thinking about visiting the locations of where some of the most recent bodies were found." Perhaps telling her this would be too much, but they knew the area far better than either myself or Silver, though we could probably manage on our own.

Stoney came in and raised an eyebrow at me.

"I can arrange a guide. When would you like to do that?" I fought between relief at her willingness to help us and the thought of having to face them again.

I bit my lower lip for a moment before I said, "This afternoon if possible. It'll give us a chance to get through some of the files and see if anything comes up."

"If you're going to give me that much time, I'll guide you myself," Sasha sounded amused. "Just come up to the estate when you're ready."

"Thank you," I said, trying to sound as sincere as I could.

"I'll see you this afternoon," Sasha said and hung up.

"Well I'll be damned," Stoney broke his silence. "You're something else."

It was my turn to raise an eyebrow at him.

Stoney turned and closed the door. "The others don't need to hear this." He came further into the room, his voice dropping to a lower level. "I got a call from Sasha late last night. She wanted to talk about you."

I looked down at my phone which was still in my hand.

"She might've called you herself, but she didn't have your number. She does now, I'm thinking." Stoney motioned at my phone.

"I was speaking with her when you came in." There had been no indication of her conversation with him about me.

Stoney glanced in the new box and whistled before returning to me. "Ketayl, I don't think you realize exactly what happened. During the meeting yesterday you ended up getting your standing above Nikolai."

My eyes went wide. "I hadn't meant to..."

Stoney raised a hand for me to quiet. "They ain't worried about you trying for dominance. Not to mention, you're not wolf. Even Sasha had a hard time explaining it to me. Rarely do they encounter someone who has the power of an Alpha, but none of the dominance. Silver and I are Alpha-types, but we don't have the dominance to match Sasha, who is still more dominant than any other Alpha out there except for Nikolai. You should see her quiet a room of Alphas with a look."

I would be curious to see that, but not so sure I would want to be in a room with that much raw power being thrown about.

"Sparky would be classified significantly lower, which was why he reacted the way he did. I think your unique position is why they chose to trust you so quickly. Though how you managed to get them to jump through hoops and provide more information like this I would love to know. Usually getting anything from them is next to impossible. They're friendly, but extremely private."

"Nikolai overheard us discussing the case at supper last night." Should I tell him he also paid our bill?

Stoney laughed. "I had a feeling the old bastard would follow you. You caught his attention pretty quick. He wouldn't harm you and yours - it was only out of curiosity."

I clenched my jaw and stared at the screen. It bothered me Stoney thought Nikolai might follow us and said nothing.

"Oh, don't make that face, Ketayl. If I told you, you would've been getting stressed out over it. I remember you ain't used to dealing with the wolves yet, despite what's happened so far."

I shook my head and continued to stare blankly at the screen.

There was a noise at the door as if someone tried it, followed by a knock.

"Sounds like your boy is back. You planning to take either of them with you this afternoon?"

I sat back and looked at the door and then Stoney. "Silver - I may have need of his specialty. If you don't mind me leaving Sparks here to work."

"He's good. Might teach my crew a thing or two in the process. Speaking of, mind if I send one or two with you? It'll be good for them to get out and in the field with someone else. I can also spare some for your lab tech if you want."

"I don't think there will be a problem," I said, unsure. I really did not know about training someone, but if I just looked at it as more help, I could make do. "An extra set of eyes could be useful, and we've got a lot of information to go through."

"I'll round up a few volunteers and have them report to you."

There was another knock at the door, this one more rapid and urgent sounding. I stood up to go answer it, feeling bad for leaving them outside, but Stoney waved me down and opened the door. "Sorry boys, needed your boss' ear for a few minutes."

I mentally reminded myself I was not their boss. Sparky raced in and over to the desk. "I've got a hit on Human DNA in the fabric."

I raised an eyebrow. It was too quick for him to have a full result yet.

Sparky did not slow down when he continued, "Okay, that's all I've got outside of some oil stains and other stuff. I'm thinking the guy might have been a mechanic or something. The tests are running right now for the full results. I'm not expecting it to be finished until almost noon. I'm not sure how I managed to pull it off."

"Neither am I," Stoney said and waved as he left.

Sparky looked back at Stoney before returning his attention to me. "Anyway, while that's running, what do you want me to work on?"

I glanced up at Silver and motioned for them to sit down. I came around the front of the desk and leaned back against it. "Old Stoney is going to be giving us more hands as this is a lot of information to sift through. I also spoke with Sasha and her people are trying to find out who might be missing, but they don't have the resources we do. We need to start comparing names to the search results starting with the most recent ones. I'd like to have something when I go to meet with her this afternoon, but it needs to be discreet. They don't want to alert these people that they might be targeted."

"You're not planning on going alone," Silver said, toying with the end of his braid. I knew that one - he would not sit this one out if I had even considered it.

"No. You're going with me, along with at least one person from Old Stoney's team. Sasha's arranging a guide so we can go to some of the areas where the more recent bodies were found. As much as I think it's going to be a dead end, I don't want to rule out a similar spell to Brown's. Sparks, I want you to stay here and see what you can come up with, given the information we have. I'll send my search results to you." It sounded like a reasonable course of action.

Both men sat there staring at me.

"What?" I bit my lower lip and reviewed what I said, trying to figure out what caused their reactions.

Silver sat forward and glanced at Sparky before turning back to me. "Don't usually see you take charge like that."

"I, uh, I didn't mean to come off as..." I trailed off and looked between the men nervously.

Silver waved me off. "It's a good thing. We need someone who can direct everyone."

I really did not want to change my working relationships with these two. If I went too far turning into their boss, I worried there would be no return to the easygoing relationship we had.

"Sparky, Campbell was attempting to make coffee in the break room," Silver said.

"Not the coffee!" Sparky quickly got up and left the room.

I looked at my partner as he got up and closed the door. That was the second time this morning. I said, "You didn't need to lie to get him out of the room."

"I didn't - she makes horrible coffee."

"Just say it," I said, resigned to whatever criticism he had.

Silver stood over me. "Why are you so hesitant to take on this role?"

"Because I don't want to change things," I blurted out. I took a moment to organize my thoughts before I explained, "The dynamic we have. I don't want to ruin that."

I caught the movement of Silver toying with the end of his braid before he took a deep breath. "Ketayl, it was bound to change someday. We both knew starting there would be points we would need a bigger team to handle something. It's one thing to be equal between the two of us, but one of us was going to need to take charge."

I crossed my arms and looked away. He had a point - I just did not want to concede.

"If it comes down to a fight though, will you allow me to take lead?" I had not expected the question.

My head snapped up to meet his eyes. "Of course, I'm..." I looked away again. "I obviously lack the skills for that."

Silver spoke softly when he asked, "You still haven't watched the video from your encounter with the slave traders, have you?"

"No," I admitted, wrapping my arms around my waist.

"When we get back, I'd like to go over it with you."

He would. Why could no one let that go? "I'd rather not see it if you don't mind."

"Ketayl..." Silver said quietly, closing the gap between us to put his hands on my shoulders. A knock at the door interrupted anything further he had to say.

Silver answered it.

"I save the coffee and you lock me out," Sparky griped at him.

This was getting nothing done. "Get yourselves settled and let's get to work," I ordered while I walked forward and grabbed a stack of files from the new box. Why was it so important for everyone to push me in this direction?

10

THE DRIVE UP to the Alpha Prime's residence was silent. I glanced in the rear-view mirror and saw Holly staring out the window looking lost. I did not know what to start for a conversation and Silver had closed himself off as soon as I chose to take her. I could tell by the set of his jaw he was unhappy about my decision.

I sighed as I pulled into the long, curved drive and parked in the same spot Stoney parked in yesterday. I turned and looked at both of them who silently unbuckled themselves. "Can you two work it out, please?" I shoved the door open and got out of the truck to gather my gear bag from the back.

Normally I enjoyed silence, but the tension had started getting to me. I had work to do, and I at least needed Silver focused. I clenched my jaw and pushed back the rising anger at the situation I found myself in. Everyone kept expecting far more out of me than I could deliver, and now I had a team to somehow control and direct on top of an investigation and having to quickly learn how to deal with werewolves.

I paused with my hands clenched into fists on my gear bag and took a deep breath, trying to calm my agitated power. Silver should be the one in charge, not me - he was better with people. I felt lacking with not having gone through any formal training.

Silver said something softly. Almost too softly for me to hear at all.

"What did you just call me?" I snapped at him.

He stepped back. "Ketayl. What did you think I called you?"

I shook my head and gathered my gear bag. Great, now I was hearing things. I could have sworn he called me by my unearned name.

"Hey, hold on," Silver said, forcibly stepping in front of me and putting his hands on my shoulders. "You need to calm down first. Look, I'm sorry I've been acting like a jerk." He glanced over at where I assumed Holly stood.

I deflated and pinched the bridge of my nose. I did not have time to babysit on top of everything else. "Just tell me I won't have a problem with the two of you."

"You won't," they both answered at the same time.

As we reached the top of the stairs the door opened. Lexi stood there smiling. "You're earlier than we expected."

I slowed my pace, unsure if we needed to turn around. "I'm sorry, if you need us to reschedule…"

Lexi waved my apology off. "It's fine. Sasha's been itching for an escape from the paperwork, though she was pulled into a last minute meeting. Come on in. Can I get any of you something while you wait? Coffee, tea, water?"

I glanced back at the two to see if they wanted anything. Both asked for coffee. "Water would be wonderful, thank you." I doubted they kept lavender tea and I forgot to pack any pre-made bags. Suddenly I started to regret the oversight.

Sasha's assistant showed us to a small waiting area across the hall from the offices before disappearing. A screen played the news on silent with captions on the bottom.

Silver stood next to me and Holly sat quietly away from us - her attention on the screen. I glared up at him and went over to sit next to her. "Hey," I said, keeping my voice low.

Holly seemed surprised by my presence. "Oh, um, look, I'm really sorry about this. I jumped at the opportunity when Old Stoney asked for volunteers to help. I didn't mean to cause an issue."

"You're fine," I said. Silver, on the other hand, needed to grow up.

I let the conversation fall there and looked up at the screen. The weather was going to be cold with a possibility of snow. Great, though there was promise of some warmer temperatures coming.

Lexi came back a minute later with a couple of bottles of water and a basket carrying coffee and other items for people to fix it the way they liked. "I'll go check on how Sasha's doing, but it sounded like it was going to be a while the last time I was in there."

I smiled at her. "Thank you. I don't mind waiting." I wanted to push off another interaction with Sasha or Nikolai if I could. After dealing with the tension between these two, I did not think myself ready to get into another staring contest too soon.

"Is there a bathroom I can use?" Silver asked.

"Yes, I'll show you. And if I'm not here and you ladies need it, down the hall on the left." Lexi pointed in the direction of the bathrooms.

I nodded. Silver disappeared with Lexi. I shook my head and pinched the bridge of my nose.

"Ma'am?" Holly asked hesitantly.

"Please, just Ketayl is fine." I took a sip of water to think about Silver's behavior. "He's such a child sometimes," I commented quietly. "I'm sorry. He doesn't seem to want to talk about it so do you think you can explain what's going on between the two of you?"

Holly fidgeted with her hands before getting up to go make herself a cup of coffee. I followed her, waiting for her to speak. Silence hung for a couple of minutes - rather long, but I was patient.

"It's... complicated. During the training session I fairly well made a fool out of myself. I clung to him or Rathal in hopes I could learn something."

I leaned back against the wall next to the counter Lexi set the basket on and waited. I wrinkled my nose at the smell of the coffee and took a step away.

"Since Brad and Darius were always working together, and frankly Savanas scares me, I tried to get to know Rathal, but he was always distant. So I looked to my classmates. Silver's smart, funny, and completely dedicated to what he does. It doesn't hurt he's handsome also," Holly said, grinning at me. "Always at the top of the class and I thought I should get to know him better. Maybe he could help me through training. I ended up falling for him in the process. And let's not talk about my track record with relationships." She gave a short laugh.

Her motivations had been different than the little I heard.

Holly continued, "I overheard conversations between him and Rathal. Found out he was interested in someone, but it didn't sound like it was going anywhere and he didn't want to push this girl. I thought I might have a chance and, well, you probably remember how I acted at the badge ceremony."

I shrugged. To me it did not matter. "I didn't know he was interested in anyone," I commented. Why would he not tell me something like that? Part of me was annoyed because of his interest in my life, but his personal life was his own. Perhaps now I had something to go back at him with if he insisted on prying.

Holly looked at me with surprise. "For some reason I thought he would have told you by now. In any case, I still care about Silver in a way, but I know he's too dedicated. I think he still sees me as the person who pestered him endlessly."

I crossed my arms and thought about what she said as well as our previous conversation.

"It's just... this might be my last chance to figure out where I fit in the TIO," Holly said quietly. "I still struggle, even now."

I bit my lower lip, trying to figure out this puzzle. "What do you like to do? There are so many options besides being a field agent."

"I..." Holly looked down at the bag she carried. She pulled out a thick pad of paper. "I'm afraid this is all I'm good at." She handed it to me.

Raising an eyebrow at her I opened the cover and examined the pencil drawing. I flipped a few pages and some of them were in ink. People and places all rendered incredibly realistically. There were a few different drawings of Silver, a couple of Rathal and the Ocean's Edge crew. More of the faces I remembered from their training class. One of me and Silver at the badge ceremony.

I paused at that one for a moment not sure what to make of the look on Silver's face while he looked down at me. I think I had been speaking with Sparky at the time. Then there were more which I assumed were from her time here. "These are incredible."

"But it's not exactly a useful skill in the TIO," Holly said sadly.

"Actually," I said. "This tells me you're very detail-oriented and probably have a photographic memory. Could you draw someone from a description?"

"I haven't tried," Holly admitted.

I grinned. I might have gotten someone better than I hoped. "Perhaps when we have time I can give you a description and see how you do." I kept flipping through the pages. There was a more recent one of just me though it looked like it was in progress. Light lines showed there should be someone else there.

"Uh," Holly said nervously.

Closing the pad, I handed it back to her. "Thank you for sharing."

Then I realized she was looking over my shoulder toward the doorway. I turned and saw Silver standing there with his arms crossed. I raised an eyebrow at him and waited for him to speak his mind, my hands on my hips.

"Damn, don't do that," Silver said, breaking eye contact and walking in.

What did I do?

Lexi stopped any further conversation. "Agent Ketayl, Sasha's ready now. If your companions wouldn't mind staying here, she wants to talk to you privately."

I glanced back at the two and Silver said, "It's fine. I have some things I need to talk about with Campbell."

I leveled a look at him that I hope conveyed my displeasure at this continuing issue. He raised his hands in defense.

Silver needed to right this.

Grabbing my gear bag, I followed Lexi. Once we were out of the waiting room, she asked quietly, "Problems?"

"There won't be when I get back," I said.

"Some personalities just don't mix. We handle all the incoming petitions, but many of the new wolves go to other packs after a period of adjustment. To change the subject, I heard something about one of yours making friends with one of ours last night." Lexi grinned at me as she opened the door.

I groaned. I had hoped it would stay between the werewolves involved and my team.

"Oh come now, Ketayl, not many can drink a wolf under the table," Sasha commented from behind her desk. "And he came back from his duty this morning with interesting stories." She seemed amused by the chain of events.

"I take responsibility for the actions of my team," I started and then stopped when Sasha held up her hand.

The Beta leaned forward smirking. "Think of it as building a relationship between our people. Is your person alright? I don't want to take Zack's claims that your man was fully functioning at face value."

"He is, thank you," I said with a short bow. "I'm still unsure how."

"That's impressive," Sasha said and waved to a seat in front of her desk. "Please sit and relax. No need to stand on ceremony."

I took the seat as suggested and put my bag down in front of me. I could sense her power, but it was nothing like the first time we met. "We haven't gotten much so far. The files we're working with may be too new for someone to have filed a missing person's report and others are coming up as deceased. Sparks managed to pull Human DNA off of the fabric, but we don't have anyone to compare it to. He's still running tests to see if we can get something to give us a lead." I handed her a folder with only a few pieces of paper in it.

"And the curse continues," Sasha muttered, looking over the report I handed her.

I blinked, unsure of the reference she made. "Excuse me?"

Sasha's head shot up. Something in her face told me she had not planned on saying it aloud. "I'm sorry, it's more of my own personal thoughts. Once upon a time becoming a werewolf was considered a curse. People would go missing and those who survived the change and returned were viewed as monsters. Now we have all these safeguards in place for those who wish to join our ranks and it still keeps happening."

"What would be a reason to reject a petition?" I asked. "I'm sorry, I've been focused on trying to match names or descriptions of the people I haven't had the time to read through the files fully."

Sasha sat back and eyed me curiously. "Usually it's because they won't survive the change. Turning isn't as simple as biting someone and transferring the virus we carry. Not only does the body need to survive having its genetic code rewritten but so does the mind."

Lexi spoke next, "A number of people who petition have terminal illnesses. We process their petitions as fast as we can, but often times their bodies are too weak to survive."

"Lexi was one of the lucky ones who managed to be strong enough to go through the process," Sasha said smiling up at her assistant. "The part a lot of people don't understand though is the mind needs to be able to adapt as well - the heightened senses, understanding shifting forms is painful and what their body goes through during it, a willingness to hunt... that's just a portion of it."

"Then there's also learning to live in a pack structure," Nikolai said as he walked in from the side door again. "Ketayl." He nodded at me.

I returned the gesture, my nervousness shooting up higher now. Somehow Sasha and Lexi had me comfortable in their presence, but I could feel the power rolling off of Nikolai. My own reacting the same way as it had last night - pushing, but not forcibly.

"I'm curious as to what you think you'll find by visiting these sites," he said leaning against Sasha's desk.

I held his gaze until he turned to look at Sasha. Perhaps there was something to Silver's observations.

Hesitantly I said, "I'm not certain to be honest. There's a slim chance there might be something arcane given what Talon reported. There is so much destruction to the bodies we're having a hard time pinpointing anything beyond another werewolf attacked them."

"It's the same one who turned them. It's hard to guess why though - it doesn't follow any of the normal patterns," Sasha said, her attention on me. "Some of the areas are difficult to get to. We'll do what we can, but I'd like your permission to bring at least one of ours in wolf form to help get your people there."

"We don't..." Nikolai began.

Sasha cut him off. "We don't need to unnerve them and keep them from focusing on their jobs."

"Hmph." Nikolai looked away from all of us.

I looked between the three werewolves before me. "I'm grateful for the assistance."

"I'll go deal with that," Nikolai said and left.

Sasha visibly relaxed once he left. "He always comes back from Council sessions so testy. He may be my mate and my Alpha, but sometimes I want to throttle him."

"Give him a few more days and he'll be back to normal," Lexi commented. "Well, as long as Marcus doesn't call him again."

"Anyway, shall we gather your people and get ready to go? It'll be probably 15 minutes to a half hour before Nikolai rounds up someone large enough to be able to carry one of you and they shift. We'll take one of our trucks to get as close as we can before heading in on foot. Between the weight and the fur, I'd like to spare your vehicle."

I stood up when Sasha did. "Sounds good."

I SHIVERED against the cold wind. I had not thought it would be cold enough for there to be a dusting of snow on the ground in places. I started to miss my gloves, scarf, and over-sized sweaters.

We waited next to a dark green truck with an open bed for the werewolf who would be accompanying us. I lost track of how long we had been out here.

"I started to think nothing actually phased you," Sasha said quietly. I found humor in her hazel eyes.

"Never did like the cold," I admitted. Though I was warmer with the new hairstyle at least on my back. So far just binding it a couple of fist spaces from the bottom worked out. A lot better than simply leaving it down. The bun had begun to feel too restrictive or severe for some reason.

Sasha laughed out loud, drawing the attention of the others. Lexi had not been standing far, but Silver and Holly were off to the side talking quietly. I started to wish I had a werewolf's sense of hearing to know how things were progressing between them. If only to know if there remained issues I needed to deal with.

At least from here it looked like they worked out their differences. It gave me one less thing to worry about. Part of me hoped Silver overheard my conversation with Holly earlier - perhaps there was a chance to fix what happened.

Mentally I kicked myself. I should not get involved in interpersonal issues like this.

Something warm bumped my side and I looked down, jumping when I saw a huge gray wolf crouching under the truck - he came up almost to my shoulder when he stepped out. Ice blue eyes stared at me intently and then he tilted his head, his tongue rolling out of his mouth.

"Oh dear," Sasha said. "Okay, let's go." She waited for the wolf to get in the back before closing the tailgate behind him.

The truck would seat six people in the two rows. I sat in the back between Silver and Holly, huddling into myself to not touch either one. We drove along a dirt path heading for the most recent site.

After a while I stiffened up as I felt eyes on me. I turned around to see the wolf in the back staring at me. Then he pressed his nose to the glass, turning his head, and letting his tongue hang out the side of his mouth.

"Hey, knock it off back there!" Sasha yelled at him. There was a whine before he turned around and laid down. "I swear your mood swings are of legend," she muttered.

"Who is it?" Holly inquired. "Oh, I'm sorry, I probably shouldn't have asked that."

"Don't worry about it," Sasha replied. The truck rolled to a stop. "This is as far as we can go. It's not too far and a fairly easy walk."

I waited for someone to let me out. Silver handed me my gear bag from the back. The wolf jumped out easily and then came around to bump my legs.

"I think he likes you," Silver mused while I gripped the truck to keep from falling over.

I glared at my partner before following Sasha and Lexi. Our wolf guide moved ahead of them, sniffing at the ground sporadically.

After about five minutes of walking, the group ahead of us stopped. "Well, this is it," Sasha said. I had my tablet out and opened the case file in question. I pulled up the picture and as soon as I stepped past the women in front of me I put my hand to my chest and closed my eyes to focus on controlling the sudden spike of power attempting to break my control. My tablet fell from my hands. What on Terra would cause this kind of reaction?

Hands pulled me back and sat me down at the base of a tree. Calloused fingers brushed my bangs out of my face. "Ketayl, what happened?"

"Is she alright?" I heard Lexi ask.

I opened my eyes to answer, but the world spun too quickly so I closed them again. My power was still agitated, but controllable now that I was away from whatever caused the spike. How did I not see what was there before I walked into it?

"What's with her eyes?" Holly's voice broke through the chaos inside my head.

"I'm not sure. I've never seen it happen in a situation like this," Silver said.

"What's that supposed to mean?" Sasha demanded.

A cold wet nose pressed against my cheek briefly and I turned to look at the wolf. I felt like I knew that stare. I took a moment before turning my attention back to the affected area. "There's something arcane-related over there."

The wolf moved to go sniff the area. I rested my forehead on my knees and closed my eyes.

"Holly," Silver said, and part of my mind noted he used her first name. "Can you stay with Ketayl? I think she's got it under control now."

"Got what under control?" Sasha asked, and I could hear her losing patience.

Silence fell for a moment and I knew Silver looked at me. He stared at me often enough when he was bored. "Me," I said. "Something set my power off."

"You're a mage?" Lexi asked. She sounded surprised.

"Arcanist," I specified. "Silver, can you tell if there's anything divine over there?" I needed to get myself back together so I could use my power to try and feel out what was there. At least if I understood what was going on, I could try to prepare myself for the chance I ran into the same phenomenon again.

I heard movement followed by Silver saying, "It's like a ghost of what was here. I've never encountered something like it before. There's not enough left to even try to piece together what it was."

Necromancer. I managed to pick up my head and looked at my partner. This had become our pursuit.

I struggled to get up and simply just slid out of the straps of my gear bag. "Hey, take it easy," Holly said and tried to push me back to a sitting position.

"Good luck getting her to do that," Silver commented. "Come on, you won't be satisfied otherwise." He held out his hand to me.

I took the offered hand as it would get me standing faster and he pulled me up too quickly causing me to stumble into him.

"Sorry, sometimes I forget how light you are," Silver said.

I pinched the bridge of my nose and shook my head. The worst of the dizziness faded. I stepped away from him and back toward the area where I hit whatever it was. I held my hand out in front of me, feeling the world through the arcane to get some kind of sense of what I had run into. There was no remnant I could analyze and yet something still existed.

"The same - it's like an echo of whatever it was." And the echo of the spell felt angry, evil - I should not encounter emotions on anything arcane. "But it feels different than the spells we encountered in Ocean's Edge. Still has some emotional responses though."

Sasha looked down at the wolf accompanying us and then glared at the ground with her jaw clamped shut.

"Is there something else?" I asked. These people had been open with me so far - it would only be fair for me to do the same.

She looked to the wolf and then Lexi before coming back to me. "Trust me, I want to ask, but I've been reminded that now is not the time. Not when there might be ears nearby."

I nodded, accepting her point.

Silver picked up and handed me my tablet before stepping into the area - whatever it was, it did not appear to affect him. He knelt down to touch the ground. "This is where the body was, correct?" His glance back at me reminded me of the device in my hands.

Dusting off the dirt, I hoped nothing happened to it during its fall. I pulled up the picture in question and walked around the edge of where the arcane echo was, trying to line it up. "Yes."

I glanced over at Holly who looked lost. Thinking quickly, I said, "Holly, can you get the camera out of my bag, please?"

She jumped and then rushed over to where I left my bag and started digging through. Mine I knew had the arcane filter already on it. She brought it over and held it out.

I shook my head. "Go ahead and tell me if you see anything. My sight and the filter may not play well together right now."

Holly raised an eyebrow at me before doing what I told her. "It looks the same." Then she tilted the camera to look at the filter on the front. "What's it supposed to do?"

I pursed my lips. I did not like the fact I could not see what it was. I answered her absently, "It allows the camera to see the arcane. If you point it at me you'll get an idea."

"Gods..." Holly said in a hushed tone. Lexi wandered over to her, likely curious.

"Well, that's worrisome if neither you nor the camera can see anything," Silver commented.

I bit my lower lip while I thought through what I knew offhand, coming up with nothing. "I'll have to research and find out if there's something which can cause an effect like this."

"Should we continue on to the other sites?" Holly asked. "I don't see anything else here that wasn't in the pictures." She paused and looked at me nervously.

I stopped and considered my earlier observation of Holly. "You're right. If you don't mind?" I looked at our werewolf guides.

"We should be able to get to two more before it gets dark," Lexi commented.

Sasha nodded, eying me cautiously. Perhaps I should have been more forthcoming about myself, but it had not seemed necessary at the time and I honestly had not wanted the weight of what I was dragging me down.

I grabbed my bag, packing away the camera, and let the others get ahead of me. I turned back to the area one more time. What on Terra was it? It had to have been tied to either the body or the attacker, but I could not tell which.

"Ketayl?" Sasha asked, hanging back. She waved the others ahead.

Shaking my head, I said, "I'm sorry. It's a puzzle I need to solve."

"About as much as the one surrounding you," Sasha commented.

I rubbed my arms and said as quietly as I could, "Let's just say I know a thing or two about being a monster."

Sasha gave me a sad smile and remained silent the rest of the way.

We managed to get through two more sites and were on our way to a third since there was still daylight. The last two sites had nothing like the first one and since we were working our way backwards, I doubted there would be anything at this one.

Holly had been incredibly helpful in analyzing each scene quickly, matching it up to the photographs, but most of the time it was moving some fallen leaves or a broken branch which had not been there before.

Soon enough we trudged through the forest again. I stayed at the back of the group as they began climbing up some rocks. I bit my lower lip while considering my options. I could use my power to get up there, but I still felt somewhat unbalanced and I was fairly certain I had unnerved the werewolves. I could only imagine the questions to come when we got back.

And to think they were worried about unnerving me.

I stared up at the rocks - I was not good at climbing and never made it past this part of the obstacle course.

Silver stood next to me as Holly scrambled up the short climb easily. "You don't think you can make it, do you?"

I shook my head. The wolf stuck his head over the edge and tilted it in question.

A hand on my shoulder pulled my attention from the problem ahead. "I'll give you a boost, okay?" His shield appeared on his left arm.

We had done this once when running the obstacle course together. That wall had been much higher, and I was able to grab the top of it before I fell back down because I could not get over the rest of the way.

"Leave your bag - I can carry it up," Silver said before he squatted down.

I nodded, putting it down next to him. I still doubted I could make it, but I could save myself with my power if I had to. Backing up to get a running start, I landed in a crouch on his shield before he pushed me up and I finished the jump off of it.

I stumbled when I landed, but I was at the top of the rock ledge.

"You need to work on your landings," Sasha mused, looking down at Silver to see what got me up here. "Huh, didn't see paladin coming either. You two are certainly an interesting pair."

Once Silver scrambled up the rocky rise, I took my gear bag back from him. "Thank you," I said quietly.

"What are partners for?" Silver smiled and reached around to pull me into an awkward half-hug. I moved away from him quickly, glaring at his amusement at the situation. Every time I thought he matured, he pulled something like this.

We followed the wolf around the ledge and up a steep, but walkable, incline. I worried we would not have enough daylight left to get back and tried to remember if had seen a handlight in my bag as we approached the site.

We spent time searching for anything new, but it was the same thing as the last two. I put my camera back in my bag disappointed. I knew coming in there might not be anything, but after the first one, my hopes had been raised.

Something arcane moving caught my attention and my head snapped in the direction it was coming from. I noticed all of us except for Holly had done the same thing. Silver called his weapons and drew his sword.

It moved fast and directly for us. Running to get in front of the group, I put my arms out and cast my shield spell to deflect whatever headed our way. Surrounding the entire group took more energy than I cared to admit.

A moment later a furry mass slammed hard into the shield and I struggled to maintain it, taking a step back to steady myself. A second furry creature also hit the shield full force and my feet slid back on the dirt. I clenched my teeth - I would not be able to hold the spell if either one struck it again. Small, yet strong hands were on my shoulders to steady me.

How did I not catch there were two of them? Two werewolves. I heard growling to my side.

The second, much larger, werewolf stood up to shake itself off and Silver moved forward through my spell, slamming his shield into it. He took off running back the way he had come. Our wolf guide gave chase.

The first werewolf labored in his breathing. Long deep gashes trailed down his sides accompanied by bite marks all over his body. I dropped my spell, not seeing a threat from the injured wolf.

Sasha and Lexi went to his side immediately. This was the one I sensed the arcane on.

Then I realized it was Holly who tried to keep me stable. "Thank you," I said over my shoulder, moving away.

"It's about all I could do. I'm a little outclassed here," Holly said, her voice wavering.

Silver still stood at the ready, his eyes searching for an unseen threat. I turned to Holly. "Did you get a good look at the second werewolf?"

"I... I'm not sure. It happened so fast." Holly sounded scared.

"Breathe. Take a moment to calm down. When we get back, if you don't mind me borrowing your skills, I'd like you to see if you can draw that werewolf for me."

Holly nodded quickly. "Yeah. Yeah, I can try."

"We need to get him back now. I'm not sure he's going to make it," Sasha said, worry plain in her voice. She and Lexi picked up the werewolf.

Our wolf guide returned by the time we got down to the rocky climb. "Go ahead. I'm only going to slow you down," I told the group. I may have only used my shield spell, but now I felt unbalanced and somewhat drained. In our hustle, I began getting winded. My gear bag felt like it weighed a ton.

There was a nudge at the back of my legs and I looked down at our wolf guide.

"He wants you to get on his back. He can make the jump," Sasha translated.

I hesitated, feeling awkward about this, but time was not on our side. Before I could move, Silver picked me up, gear bag and all, and put me on the wolf's back. I wrapped my arms around the furry neck as he started to move and tucked my legs along his sides, hanging on as he bound down the rocky climb. The wolf did not stop there and continued running. I kept my eyes closed and my head against the back of his neck as he ran, holding on for dear life.

Once he stopped at the truck, I shakily got off and said, "Thank you. I guess I'm not as strong as everyone thinks I am." I rubbed his head.

He put his nose under my chin and pushed my head up before taking off in the direction of the group.

A few minutes later he returned with Holly and the rest were not far behind. I had already loaded my gear bag in the backseat and opened the tailgate by the time they got to the truck.

This was not what I expected when I set out this morning. I only hoped it brought us closer to solving this.

11

____

"I NEED someone to meet us outside with a stretcher," Lexi ordered over the phone as Sasha drove. We had to be getting close to the estate. I was not sure how much more of this ride I could handle.

Sasha sped faster down the dirt paths than I was comfortable with and I closed my eyes, holding onto the seat in front of me. The truck barreled through the open gate a few minutes later and slid to a hard stop in front of a side door. Lexi hopped out before the truck stopped and Silver before Sasha put it in park.

Two werewolves bounded out the door with a stretcher, immediately heading for the bed of the truck. I managed to keep the group in sight to know where to turn next in the estate.

A large, thick metal door sat open and inside was the most basic room possible. They set the wolf down on the table in the room and I moved out of the way for the person rolling in a tall, enclosed cart.

Holly remained near the door while Silver shed his armored jacket and stood next to the table. I put my bag in the corner and removed my coat as well, pushing up my sleeves. I did not have time to be distracted. There was something arcane on this wolf and it felt as dark and twisted as the necromatic spells I encountered before.

"He's too weak to take healing - I'd end up killing him," Silver said. "I don't know how he was running at all."

"Adrenaline," Sasha commented. "A werewolf is tougher. Try."

Silver touched the unknown wolf's head and it snapped up at him weakly. He grabbed the wolf's muzzle and held it down. "I'm trying to heal you so knock it off."

My camera - I quickly dug it out of my bag and began taking pictures. The injuries to this wolf were far less severe than the others though running headlong into my shield spell did not help. I could not see what was arcane about him - the spell buried deep in his body.

I clenched my jaw in frustration. How was I supposed to take images of the spell?

"Something is blocking my attempt. Ketayl?" Silver gave me a desperate look.

I handed the camera to Holly and approached the table next to Silver. "It's in his body out of my sight. I'm not sure if I can dismantle it." I was not even sure the spell was tied to Silver's problem.

I had my hands out and over the wolf before Silver could tell me. I followed the various twists and turns of the spell woven throughout his body. If the spell had been in full effect, he would have been little more than a puppet. Eventually a thread led me to his mind - it was partially disconnected, which might explain how he broke away from whoever cast this on him.

I was right that it was for control, but there was something else built into the spell I could not see. "Silver, focus on his mind. I'm only seeing part of the spell."

There was silence for a few moments. The werewolves worked to try and save the affected werewolf through conventional means. I broke apart the threads to try and weaken the main spell. As soon as I broke one of the threads down, another took its place.

"This is insane," Sasha said. "His body should have started some healing on its own by now."

Silver spoke again. "What I can get is something is draining his life. Might be stopping his healing abilities."

"I can't break the spell down fast enough. It keeps regenerating," I said.

"Can you disrupt it long enough to let me heal him?" Silver asked, his voice making it sound more like an order.

I shifted my attention back to the main part of the spell. I wrapped my power around to contain what I could and began pulling the spell away to disrupt it. I clenched my teeth at the strain of trying to hold the whole spell. A few of the puppet strings snapped.

"I still can't get past whatever is blocking it," Silver called out.

Stretching my rapidly depleting reserves, I tried to pull harder. Maybe if I pulled far enough it would break.

"That's it, Ketayl. The block is lifting. Just a little more," Silver encouraged. I had to hang on.

"We're losing him," someone said.

I could not fail here. I would not fail. I just needed more power and I could make it. Seconds which felt like hours ticked by as I pulled as hard as I could to disrupt the spell.

"He's gone."

I refused to let up despite becoming lightheaded from my attempt. There had to be something that could be done. I was not sure how much longer I held it until someone put their hands on mine.

"It's over," Silver said softly. "Let go."

The necromantic spell dissipating actually caused me to stop and what remained was a stronger version of the echo we encountered in the forest, but my reserves were too depleted to be affected by it.

The unknown werewolf was really gone. I stumbled back a few steps until my back hit the wall and I stared at the dead werewolf on the table.

I failed.

My chest heaved, trying to catch my breath from the exertion. I looked down at my shaking hands and ignored the feeling of being almost completely drained. What now? Was there nothing else I could have done?

People were talking, but I understood none of it. I had failed.

Evidence. I needed to gather evidence to bring back to Sparky. There was still work to be done. I took a shaky step forward and stumbled.

Someone managed to catch me before I fell too far. "Ketayl, dammit, go sit down. Even I could feel the sheer amount of power you were using," Silver said. "Holly, can you point that thing over here? I need to check her levels."

I just stayed where I was. I did not have the energy to push myself away.

"What?" Holly asked.

"You had to have felt how much arcane energy Ketayl just used. The camera's filter will let me see how low she is," Silver said firmly.

The camera clicked a few times before I sensed someone else coming closer. It was warm here and damned if I could move right now.

"I don't think it looks good compared to earlier," Holly said quietly.

"Damn," Silver cursed quietly. He shifted and I tried to move again, only succeeding in bringing my hand to his shoulder. I weakly pushed against him. Arms tightened around me. "If I may make a request on her behalf?"

Who was he talking to?

"Go ahead," Sasha responded after a moment.

Silver shifted. I needed to move away and stand on my own. "Is there some place Ketayl can rest? I would also like to call our lab tech and see about getting him and those assisting him out here to start processing evidence."

"You have the girl," Sasha noted.

I more felt than heard a low growl emanate from Silver. "She's already received her orders from Ketayl and I believe I'm the only one here who knows how to care for my partner."

I managed to push myself away from Silver this time. "I can care for myself." I wobbled on my feet and he quickly grabbed me again.

"Like Hell," Sasha snapped. "I'm fairly certain everyone in this estate could feel the sheer amount of power you used. Lexi, show them to the lounge - it'll be the quickest place to get to. And make your call. Your team protected me and mine and did everything within your power to try to save someone none of us knew."

I looked down at the wolf who had been part of our guide. He sat in front of me with his head tilted before touching his nose to the floor.

"Nikolai says 'thank you' and... Would you just go shift already?" Sasha pointed at the door. "I'm tired of relaying stuff for you."

The wolf turned his head toward Sasha and rolled his tongue out. Wait, this wolf was Nikolai?

"You're impossible. Fine, whatever. I've got stuff to do," Sasha threw up her hands and signaled for the others to head out. I had barely paid attention to the two other werewolves who carried the body in.

Lexi picked up mine and Silver's bags as well as our coats after she washed her hands at a sink hidden behind a closet door disguised as part of the wall. "If you'll follow me," she said somberly.

Nikolai hung at my side as much as he could, but three of us could not fit through doorways and Silver refused to let me walk on my own. I supposed I was lucky he decided not to carry me.

I stumbled far too many times for my liking, which only slowed the others down from being able to get rest. I pushed myself away from Silver and leaned against the wall in the hallway. "Go ahead. I'll catch up."

"Stop being stubborn," Silver chided. "I'll carry you."

"Don't..." I started shaking from the exertion of trying to keep myself upright against the wall.

Nikolai whimpered.

Silver picked me up despite my protest. It seemed in a blink we were in the lounge. Plush chairs and couches dotted the large room. A fireplace sat along one wall and a giant screen dominated another. There were tables with games off to the side.

Nikolai padded over to a chair and put his paw on it.

"Are you sure?" Lexi asked. He pawed at the chair lightly and she went over to put the footrest out and shift it into a reclined position. "Okay, but don't forget you were the one who said she could rest in your chair."

Nikolai nudged a nearby cushioned bench over to the side of the chair with his nose. I closed my eyes and tried to ignore what was happening. I could be embarrassed about all of this after I got some rest.

"Feel free to take a seat anywhere. Nikolai is the only one who is territorial about his chair," Lexi said. I heard a door open and close a moment later.

I barely noted the change from being held to being in the chair. The weight of a blanket being thrown over me was the last thing I managed to stay awake for.

"I TAKE RESPONSIBILITY," I heard Silver's hushed voice. "I thought to sit back and let her take full lead and what Ketayl needed was a partner. I'm not making that mistake again so until she's back on her feet, I'm in charge of this investigation."

A weight rested across my hips. Whatever it was, it was warm. I heard the faint scratching of a pencil on paper.

"Boy, you don't want to start this contest with me," Stoney said, also keeping his voice down. "And why wasn't the agent I assigned taking care of collecting evidence?"

"Ketayl assigned her a duty and currently she is doing it," Silver said sharply.

I still felt exhausted, but cracked open my eyes to look over at the two quietly talking in the doorway. The weight across my hips shifted and I got a hand out to pet the wolf. The head seemed overly large for Artemis.

"I don't care what you think, boy. You ain't got the seniority." Stoney's volume rose as he spoke.

"Enough," I managed to get out. My voice barely above a whisper.

Both men turned toward me. I struggled to sit up and then realized the wolf's head across my lap belonged to Nikolai and not Artemis. I would have to apologize later.

I rubbed my eyes, still feeling tired. What had I missed? What time was it?

"Oh, and you're one to talk," Stoney said at a regular volume. "You've got someone in here drawing instead of collecting evidence as is her job."

Nikolai turned his head and growled at Stoney. The Dwarf took a step back, eying Nikolai cautiously. I felt the power rolling off of him, but it seemed focused elsewhere.

I did not have time for dominance games. "I gave her a task based on her unique skills. Or would you rather I wasted the talent you have loaned me?" I swung my legs off of the footrest and stood up, dropping the blanket back on the chair. "Sparky and the two working with him should be more than capable of collecting and processing the evidence we need. I trust my team to know their jobs and take charge when needed."

Stoney's attention was on the wolf growling at him. "What do Nikolai or Sasha think of this?"

I looked down at the wolf who still had his teeth bared at Stoney. "I can't understand him, but I think Nikolai might not be happy with you right now."

Sasha appeared from another doorway. "What is...? Come on, can we not do this?"

"Ketayl?" Holly said quietly coming up next to me. "This is the best I can do. I'm afraid the details are fuzzy."

I took the pad of paper she handed me. It was not the same one from her bag that she had shown me earlier. She had drawn a rendition of the second werewolf. As clearly as I could remember it at least. It was from when he stood up after hitting my shield. "Good job. Now we have an image of the attacker."

"You have what?" Stoney walked forward, keeping his eyes on Nikolai. I turned it around so he could see it. "This is far better than any composite I've ever seen. Still, what in the Hells happened to take you down?"

"Ketayl did everything in her power to try and help save that wolf down the hall before he became evidence," Sasha growled at him.

But it had not been enough. I looked away, but only far enough to keep what was going on in the corner of my vision.

"Does Ketayl still have your support?" Stoney refused to meet either Sasha's or Nikolai's gazes.

"It never came into question," Sasha said. She nodded at the werewolf standing before Stoney. "His words, but I agree."

"Then I will respect that." Stoney turned and left.

I took a deep breath and handed the pad back to Holly. "Silver, can you give me an update?" I asked, taking a seat on the cushioned bench next to the chair. I rubbed my face with my hands.

Silver came over and knelt in front of me. He said softly, "Only if you tell me how low your arcane energy levels still are."

I glared at him.

"Or I can go get the camera and leave you wondering." Silver smirked. I knew he would hold true to what he said.

I rolled my eyes and shook my head. He could be such a pain. "Don't ask me to do much for a few more hours."

"Would you go shift already?!" Sasha yelled at Nikolai. "We need to have a conversation and it works better when you can speak."

Nikolai came over and put his head on my legs, pushing Silver out of the way.

"Oh you have got to be kidding me. I swear you're nothing but an overgrown pup." Sasha sighed and explained, "He doesn't want to shift because you're willing to pet him."

"I, uh..." I looked down at Nikolai who nudged my knees with his nose before planting his head back on my lap. "I'm sorry. I hadn't thought about what I was doing earlier. When I woke up I thought he was my friend's animal companion."

Sasha just waved at Nikolai as if she gave up trying to argue with him.

Tentatively I put my hand on his head and started rubbing it. His eyes closed and he looked as content as I had ever seen a wolf.

Sasha took a seat and signaled for the others to do the same.

Silver started, "I called Sparky about getting him, Mark, and Danny out here. They're collecting evidence as we speak. You unfortunately woke to the disagreement between myself and Old Stoney."

"I've never seen the old man act that way before," Sasha commented. "I've also never seen him question another's authority. Especially someone not wolf."

"It's probably expected when you end up with another dead body," I commented quietly. "I've not exactly been the person everyone thinks I should be."

Suddenly Nikolai snapped his jaws at me before returning to his previous position.

"He's right: you need to stop that. And he still wants to be petted. Do you want to take him home? He'd make a great pet. I promise he's house broken," Sasha said smiling. She laughed out loud when Nikolai turned to glare at her for a moment.

I ran a hand through the soft fur on his head. If I did not think about the fact this was the Alpha Prime of the werewolves, I found petting him to be calming.

"Ketayl," Silver said softly. "What forced you to use so much arcane energy? I didn't think you'd end up draining yourself like that."

I ached thinking about it. "It was the only way I could try to contain the spell. There were threads throughout his body that would have worked like puppet strings if the spell hadn't been partially detached. The main part of the spell was in his mind and I could only see pieces of the other part, which was why I asked what you saw."

"That there was something draining his life. What else?" Silver did not often get this inquisitive.

I closed my eyes and thought for a moment, trying to slowly go back through it. "For every thread I destroyed another took its place. I wasn't strong enough to attack the main part of the spell. Containing it to force a disruption took nearly everything I had." I turned my attention to the floor - it had not been enough.

"I..." Holly started and paused. I signaled for her to continue. "I hope I wasn't out of line, but I tried to take images of the event."

"Someone needed to document - the rest of us were too focused on what we were doing," Silver said.

"May I see them?" It would be hard to make out much detail on the camera's tiny screen, but it would give me an idea of what we were working with.

While Holly went to get the camera out of the bag, Sasha eyed myself and Silver. "I've got to ask: what is the deal with you two?" She pointed between me and Silver. "I've never seen a functional team with such polar opposites in terms of types of power."

Silver looked at me and I waved at him to go ahead. I was too tired to explain. "Ketayl and I started working together almost a year ago. I was brought in as a divine consultant on a case she was working on."

Holly handed me the camera. "Thank you," I said. I turned it on and started reviewing the images while Silver explained how we came to have formed our current team.

Nikolai nudged my hand and I juggled the camera so I could hold it one-handed to review the images. I half-listened to Silver speak about the first case we were on involving a necromancer.

I paused at one of the last images taken in the room. In the small image alone I could get a strong sense of the amount of power I used. I had managed to pull the spell up and out of the unknown were-wolf's body. Once it got blown up, I could start piecing together what it was. With any luck, Silver's aura illuminated the rest and these images showed the whole spell.

"A necromancer?" Sasha asked.

"The spell on the werewolf was a combination of arcane and divine - it's the general definition though not the most accurate," I explained. "It also has to toy with another's life."

Sasha looked down at Nikolai, whose eyes were open. I removed my hand from his fur. There was a long pause before she said, "Well, yeah, it makes sense why these two are working together now. But how do we combat someone like that? Not to mention we have to find this necromancer first."

I turned my attention to Silver who simply shrugged. Holly

pulled out her sketch pad and set about drawing. She deserved the break.

"You know, I missed that," Sasha said. She took a deep breath and then looked at us, but not before shooting a comment at Nikolai. "Now go shift. You've pestered Ketayl long enough." As he padded out of the room, she returned her attention to us. "Does Stones understand the purpose of your team?"

I glanced over at Silver and shrugged. It had never come up. "He might not. I'm not sure how much Lockonis told him ahead of time. We were basically sent on the off-chance we would find something."

"I think her other motive might have been our specialties. Even if it wasn't something specific for our team, we'd still be of use," Silver added.

Sasha snorted and hung her head. "Sometimes I wonder about Lockonis' foresight - most of the time I assume she's doing something to amuse herself, but she's always several steps ahead. In any case, it sounds like we're going to need both of your specialties in conjunction with our abilities to try and pinpoint where this bastard is. The hard part is you're not pack, so when we're in either wolf or even hybrid form it'll be next to impossible for us to communicate. And those forms are far stronger than this." She gestured to herself. "I just can't think of who might be turning these people and why a necromancer would be involved."

"They could be one and the same," I commented, not really thinking it through. Everyone's attention turned to me. "It's just a theory - I've got nothing to back it up. And likely far-fetched since I didn't sense any arcane on the other werewolf."

Sasha pinched the bridge of her nose. "It's probably better if we wait on throwing theories around. Your team is better at running those types of things than I am. I've got some stuff to catch up on and I should let you get back to work. If you need anything, don't hesitate to ask." With that she left.

"We should go check on Sparky," Silver said. He came up next to me and started trying to help me up.

I glared up at him and moved away, slowly bending down to collect my coat and bag. Then I signaled to Holly to follow us. I was still exhausted, but the team could not afford to have me down at this point. Silver took the bag from me.

"After this, supper?" Silver asked.

I glanced at my watch and nodded. "We can't starve Sparks for too long."

Holly laughed lightly.

As we left Silver commented, "You do realize you were petting the Alpha Prime, right?"

I clenched my jaw, fighting down the heat rising to my face. "Don't remind me."

"MAN, I hope the boss recovers soon - I'm starving!" Sparky's voice carried out of the room and into the hallway.

"You could always go check on them. We're done here," a male voice said - I recognized it as one of the people assigned to us, but could not remember who exactly. "Just need to pack up."

Sparky gave a shaky laugh before he said, "Hells no. The werewolf guarding her could probably swallow me whole. I'll wait."

"Sparky afraid of the big bad wolf?" Another man teased.

Silver signaled for us to wait a moment and he strode in. "When the werewolf is the Alpha Prime, he might have reason to."

I heard cursing from the other two. I turned back to Holly to find out if she understood this. She covered her mouth with her hand and laughed softly. Must have been something from training. I resigned myself to not understanding what just happened.

Sticking my head around the corner, I took in the scene before me. The body had been removed, but blood still covered the surrounding floor.

"Oh, hey, boss, feeling better?" Sparky asked when he spotted me. "You don't look so good still."

"A little." I paused, reaching out with my power and finding the same effect as in the forest. "You'll have to forgive me if I stay out here. I don't want to run into that effect again today."

"What happened?" Mark asked.

Silver glanced back at me before answering, "It's somewhat complicated to explain right now." He closed his eyes and reached out toward the empty bed. "I should have checked for it first. I can't sense it unless I'm actively searching." He tossed me an apologetic look.

"Agent Ketayl?"

I turned to see Lexi standing behind me in the hallway wringing her hands. "They're requesting your presence in the office. Agent Silver's as well."

I nodded and signaled at him to follow. I turned to Holly and asked her, "Do you mind helping them finish up?"

"Of course not." Holly rushed in.

We followed Lexi down the hall. I asked her, "What's going on?"

"They're in a conference call and unfortunately that's the most I know. The offices can each be sealed off so no one can listen in," Lexi said quickly.

I took a deep breath and tried to calm myself. How much trouble had I managed to get myself into in the last 24 hours?

Lexi knocked on the door when we arrived. Sasha answered a moment later and ushered us in with a quick thank you to her assistant.

This was not Sasha's office. I glanced around at the more utilitarian room. Nikolai, in his native form again, stood before a large screen on the wall.

Video conference call, great. We had to come fully around to see who was on the screen. Lockonis sat on one side of the split-screen with Stoney on the other. It looked as if the Dwarf was still in his vehicle. Thankfully it was not moving.

"Ket, you look like Hell," Lockonis commented.

Thanks, really. I ran a hand through my bangs, my fingers getting caught on the tangles in the ends. I tugged a little harder to free them.

Nikolai glanced at us quickly before returning to the people on the screen. "Can we get back to the matter at hand?"

Which was?

Lockonis looked over in my direction. "Tell me what you've got."

I glanced up at Silver for a moment before starting my recount of the day. My partner filled in on what he knew.

"No wonder you look like Hell," Lockonis commented offhandedly. "Stoney, this falls under their team's jurisdiction. No more trying to take over their investigation, got it? And don't forget they have the werewolves' support."

"Ketayl has the werewolves support - that kid is a rookie. He's not ready to take charge," Stoney said.

"Time doesn't equal wisdom," Sasha said. "Nikolai and I were present when everything occurred. It was a seamless transfer of power and frankly Silver is more than competent to handle things in Ketayl's absence. The small one has also handled the people with him well and earned the respect of our pack."

I turned my attention to the floor and cringed at my failing. I was the one who should be questioned for my competence.

Stoney crossed his arms, frowning. "Fine, I can assign more qualified people to help them."

"No," I said quickly. Everyone's attention turned to me. I paused for a moment, biting my lower lip. I took a deep breath and forced myself to continue. "Look, I may not have the most experienced or qualified people - however that is quantified - but changing them out now will mean we have to catch up a whole new set of people. And I want to give them a chance. They've all done good work so far."

"But Holly..." Stoney started.

I cut him off. "Has an incredible talent which I intend to fully utilize. Beyond her artistic skills, she is incredibly detail-oriented to the point I think she might have a photographic memory."

"She can't remember simple orders," Stoney argued.

"But she can remember, with incredible clarity, people, places, and events. Without anyone telling her, she took images of what was going on while we tried to save the affected werewolf, which will give me a chance to analyze the spells being used to figure out what level of caster we're dealing with. Holly knows her job - she just needs to be able to do it." My power pushed at me like a gentle tide. The last time I got this argumentative was when one of the branch lab techs verbally attacked Sparky.

"Wait, is this the Holly Campbell I keep seeing reports about?" Lockonis raised an eyebrow.

"Yes," Stoney said in resignation.

Lockonis turned in my direction. "You would manage to find her niche."

I shrugged. All I did was talk to her and listen.

Lockonis gave a loud sigh. "Stoney, leave them alone and let them work. I'm sure you've got other things you can focus on. Don't forget you called me about getting someone out there to deal with that case. I already explained when I said joint it was because I wanted Ketayl and her team to have full autonomy, but that they would need your support. You cause them problems, however, you get to deal with me."

Stoney reached forward and punched a button cutting his connection. Now I was confused - I thought it had been Lockonis' idea to send us.

Sasha commented, "I know he's been thinking about retirement, but I don't think he's ready to let go."

Lockonis sighed. "Yeah, I'm not looking forward to finding a replacement for that branch. There aren't many who can run a training team and keep up relations with a werewolf pack."

"Fewer who can deal with this one," Nikolai said. "She does fairly well." He tilted his head in my direction.

My eyes went wide. No. No, no, no. I could not take another change right now.

"Sorry, Niki, I'm keeping Ket." Lockonis paused. "I'm interested in hearing what you have to say later, kid. For now, have your team get the case file updated and get yourself some rest. Something tells me you're all going to need to be at full strength." Then she waved and cut the connection.

Sasha snorted. "That woman moves in mysterious ways."

Nikolai crossed his arms and stared at the screen which showed the video call program. "I've seen plenty of petty bickering over control, but I think that might have been the worst."

"I've really never seen Stones like this," Sasha said. "Perhaps he has been at the top for too long."

"It is not for us to determine," Nikolai said before turning to me. "And thank you for indulging me earlier. Most are too afraid to come close."

I looked away, feeling the heat rising to my face and he laughed.

"We shouldn't keep you any longer," Sasha said. "I'll escort you."

Nikolai remained in his office and shut the door behind us.

Sasha shook her head. "In truth we all get that way when in wolf form. It's like being an over-sized domesticated dog."

"I... uh..." I gave up and shut my mouth.

"Really, it's fine. A good thing actually, otherwise we'd still be dealing with a grumpy Nikolai. It takes him a week or two to fully settle down after a set of Council sessions. He doesn't like being a politician." Sasha paused momentarily, laughing to herself. "You might be getting a visitor occasionally now though."

We gathered up our remaining team members and headed out to

the now two vehicles. Nikolai waited outside the door at the top of the stairs. "Silver, a word?"

I kept the rest of them moving. Soon the trucks were packed, and Holly looked lost while Silver spoke with Nikolai.

"Hey," I said, "If you want to head back with the others then go ahead. Maybe you can fill them in on what we found. I'd like it if you could upload the images from my camera to the case file. I'll wait for Silver."

"Okay. Yeah, I can do that." Holly's confidence seemed to increase. I got my gear bag out of the truck and gave it to her.

What happened to cause so much change in her between the ceremony and now? Granted, that meeting was too brief to have gotten to know her at all.

I leaned against the driver's door on my loaner vehicle and waved the others for our team off. Sparky knew what needed to be done. Hopefully Stoney would let them be. I did not think he would defy Lockonis, but I knew better than to blindly trust the thought.

I opened the door and slid slowly into the driver's seat hoping to warm up while I waited. This was going to be a long drive back. A hand stopped the door before I could close it.

"You're not driving," Silver said looking down at me. He held out his hand expectantly.

Glaring up at Silver, I dropped the keys in his hand and got out. Fine, he could drive then.

12

I SILENTLY WATCHED the trees go by as Silver drove. I jumped when my phone rang. Digging it out of my pocket, I mentally groaned - I had been so caught up in everything I forgot to call Kitteren again.

"*Hello?*" I answered, using the odd dialect of common my sister and I spoke. It was about the only way I could try to keep the conversation private.

"*Ket, what's going on?*" Kitteren immediately sounded worried.

Pinching the bridge of my nose to try and keep myself focused, I said, "*I'm sorry, I just got caught up with everything.*"

"*You sound exhausted,*" Kitteren observed.

That was putting it mildly. "*Long day.*"

Kitteren paused. "*Sounds like you're driving.*"

I rolled my eyes. Trackers were far too observant. "*I'm not, but we're on the way back to the office.*"

"*Who's with you?*" Kitteren asked. She was going to have a lot of questions and I did not have the energy to answer them all.

"*Partner,*" I said. Silver would understand I spoke of him if I used his name, even heavily accented. I felt a little guilty about it, but would rather not have to answer as to why his name came up.

Kitteren snorted. "*Tell him I'll wipe the floor with him if he doesn't make you take care of yourself.*"

"*You tell him,*" I shot back at her.

"*I might just do that. Ket,*" Kitteren said softly, "*Just be careful, okay? Come back safe.*"

"*I'll try.*" It was the most I could promise.

Kitteren sighed loudly. "*Okay, give me a call when you're not neck deep in a case or exhausted.*"

"*I will.*" Part of me wished our conversation had been longer, but I was too tired to do much more and I think she knew also.

"*Love ya, sis. Bye!*" Then Kitteren hung up.

"Kitteren?" Silver asked.

"Yeah." It should have been blatantly obvious.

Silver gave me a sidelong glance. "She's just worried about you."

I closed my eyes. I was too tired to think straight.

"Why don't I just drop you off at the hotel? I think I can keep them moving," Silver offered.

I leaned forward and pressed the heels of my hands against my eyes. "No, I need to get my report in about the spells used and analyze the images Holly took."

"Ketayl..." Silver started and then sighed. "Okay, but at least consider an early night? You really need a full night's sleep."

I simply leaned back and stared out the window. I refused to give an answer one way or another.

"I'm sorry I haven't been there for you," Silver said so softly I almost missed it.

"What?" I asked and turned to look at him.

It was hard to make out Silver's face in the dim lighting, but I thought perhaps he had not meant to say it out loud. "As a partner. I got caught up with trying to push you into what I thought everyone expected and then in my own issues. I haven't exactly been here to support you like I should have."

His earlier conversation with Stoney referenced the same things. "It's fine - you followed your training."

"No, it's not. You were doing so well in the role I forgot I wasn't just a soldier taking orders." Silver paused. "And thank you for standing up for Holly. Especially when no one else was."

"She just needed someone to listen." What else could I say? And why had no one else done it before me?

Silver let out a long breath. "And that's something I didn't do and it's something I used to pride myself in. Look, I overheard the conversation the two of you had in the waiting room."

I had a feeling he just wanted an excuse to escape.

"While I don't have romantic feelings toward her, I should have been there to help her along during training and there's nothing I can do to make up for it." The sincerity in his voice surprised me. For some reason I expected the words to be shallow, but I reminded myself Silver would not patronize me.

I yawned. "Could try being her friend."

There was a long pause and I could sense Silver's attention on me, which should be on the road, before he said, "Yeah, I suppose I could."

Silence fell between us for a few minutes before I found something else to talk about. "So who are you interested in?"

I sank down in my seat and closed my eyes. Silver had turned the heater for my seat on before we left and I just wanted to curl up in the warmth.

"I..." Silver paused. "I kind of wish Holly hadn't said anything. Look, she's not interested so there's no point."

"Not like you to give up." Did that make sense? I needed to stay awake. Maybe I should have him swing by somewhere so I could pick up something to help.

"I didn't say I was giving up. I'm just not going to push her," Silver corrected.

"Maybe she needs a little push." What was I doing? This was not a topic of conversation I should be in. "I shouldn't be trying to talk about this, I'm sorry. I have no experience in the matter." I sat forward and pinched the bridge of my nose. Something, anything to stay awake.

Silver gave a short laugh. "You're also exhausted."

Thank you for stating the obvious.

"Why haven't you pursued a romantic relationship?" His question caught me off-guard.

I stopped and tilted my head at Silver. I thought we had been through this already. "It's not safe for the other person involved. I could inadvertently hurt or kill them. I'm too dangerous."

"You could try. Just take it slow." I rolled my eyes at his suggestion.

I remained quiet for a moment and turned my attention back out the window. No one wanted a monster anyway. Finally I said, "No. I won't take the chance with someone's safety. Especially not someone

I obviously care that much about." What I kept silent was that I had already gotten too close to too many people.

Silver remained quiet and I refused to look in his direction. Of all people, he should understand. He had a front row seat the last time my power went out of control.

A calloused hand reached under my hair and started rubbing my neck. I closed my eyes and just let him. I was too tired to fight. No matter how hard I tried to keep him at arm's length, he always pushed past it. I feared letting him in too much closer. I still vividly remembered what happened during our most recent training session.

I may not have hurt him, but Lockonis showed I had abilities I was not even aware of. I think the only reason it ended the way it had was because part of me did not believe Silver would actually hurt me.

Granted, the bruises said otherwise, but they were not the first I received in training and I doubted the last. I decided to let the world fade away for at least a few minutes. We still had the better part of an hour to get back to the office.

"I can't believe you let me fall asleep," I grumbled at Silver. I fumbled with the keys while we walked, nearly dropping them a few times.

He took the set from me and grinned broadly. "It's rare you don't give me any grief about touching you. Besides, you needed it."

"Not that it helped," I said. I was still tired. I may have to give serious thought to turning in early tonight.

Silver frowned. "I'm sorry. Coffee?"

I shook my head a little too quickly and needed to take a moment to get the dizziness to go away. "Ugh, I can't stand the smell of it - I don't even want to try it."

Silver laughed loudly. "I wondered why you always moved away when I had a cup of coffee in hand." He stopped me in the hallway on the way to our temporary office and brushed my bangs back. "I'm glad you're loosening up with me. Sometimes it's hard to read you."

I rolled my eyes and moved away. I still did not understand why he insisted on trying to break through the walls in place for people's safety. His armor could not protect him from everything.

"Take an hour to get what you need in order and then we're going to get something to eat. After that I will drive you back to the hotel and you will take a full night's sleep," Silver ordered.

"Bossy," I said, but did not argue further. "What are you planning on doing?"

Silver seemed confused for a moment before he answered, "For now, I'm going to see where everyone is. When I drop you off I need to run a quick errand and then I'm coming back."

"Errand?" Silver had not mentioned needing anything prior.

He paused for a moment before he said, "I need to go to a store - replace something forgotten."

"Oh. Okay." I found his wording weird, but I was tired and not necessarily understanding correctly.

"You're really not fighting me on this?" Silver asked as he unlocked our temporary office.

I admitted, "Silver, I'm tired and I can't think straight. Trust me, I want to, but even I can accept there's a limit."

I had barely stepped in and hit the light switch when the world spun quickly and suddenly my face was pressed against something solid and warm. I felt pressure on the top of my head.

It took me a moment to realize Silver had turned me around and hugged me. "What are you doing?"

I heard him take a deep breath. "Just happy you're starting to understand your limits."

"Could you be happy in a less physical way? I still don't like being touched." I tried to move away from him.

I felt a pressure on the top of my head again while he laughed before he let me go. "Well, too much more and I was probably going to need to start worrying."

I shook my head and moved away. Obnoxious big brother indeed. "Go check on the others. I assume they're down in the lab."

"Yes, ma'am," Silver saluted and turned on his heel.

"Don't start that," I grumbled.

Silver laughed loudly as he headed down the hall.

13

<hr>

SILVER HAD BEEN GONE for over an hour, but I would not complain. I managed to finish my report and now attempted to analyze the images Holly uploaded. I tilted my head at the screen. The problem I had now was I did not know if it was the screen that was fuzzy or me. I glanced up at the projector attached to the ceiling. Maybe a different source and a larger image would help.

I picked up the remote on the desk and pointed it at the projector. Nothing happened when I hit the power button. The remote lit up telling me the battery in it was not dead. I got up and stood as much under the projector as I could and pushed the button again. With the tables full of files directly below it I had to lean into the center.

Still nothing. I leaned on the table and twisted to look up at the projector. It was plugged in.

"The remote never worked on that thing," Stoney said from the doorway. "We've kept the tables in the center to be able to reach the button."

I frowned at the remote and then put it down on the table in front of me. The tables were covered in files and I did not want to disturb them. I glanced around the room to see if there was something I could use to reach it.

Then I remembered the weapon attached to my thigh. Pulling it out, I extended the staff and used it to press and hold the power button. The projector began powering up.

"If Coburn saw that, he'd lose it," Stoney laughed. "But I won't talk, I use my warhammer as a paperweight when I have the windows open in the summer."

I pinched the bridge of my nose while I waited for the projector. If he was here for a reason, I wished he would just come out and say it.

"Ketayl, I need to apologize. I could sit here and make excuses for my actions, but, well, I guess I should seriously start considering retirement. I'm losing sight of what's important and that's no good for anyone." Stoney entered the room fully, glancing at the image displayed on the wall. He whistled. "And damn me for questioning your abilities. You ain't doing this to rub it in I hope."

I shook my head. "I'm trying to analyze the spells used. The camera had a filter on it for the arcane and Silver's aura shows the divine. I'm just having a hard time looking at it on the screen." I made the gesture to expand the area I wanted a better view of and nothing moved. "Not my office," I reminded myself and went over to the computer to zoom the image in.

"First of all, you probably ain't seeing straight because you're barely standing. Second, the projector may be good, but it's still just a projector. Training facilities aren't high on the list for upgrades." Stoney crossed his arms and then tilted his head at the area I zoomed in on. "Glad you're here - I can't make heads or tails of this."

"This part here," I said once I got back to where the image was being displayed, pointing to the sickly green colored mess of the main spell and its hundreds of threads, "Is the arcane part of the necromancer's spell. The rest of what you're seeing in this section is my attempt to disrupt it."

"Hm." Stoney stroked his beard. "Not a one of us here would have seriously thought there was magic being used, never mind something at this level. Even Talon second guessed what he sensed. Speaking of, and I'm just curious, what's your rank?"

"I don't have one," I replied - my attention on the image in front of me.

Stoney crossed his arms and looked up at me. "You can't be telling me you're still a student."

I should have thought that through. "It's complicated. The short answer is I need to satisfy the EAC before they'll reevaluate my standing."

"I can only imagine the rocks you need to break for them," Stoney said offhand. He stroked his beard while he studied the image I should be analyzing. "I'd say talk to the Arcane College, but they're not quick to do things either and the DAC would probably give you the same grief as the EAC, though I know a few folks there."

"I was previously a Researcher with the Arcane College," I said, tilting my head to get a different perspective. "The Director wanted my rank reevaluated."

There was a pause before Stoney said, "You're right; it sounds complicated. I wouldn't want to be stuck between those two schools."

It looked as fuzzy here as it did on the screen. I squinted in hopes something would make sense.

"You need rest. Shut down and pack up. And that's not an order, but you ain't doing your folks any good being this tired."

"She might listen to one of us," Silver's voice came from the doorway.

I thought I had not argued with him about this earlier.

"Sorry, I lost track of time down in the lab. Sparky ran the DNA through RIGs, but came up with nothing again."

I took a deep breath before asking, "What else?"

"No," Silver said sharply. "I tell you and then you'll be thinking about it all night."

"He's got you pegged, girl. Might as well give in now." Stoney laughed and waved as he left.

Silver picked up the remote and tried to turn the projector off. I told him, "Doesn't work." Then I pulled out my staff again to reach the power button.

"That's not what that's for," Silver chided.

I shrugged and moved to collapse in the chair in front of the computer. What was I supposed to do again? I was hungry and tired.

Silver sighed loudly. "Ketayl, shut it down. I've already sent the others off to go eat. For as much as Sparky complained about wanting food, he couldn't tear himself away from his work. I really hope he doesn't start picking up on your habits."

I shot a glare at Silver before setting about my task.

"Do you want to just head back to the hotel and I'll run and get food for us?"

The idea was tempting. I shook my head. If I went back, I would fall asleep first.

Silver hung behind me. "Do you want to take a shower downstairs before we leave then? Look less like you've walked through a level or two of Hell? It might also help keep you awake for a bit longer."

The computer was thinking about shutting down and I stopped and stared at him, tilting my head. What in the Hells was he talking about?

Silver pulled out his phone and fiddled with it a moment before turning it toward me. The front-facing camera was active and I was a mess. My bangs were stiff at the ends from dried sweat and I looked like I had not slept for a week.

"Oh. I'll go clean up." Why had I not thought to use my phone that way? Why had Silver? Those questions were inconsequential and could be ignored. I found my way to the nearest bathroom - a shower would take too long.

I put my hands on the long counter where the sinks sat and hung my head. Now that I had nothing distracting me, I ached. I was tired, I was hungry, and I hurt. I could not remember a time when using my power hurt.

And I had still failed.

Pulling myself together, I stood up and used my power to clean off as much of the day as I could despite feeling exhausted. I did not want to waste the time right now on anything longer. I did not appear much better when I was done and cupped my hands under the cold running water to splash it on my face. Food then bed. Sleep would help the rest with any luck. Just not my failure.

ONCE SILVER MADE sure I went back to the suite after we ate, he excused himself and left. He never did give me back the extra set of keys to the branch office. I would have to reclaim them in the morning.

I changed and curled up in bed, figuring I could get some reading for school done before I started falling behind. I liked staying ahead, but I had a feeling this case would tax my being able to juggle even this workload. How would I handle the practicals?

Figuring it was a conversation I would need to have at a later time with Lockonis, I arranged the pillows behind me so I could sit up. I settled my tablet on my lap and got to work.

"Oh, hey, sorry, didn't mean to disturb you," Sparky's voice came from the doorway. Ironically, he had come to the bedroom door, so he planned on talking to me about something.

"You're not. What do you need?" As much as I wanted peace, I had to remain strong for them. Going to bed before the others was bad enough.

Sparky looked a little nervous when he said, "I was about to head back with the others when I saw Silver leaving with Holly. Is there something we need to know about?"

I paused, trying to think why that would be. "Silver said he needed to go to a store to get something. Holly is familiar with the area."

The Halfling seemed surprised by what I told him. "Oh, okay. You're fine with this?"

I raised an eyebrow at Sparky. "Why wouldn't I be? He gave me a rough schedule for the rest of the night. He'll be rejoining you back at the office when he's done. At least they're able to work together."

"I think it might end up being more than that," Sparky commented. I could not figure out if he was still nervous or simply not happy about the situation.

I pinched the bridge of my nose. I was too tired to deal with this. "If that's the case then it's their business. As long as it doesn't interfere with the investigation."

"You're the boss," Sparky said sharply and spun on his heel.

Why did they all have to bring up non-issues with me I had no control over? "Make sure you get rest!" I called after him.

"Like you're one to talk!" He shouted back before I heard the suite door open and close.

I sighed, looking at the tablet on my lap. Between the case and the relationships, I worried I would be too distracted by everything going on to focus. If Sparky brought it up as a concern, should I be? I could not recall any reason to have tighter control over what everyone did. And how would I go about that anyway?

I pinched the bridge of my nose - it was going to be a long night.

"GEEZ, Sparky, can you not make something out of nothing? I asked Holly to show me where I could get something we needed and she offered to drive me." Silver's voice carried through the suite into my room and startled me awake. I was still sitting up against the pillows with my tablet on my lap.

Rubbing my eyes, I looked around and tried to figure out what time it was. It was still dark out.

"I don't think you're being fair to the boss running off like that," Sparky said angrily. "You can't keep stringing her along."

What were they talking about? It mattered if it would affect their ability to work on the investigation.

"I told her I was going. Now keep your voice down - I don't want to wake her," Silver said in a loud whisper.

It was a little late for that. The world seemed off and I really just wanted to curl back up and fall asleep.

"Don't tell me you've been up this whole time," Silver said, standing in the doorway with his arms crossed.

"No, you two are loud," I mumbled. My tablet disappeared from my lap. "Give that back."

"Sorry we woke you and no," Silver said and stood over me. My tablet far out of my reach. I tried glaring at him, but it did not seem to work.

"See what you did, you freakishly tall ass," Sparky said. I cringed at his volume. "You need to apologize to the boss for sneaking out on a date."

Silver rolled his eyes and turned back to the Halfling to tell him, "It wasn't a date."

"Enough," I managed to say firmly. "I don't know what time it is, but you both need sleep." I closed my eyes and rubbed the back of my neck. Must have fallen asleep in a weird position. At least I felt better in terms of my arcane energy levels. Physically I still felt exhausted.

"Sparky, go ahead. I'll be in shortly," Silver said quietly.

I heard heavy footsteps leading away from my door. Suddenly there was a weight on the side of the bed.

"Let me take care of that for you," Silver said softly. I opened my eyes in time to see him reaching for the back of my neck.

I moved away from him. "No, I'm fine."

"Ketayl..." Silver sighed. "This isn't about what he said, is it?"

"What? No, I want to be left alone. Go get some sleep." I huddled down further in the bed and pulled one of the pillows over my head.

"Alright, goodnight then." Silver shut the lights off and closed the door when he left.

Finally, some peace and quiet, but now it sounded like I had a bigger problem to deal with than I previously thought. I only hoped they would be in a better frame of mind after they got some rest. If not, I might be asking for help on how to manage team members who were angry with each other.

<hr>

THE NEXT MORNING I was up, dressed, fed, and ready to go before I saw either of the other two. A fresh dusting of snow coated the ground. Why had I not thought to check the weather for this region before we left? I already felt cold looking at it. Silver insisted I pack the new shirts I bought from when Mother dragged me out on a shopping trip. They would have been fine for the little I ended up going outside at the main office, but not here.

"Ketayl," Silver said quietly as I reached for my coat. "Here." He handed me a small white box.

Raising an eyebrow at him, I slowly opened the box. A pair of black fingerless gloves lay inside. It looked like they would come down over my wrists. I paused, unsure what to think of the gift in my hands. I looked up at Silver hoping for an answer. "Why?"

Silver fidgeted for a moment. "You forgot your gloves. These will be easier if you need to use your staff. It's what I asked Holly to help me find."

I caught Sparky staring at Silver as if he did not understand. Silver's reasoning seemed straightforward enough.

"You really didn't have to." I touched the gloves and it felt like the same soft leather my coat was made of.

"It's the least I could do. I'm not sure how well the enchantment will work to keep your fingers warm. This is the first time I've tried it. In any case, we should get going." Silver sounded nervous.

Who was I to turn down a thoughtful gift? "Thank you," I said quietly and put them on before sliding into my coat.

"Now she looks like a bad ass mage," Sparky said laughing lightly. "She makes your poor sense of fashion look good."

I rolled my eyes and shook my head. Hopefully they worked out their issues. I was not good at this babysitting thing.

Silver still insisted on driving, and frankly I did not care. I was going to be spending part of the morning catching myself up on what the team found anyway and took advantage of the free time to start doing so on my tablet.

When we got in Sparky quickly rounded up the other three and headed down to the lab where they had set up to work. Silver and I returned to our room.

About an hour passed while I paged through another report on the computer.

Silver asked, "Were you able to finish analyzing the spell last night?"

I did not bother looking at him. "Hm? No, everything was fuzzy and I couldn't focus. I just want to catch up on what's gone on in my absence first." The silence following drew my attention over to him.

Silver toyed with the end of his braid. "The short answer is more dead ends. The werewolves tried tracking the paths the unknown werewolves came through, but the trail up and vanished again."

I sat back in my chair. "Thinking magic?"

"Possibly. There weren't any vehicle tracks." Even Silver sounded unconvinced magic was involved. "It's probably too late to try and get out there to see if there's a remnant."

Quickly I calculated the time in my head and nodded. "It likely would have degraded too far before we could get out there. But why? And who? It doesn't make sense. I can't figure out a motive for doing this."

Silver sat forward quickly. "Ketayl, stop for a moment. Think about it - necromancers seem to want one thing."

Glancing at the report on the screen, I said, "Power, yes, but why drain the life of a werewolf while using them as a puppet? It's like they can't decide if they want an army or a source of power."

Silver sat back and stroked the patch of hair on his chin. "Why not both?"

I stopped and tilted my head at him.

He sat forward and said, "How many names were in the search you ran? We can't assume all of them were rejected petitions, right? And we don't know how many affected werewolves still exist."

There were a few dozen names. Some of them traveling together in groups. "But what purpose would it serve to slowly drain the life of a werewolf? And I didn't sense anything arcane on the other one."

"Nikolai said he was much older. Not as old as he and Sasha though." That part I had not been told. "If he's the Alpha of the pack, he might not have the same spell on him."

I tapped my finger on the desk while I contemplated. "The hard part here is we don't know much about werewolf physiology. Stoney provided an excellent primer on their culture, but I think we need to know more about the science involved."

Silver stopped and looked at me like I had gone crazy. Perhaps I had. "You start talking science and we're in trouble. That's leading toward a very intelligent adversary if they're mixing it with magic."

I briefly wondered what his thoughts were whenever I copied files using magic onto the computer. Perhaps I should not do that around him anymore.

"Think about it. If the unknown werewolf turning and the necromancer were one and the same, I would have sensed an arcane presence. Provided they hadn't figured out how to mask it completely. If they are separate individuals then there's got to be some motivation to work together," I commented.

He stroked the small patch of hair on his chin. "Are you thinking we need to go talk to the werewolves again?"

I paused, unsure after yesterday's events. "I'd rather exhaust all of our options first."

"You just don't want to end up petting the Alpha Prime again," Silver said with a broad, teasing grin on his face.

I sighed and shook my head, returning my attention to the report I had been reading.

"Can you pull up the image you were analyzing last night?" Silver got up and reached for the power button on the projector. He managed it without help. I mentally cursed my lack of height.

This was not our office. The projector only displayed what was on the screen in front of me. Quickly I pulled up the image in question. I could read the report on my tablet just as easily.

I dug my tablet out of my bag and started searching for the report I had been reading.

"Ketayl, what's this?" Silver asked pointing at the something in the image displayed on the wall.

I glanced at the area he pointed at and then at it displayed on my screen. It was not as fuzzy as it was last night, but I still needed to zoom in to try and make out what caught his attention.

This was not something I had ever seen before. I zoomed further in on it, trying to read the tiny bands of arcane text. The image began to distort. "I can't tell."

"Do you remember sensing it?"

I closed my eyes and took a moment to go through my memories. "With as much as had been going on, I'm surprised I found out what I did. This looks like it's hidden deep in the main part of the spell."

"Can you back it out?" Silver asked, staring at the image on the wall.

I sighed, resigned to the fact I would not be finishing the report right now. Silver rarely got this involved in something. Most of the time he seemed bored.

Indulging him, I figured I could at least sit here and operate the computer. He still struggled with some of the technology though usually he managed to get what he needed done.

Silver flipped the end of his braid back and forth while he studied the image again. "Yeah, I can see why you would have missed that. I would have been completely lost if you hadn't been there."

I sighed and picked up my tablet to keep reading until Silver needed something else. Might have been better with a different mage. Someone stronger than me. I inadvertently made a sad sounding noise and tried to pretend nothing happened.

"Ketayl, don't." Silver came over and brushed my bangs aside. "You tried with everything you had. Don't dismiss what you did. Now we have to find this bastard and stop this from happening to anyone else."

Pausing for a moment, I said, "What about the people already affected? I didn't let go until the spell dissipated, which was after he died. How are we going to free them?"

"One thing at a time. For all we know, ending the necromancer will end the spell." For some reason I did not expect the gentleness on Silver's face.

"Or it could immediately kill them," I countered.

Silver held my head with both hands. "Exactly. We don't know, and I need that incredible mind of yours to start trying to analyze what you can. I'll let you know what I find out."

I could not stop worrying about everything else, but he was right -

I needed to focus and get to work. Except now we traded positions and he took lead. I closed my eyes and took a deep breath, hoping he would let go and move away without me having to say anything.

"What's wrong?" Silver brushed my hair away from my face again.

I leaned back to pull away from him. "I'm not exactly doing what is expected of me."

"And you started fine, but when this case came under our team's jurisdiction, I needed to step it up and I didn't. The failure is with me. Ketayl, if you hadn't forced the issue, I would've driven Holly away instead of standing up for her and we would have lost the opportunity of using her abilities." How could he remain so gentle with words like that?

I pointed back at the image displayed on the wall. After he moved away, I asked, "How was your time with Holly last night?"

Silver turned to look at me, surprise on his face.

I shrugged. "She seemed happy this morning when I saw her. I'm sure she needed a friend to talk to after yesterday's events."

Silver tugged on his braid nervously. "Oh, um, well, I asked her where I could find the gloves and she wanted to stop at the art supply store also. I bought her a new pad and pencils as an apology for acting like a jerk."

I returned my attention to the image on the screen. "That was nice of you."

He sighed loudly. "We just talked and caught up. Ketayl, honestly, we just went to a couple of stores and came back to the office to work."

I stopped and looked up at him. Silver appeared desperate - as if he silently pleaded with me to believe him. "I know. I was just curious. You like small talk and I should probably get better at it." If he did not want his usual small talk to fill the silence, then I would focus my full attention on my work.

"Sorry, guess I'm a little testy after Sparky giving me grief last night."

I hummed in acknowledgment, not really paying attention. I grabbed a pad of paper and started marking down my observations. I lost track of time as I wrote, theorized, scratched out what I had and started over - slowly making my way toward the truth. Occasionally I referenced my library on the tablet, hoping to find some kind of answer.

Silver came over a couple of times to zoom in the image as he needed.

I crumpled up another piece of paper, tossing it in the direction of the trash. The ball of paper bounced off the edge and fell on the floor. There had been a number of those.

I ran a hand through my bangs in frustration. I had to be missing something. What could that part at the central axis be?

"Central axis. Central axis." I tapped the end of my pencil on the desk. "The last necromancer's spell was feeding power through the central axis," I said quietly.

"You think this was doing the same?" Silver said and I jumped, not expecting to be answered.

"I don't know. You said it was draining the werewolf's life. It's possible I guess." I could hear the uncertainty in my voice. If I could hear it, Silver would be on me for doubting myself again.

Silver opened his mouth to say something, but did not get a chance before Sparky popped his head in the door. The Halfling asked, "Hey, me and the others were thinking of heading out to lunch. See if we can't come back fresh at this. Is that okay with you, boss?"

"Yeah, go on. Take at least an hour," I said. My mind was mostly still on the problem at hand.

"Actually, why don't we break for lunch as well," Silver said before Sparky left. "Do you mind if we join you?"

"Nah, the more the merrier. Come on! We'll meet you outside." Sparky waved and left.

"Ketayl," Silver said and came over to where I still scribbled.

"You go on ahead. I'll go get something later. I think I'm close." I had listened to the conversation, but I could not afford to break my chain of thought.

My gloves fell on top of what I had been writing. I glared up at Silver. "You're going now with the rest of us. If you don't then you'll be at this for hours. You need a break too."

When he got this way, there was little point in arguing with him. I put my gloves on and tossed the pad of paper and pencil in my bag along with my tablet. Fine, I could work and eat.

14

"GIVE IT A REST, BOSS," Sparky said. He was looking over my shoulder from the booth behind me.

They decided on the Wandering Drummer again. Apparently it was the best food in town. It mattered little to me.

Silver sat with the other group. He said, "Someone take that away from her please."

Mark, who sat across from me, reached for it, but Holly stopped him. She said, "I wouldn't try it. You saw the images."

"Oh, yeah," Mark said and withdrew his hand.

I stopped and looked at the two of them. Now they were scared of me? I shook my head. I could not win. I guessed I was as cursed as the werewolves. And the ones who were being used must feel twice cursed.

"I don't think I've ever seen anyone write so straight without lines on the paper before," Holly commented.

"Decades of practice," I muttered. And I had to learn fast - the Arcane College did not appreciate sloppiness.

Last time the connection to draw power had been on the divine side. This time it was arcane. I tapped my pencil against my cheek.

Sasha said something about how the affected werewolf should have been healing himself by the point we had him back at the estate. What if the spell to drain was attached to the werewolf's ability to heal? That would make sense if their regeneration abilities were as powerful as suggested. The spell would interrupt their natural healing ability, drawing away life energy, but leaving them able to function normally. I would have to run the thought by Silver later.

But still, what would the part of the spell at the central axis be? Some kind of connection to feed the puppet spell? If only I had been able to analyze the puppet spell on James during our last encounter with a necromancer.

Though that spell came across more as a command-type of spell rather than making someone a puppet. Either way, I had some research ahead of me. I jotted down notes in my tablet to remind myself later.

Someone sat down on the bench next to me and took my pad of paper and my tablet away, sliding food in front of me. I glared up at Silver and said, "I was working."

"I know, and that's the problem. Break, remember?" Silver held out one of the breaded cheese sticks toward me.

I rolled my eyes and snatched it from him, dipping it in the sauce. "You're impossible sometimes."

"Glad to be of service." Silver then got up and went back to his table taking my pad and tablet with him. "And you know, you can take your gloves off," he tossed over.

I looked down at my hands. I had not even realized I left them on. I had been cold when I got in here and with them being fingerless, they did not interfere with my writing.

Holly laughed behind her hand while the others showed their amusement more openly. I wiped my fingers and then took the gloves off. I thought about pulling out my phone to spite them all, but gave in and decided to try and be sociable for the remainder of lunch. *"He's such a pain,"* I muttered, switching my dialect.

"If you're going to curse me in common, at least use a dialect I can understand so I can enjoy it," Silver tossed over from the booth behind me causing the others to erupt in laughter after a moment.

I rolled my eyes - I was not going to win. This break felt wrong. Like I would miss something by not continuing to work.

"Ketayl, I think we need to consult the werewolves again," Silver said after I explained the theory I came up with over lunch. "You're probably right and we should confirm it."

I really did not want to go visit the werewolves again.

"How about if we come to you this time?" a female voice came from the doorway. Lexi stood there wringing her hands.

I waved her in. "That works as well. Is it just you here?"

"Yes. I needed to run a few errands in town and Sasha asked me to extend a dinner invitation to you and your team. We're..." Lexi trailed off as if she was searching for how to word what she wanted. "I guess the best way to put it is that we're not used to sitting back and not taking action. Usually we take care of our own. They'll be curious as to what you have."

I knew they were going to want an update. "Do you think you can help us out with something?"

Lexi hesitantly took a seat at the tables full of files Silver and I sat at. "I can try. I'm nowhere near as old and familiar as Nikolai and Sasha. I was turned only a few years ago."

I smiled to help put her at ease. "It's okay. You know more than we do. Silver, do you want to explain your side?" It would be easier for her to get the idea about something potentially draining a werewolf's regeneration capabilities.

Silver went through his explanation and I finished with mine.

"Well, we'll usually heal from small cuts and scraps in seconds. Deeper cuts or broken bones in a matter of minutes depending on how severe it is. Also, age is a factor - younger ones like me take longer, but that only lasts about five or six years. You could hit someone like Nikolai with a freight truck and you'd think you hadn't hurt him."

"The general age range on these werewolves is several months to a year, isn't it?" I asked, and picked up a random file in front of me, flipping it open to confirm. "How can you tell the age of a werewolf?" There was a claim on roughly how old the rogue was, but I hoped there would be something to explain the reasoning.

Lexi bit her lower lip for a moment. "It's hard to explain. For us it's instinctual to recognize age. When you get to someone like Nikolai or Sasha, it's less distinct, but you know they're old. The werewolf who ran - he felt old, but not as old as them if you get what I mean."

I nodded, understanding the basic concept. Elves were often the same way, but it was even less distinct - without confirmation, I knew Silver was about my age and could get a general idea if another Elf was significantly older or younger than me.

"Plus being this young, they're smaller. It takes a couple of years before our wolf form gets to its full size."

I looked to Silver. He grabbed one of the files on the table and opened it. "I'm not sure where else to go with this. What I can't figure out is why go through the trouble of turning people if you're in the Alpha Prime's territory? Why not go after his werewolves?"

Lexi looked between us like we were crazy. "Someone would have to be insane to directly attack the Alpha Prime's pack."

"That's usually what necromancers are," I muttered, thinking. "I have a feeling it has something to do with the spells being cast. How resistant to magic are werewolves?"

Lexi paused for a moment. "It'll hurt, but our regeneration helps."

Silver eyed me for a moment. "What's going through that head of yours, Ketayl?"

I bit my lower lip for a moment before I said, "A lack of under-standing of pack magic. Nikolai was telepathically talking to Sasha while in wolf form. That shows a connection of some sort. It wouldn't matter what pack the necromancer attacked - I'm thinking someone would find out. Create your own pack..."

"And you don't run the risk of having a whole bunch of powerful werewolves after you," Lexi finished. " The reason I had to call and relay the orders was because for someone like me in my native form, I'm not capable of clear communication and Nikolai and Sasha were too occupied."

I tapped my finger on the table. "But why have the puppet spell?"

"In a pack, we're resistant to forcible commands from outsiders and even inside, if it goes against everything the individual believes, they can fight it. I'm not sure if you knew Nikolai was trying to connect with the wolf and force his healing abilities to work, but it's a lot harder without him being in the pack."

"Maybe the spell has to be cast before turning them?" Silver tossed out.

I shrugged. "More questions and no answers," I said with a sigh, sitting back in my chair.

Silence hung for a long moment. "Agent Ketayl," Lexi said quietly, "Can I speak with you privately?"

I glanced at Silver. He said, "I should probably check on the crew down in the lab." He closed the door behind him.

Lexi's attention was on her hands in her lap.

"You can just call me Ketayl. I've never been one for titles," I said softly.

"I'm sorry, it's just... this is very odd for all of us. We've never had a non-wolf do so much for us. I..." Lexi paused, and I waited for her. "Sasha told you I was terminally ill when I was turned. My family and my boyfriend at the time actually pushed me in this direction - so that I could live. My boyfriend." Lexi paused laughing lightly. "He said it would be like having a girlfriend and a dog all in one."

I folded my hands over my lap, giving her my full attention. It sounded like this was hard for her to talk about. Listening was about the only thing I felt good at lately.

"We went over everything together, including how involved I would need to be with the pack. I mean everything. Then it happened and I was cured. Except I traded it for this curse. Suddenly I had become a monster to them. Who I am didn't change, but they couldn't see past the fact I was now a werewolf. I haven't spoken with any of them since shortly after being turned."

How could they just abandon her like that? There must be a reason she told me this.

Lexi fiddled with her hands before clutching them together and continuing, "Then you and your people came along and didn't even look at Nikolai in one of his foul moods as a monster. I guess you gave me hope. I've been kind of lost since my family rejected me. It's why Sasha keeps me close."

"I'm not going to say Nikolai and Sasha didn't scare me," I admitted.

Lexi laughed lightly. "Even I could smell that, but you held your ground. It was weird, but I got the sense you were more concerned about them as the heads of an organization rather than as were-wolves. I'm still working out how I can understand things like that."

I pursed my lips and thought about it. "That sounds as accurate as anything else I thought of. Though there was a lot of raw power in that room I still can't explain."

"They were exerting their dominance."

I bit my lower lip. That had been my guess at the time, but it was nice to have it confirmed. But why?

"Do you...? I'm sorry, I should stop taking up your time," Lexi said and stood quickly.

I shook my head and said gently, "I think I need a break from what I was working on anyway. What did you want to ask?"

Lexi bit her lower lip. "I mean, it was just a passing thought since I want to help, but I was wondering if maybe there was a place for me in the TIO? I'm pretty good with computers. I don't know about this stuff you're working on though."

I looked down at the files spread out. We should really pack them up since the others were using the digital copies. "Silver and I are an oddity, but Lockonis usually oversees the cyber team. I can ask her if you want."

"You would? I mean, there's a lot that would have to be arranged, but..." Lexi bit her lower lip again. "It's just I want to help. I guess you've kind of inspired me. For so long I felt the label of werewolf weighing me down, but we didn't even realize you were a caster until you ran into whatever that was in the forest and then the power you used trying to save the stranger. You don't seem to be defined by the labels and titles."

I stared at her dumbfounded. I constantly felt the weight of being defined as an Arcanist. Should I explain that to her?

"I, uh, I better go. I'll see you this evening. Dinner is to be served at 1800, but they've asked that you and your partner arrive an hour or so early. Casual attire is fine. Thank you again, Ketayl." Lexi quickly let herself out.

What just happened? I should contact Lockonis and tell her I had a werewolf interested in joining the TIO and leave it at that.

Silver came back a few minutes later. I still had not wrapped my head around what just happened. "You okay?"

I blinked and shook my head to clear the confusion so I could refocus. "Yeah, I need to send a message to Lockonis." I got up and grabbed my tablet, quickly typing up the short message. I gave up trying to keep track of what time it was back home - she could read it at her leisure.

"What happened? You seem out of it." Silver stood over me at the desk.

"Lexi asked about joining the TIO," I said absently. Her words still would not compute in my head.

Silver leaned against the desk. "You've made quite the impression on the werewolves."

I rolled my eyes. "I'm not trying to."

He shrugged. "Sometimes it's best if things happen naturally rather than try to force it. I'd prefer someone genuine rather than someone with an agenda."

I raised an eyebrow at Silver not understanding what he was getting at.

"Perhaps we should discuss this at a later time. Sparky could use some help in the lab - he thinks he has something, but he can't figure out what." Silver moved away.

Finally, something I could focus on. I put my tablet away and followed Silver out the door.

15

"WHAT DO YOU HAVE, SPARKS?" I asked as I entered the lab. All four looked up at me and I slowed my stride. I forgot the others were here with him. The three on loan to us were sitting around a table on laptops. They appeared to be going through the information available to us. I glanced at the closest one and saw he was running names still. Without their help, we would be drowning in information.

"I, uh," Sparky said, pausing and then looked over my shoulder where Silver stood. "I'm not sure. I managed to separate the virus which causes the change, but the samples look different. I just couldn't tell you how."

"May I?" I gestured to the microscope he had been using.

Sparky looked at me nervously before moving out of the way. "Um, yeah."

I took the opportunity to look at the sample he had been examining and then swapped to one of the others on the table. I stood up and stared at the microscope, pursing my lips. This was odd - it felt like looking at the same color but off by a shade.

"I was wrong, wasn't I?" Sparky sounded depressed.

I shook my head. "No, I'm seeing it too, but it's hard to describe. What other tests have you run on this?"

That seemed to perk the Halfling up. "Nothing yet, just thought to take a look and see if there was something in the virus itself."

"What are you thinking, boss?" a male voice from behind me said. I could not remember which of the Human men it belonged to.

I turned, not expecting the question. "I don't know." I returned my attention to Sparky. "It's extremely subtle. It should look the same from multiple sources if they're being bitten by the same werewolf."

"More than one?" Holly asked.

I shook my head and stared blankly toward the floor. "Too close even if they were siblings. It looks more like it's been altered slightly."

"I can run a sequencer, but it's going to take a while. This equipment is old," Sparky said.

I sighed and looked at the out-of-date technology around us. Outside of lacking a lab tech, it was no wonder Stoney sent his stuff to the main office to process. Even with the travel time, Sparky or I could get it done faster. "There's nothing we can do about that, unfortunately."

Silver spoke next. "Just do what you can. We're all expected over at the Alpha Prime's residence tonight at 1800 for dinner. Ketayl and I will head up beforehand. No need to change - they said casual is fine." En route down here, I had informed Silver of the details regarding the invitation.

Silver really fit the leadership role better than I did. I just hated the idea of arriving with more questions than answers.

"And let's get a quick training session in before we go," Silver said with a broad grin on his face. I glared at him while everyone else groaned. Perhaps letting him take charge was not the wisest idea.

<hr>

SILVER ABSOLUTELY INSISTED on squeezing in a training session before heading to dinner with the werewolves. He even ran back to the hotel to get our clothes.

Stretching as I walked, I started to get warmed up while I waited for Silver to finish his preparations. Last I saw him, he was already dressed and putting together a workout.

I had not bothered to find out what physical training facilities this branch had, but this was something important to Silver. I imagined this was one of the first places he located.

Sparky managed to get out of the impromptu training session citing tests he needed to complete. Mark and Danny talked quietly on the other side of the room. Holly jogged lightly on a treadmill, her curly, dirty-blond hair that she had pulled up in a messy bun bounced with each step. She wore an outfit similar to what Kitteren would in the warmer weather - very short, tight shorts and a sports bra. I felt scrawny in comparison to the woman - she appeared to be mostly lean muscle.

At least the outfit Kitteren bought for me hid most of that. Tightening up my ponytail, I walked over to Holly, figuring I could check and see how she was doing before Silver showed up.

Holly smiled at me, dialing down the speed of the machine to a walk. "Should I ask what Silver's training sessions are like?"

"Mostly me on the floor."

She laughed lightly. "Sounds like any training session where we got partnered up. I could only ever beat him on the shooting range."

I shrugged. "He prefers to fight in close quarters, though I still have to watch for his shield. He can throw it from pretty far. I have no idea what he has planned." I glanced at the setup of the room. Most of it was open space with only a few machines and rigs along the outer walls. A rack of free-weights sat tucked against the wall in the corner. "What do you usually do here?"

"It depends. Most of the time we're on our own for physical training. It'll be on our schedules, but there's no direction like in the basic training. Not that Faring ever really seemed to know what she was doing."

"I can only imagine what that looks like now. My sister transferred to that position for this session." Kitteren had taken the temporary transfer to Ocean's Edge despite her differences with Savanas.

"You have a sister? For some reason I didn't think you did."

I shrugged. "I need to remember to call her at some point, but she enjoys this stuff. I don't."

Holly laughed lightly again as Silver strode into the room. She quickly ended her warm-up and moved to stand next to me. For once I did not feel short since we were the same height.

Silver came over and held out my shrunken staff. I took it and glared at him. This was going to be horrible. He patted me on the head and I swatted at his hand. *Patronizing jerk.*

Moving to a board he could write on, Silver began directing the others with a warm-up of his design that would be a full workout alone for me. As the others began, Silver pulled me aside. "Have you warmed-up at all?"

"Not really. I don't think this is a good idea - I need to have something to bring before the werewolves later."

"You need a break. You didn't want to take it at lunch so I'm pulling you away now. You'll never see the big picture if you stay so buried in the details."

I made a face of annoyance at him. I had tried to be sociable at lunch, but I was still working through theories in my head. I hated the fact that even from the other booth he could tell.

"Come on. They'll be finished with the warm-up soon. I have a feeling we're not getting through this case without a fight."

Clenching my jaw tightly at the thought, I followed him to the middle of the floor. I continued to hope his instincts on this were wrong.

"We'll take it slow. Just go through one of the sets of movements Kevin taught you and I'll parry." Silver split his attention between me and the others who were running laps around the room.

Taking a deep breath, I extended the staff and waited for him to draw his sword and shield. I went through the movements mechanically, slowly developing a more fluid rhythm as we went. Silver met the staff with his sword and occasionally shield, but never pressed his strength into it.

After several minutes, we stopped so he could direct the others further. I pulled at the collar of my tank top - it had gotten overly warm in here and the others went through a far more aggressive workout than I had. Mark and Danny had both gotten to the point of taking their shirts off. At least I was not the only one who thought it was warm.

"Yeah, the air flow in here isn't very good," Holly commented. "It's worse in the summer. Most of us have gotten comfortable wearing minimal clothing."

"Maybe it'll be good in the dead of winter," Mark said. He had gone to a control panel on the side of the room and looked up at the large fan hanging from the ceiling as it began to move.

Danny wiped his face with his shirt. "You know the fan doesn't help much, right?"

"It helps a little."

Silver tossed me a bottle of water. "Drink before you get dehydrated - it is pretty warm in here and we've barely gotten started." He shed his shirt after I caught the item. His necklace with the sun pendant caught my attention. Most of the time I forgot he wore it, but it always made me curious about what it meant to him whenever I saw it.

I turned away from my partner and pulled at my collar repeatedly to get some airflow. Silver needed this "break" more. Exercising helped him think. Did he have to drag me along with him though?

I jumped when I felt the back of my shirt get tugged at the collar. "You've got something underneath if you want to take this layer off," Silver said, his voice even. His lack of tone made it sound off to me.

"You won't bother us," Danny said. "We've all been in here when Old Stoney takes his shirt off. Can't get worse than that."

The others laughed and I hid my conflict behind taking a drink of water.

"I'm fine, thanks." No one needed to see my scar. Or how scrawny I was in comparison.

Silver got the three started on their workout before coming back to me. "Care to repeat the training session from before we left?"

"No."

He laughed. "Too bad. I want to see where you can take mixing your power with the staff."

I sighed and put my bottle of water under the bench to the side. Did he have to do this with an audience? And this room was not really built to handle me using much in terms of spells. At least offensively.

For the next several minutes Silver chased me around the room. I mostly avoided, keeping to defensive spells like my shield. Even then, I used it sparingly.

It became far too hot in the training room and I was still not fully recovered from yesterday. Between the two, I found it difficult to keep up with my partner's increasing speed. I swung wildly at Silver's sword and fell to my knees, trying to breathe.

"Stop!" Holly called out. Suddenly she was kneeling next to me. "Pay attention, dammit. She's overheating."

My bottle of water appeared in front of me. I took it and nodded, downing most of its contents quickly, but it was still stifling in here.

"Come on. The locker room will be cooler." Holly got under my arm and stood up with seemingly little effort, dragging me with her.

I pulled away from her. "I can manage, thank you."

Holly walked with me anyway. She remained silent until the door closed behind us. "Guess he hasn't changed much. Silver always got so into it that he stopped paying attention to who he was partnered with after a while."

"It's how he thinks. I just wish he picked a better time to do it or at least not drag me along." It was cooler in here, but not by much.

Holly laughed and went to a locker. "We look to be about the same size. I think I've got a clean pair of shorts you can borrow. That quick-dry stuff for clothes doesn't work well in here. You should probably also take your shirt off. To be honest, most of us keep memberships to other places because it's so bad and only come down here when we have to."

"I'm fine with what I've got." But she was right - my tank top was soaked and I would never cool off enough with it on. Turning away from her, I pulled it off, hanging it over the bench nearby, revealing the purple sports bra I had on underneath. I still felt drenched even with the offending garment off.

"Like purple?"

I shrugged, not turning around. "My sister bought the set for me."

"That's sweet of her. My brothers are too full of themselves..."

The sound of the locker room door opening stopped any further conversation. I twisted to look over my shoulder and saw Silver sticking his head in. I forgot there was only one locker room.

"Everything okay?" he asked, stepping in fully.

I turned away and hung my head, letting my ponytail fall forward so I could get air to the back of my neck.

"Geez, give her a chance to cool off," Holly said.

There was silence for several seconds before Silver spoke again. "I just wanted to make sure it hadn't gotten worse. Head back out with the others. I'll keep an eye on her."

The door opened and closed sharply. Now the roles were reversed and Holly was angry at Silver. It had to be the heat making everyone weird.

"I'll be fine, just go," I said.

The sound of water running preceded a cool, damp towel being pressed up against the back of my neck. "Not until you're ready to continue."

I refused to turn around. "I think I'm done."

"Not until you push more. You're holding back on me."

"Why is this so important?" Why could he not see I held back for his safety?

Silver moved to stand in front of me and I brought my arm down over the scar. He had seen it a number of times, but it bothered me right now.

"You know, you only bring attention to it when you do that. No one is going to notice otherwise." Silver tugged lightly at my arm. "And it's important because we need to know how to fight together. While I don't need you going all out when it's sparring between the two of us, I do need to have a general idea of what to expect."

He held the damp towel out to me. I took it, wiping my face and neck down to the front of the top. I felt better at least. I picked up my shirt from where I had hung it over a bench. Suddenly it was gone from my hands.

"Leave it off. You look fine. Great, actually. Can you just wear this when we train from now on?"

I looked up to find him giving me a mischievous smirk. I rolled my eyes and shook my head, walking away. *Such a child.* He must have spoken with Rathal recently. Always with the odd comments after they had talked.

"Full set now!" Danny called as soon as I entered the training area again. "I was starting to feel like a wimp earlier."

"She still outlasted you!" Mark yelled back at him.

I stopped at the other side of the room. An idea crossed my mind and I wondered if I could pull off. It would take some creative manipulation, but it would save me from all the running around for a minute or so if I was lucky. Timing would be key.

Standing as still as possible, I created an illusion of myself and went invisible at the same time, remaining in my spot. If I moved too early, Silver would not take the bait. I still wondered how he managed to sense me when I used my invisibility spell.

It was a simple illusion, but it should be enough.

As Silver came forward to attack, I fell back while my illusion circled around him. I continued to move it just out of his reach, but kept the movements looking natural. I maintained this dance with him for a while, but did not attack or block - just evade.

I could see the frustration on Silver's face. I grinned to myself, wondering if he knew I was basically wearing him out without having to expend much energy. Though I would have preferred to go to tonight's dinner with full reserves. At least it was a long drive so I would have time to recover some.

"Come on, Ketayl. At least you were fighting back before." Silver's attention was on my illusion.

I found far too much amusement at the situation, but stayed silent as he came back around. As he stepped past where I stood, I missed seeing his left arm go back before his shield flew through my illusion, dissipating it. It made my partner stop short.

Quickly stepping behind him, I kicked him in the back, releasing my spells at the same time. He fell to his hands and knees.

"What in the Hells?" He turned back at me. I heard laughter from the other side of the room.

I folded my arms and stood there looking down at him. Apparently I did have options. At least ones to give myself a break.

Silver picked himself up off the floor. "That'll teach me to only follow my eyes." He seemed amused by the events. "Nice trick, but I won't fall for it again."

I shrugged and glanced at my watch. "We need to wrap this up."

He raised his sword, pointing it at me. "I'm not done with you yet."

I used my staff to move the tip of his sword away. It started making me nervous and I preferred to not repeat our last training session.

Silver sheathed his sword, still grinning. This would not end well.

Next thing I knew I was on my back on the floor, my staff rolled away when I dropped it from the sudden impact. Silver knelt over me, pinning my wrists. I pushed back, but there was no way I could move him. I glared at the man above me. I hated it when he pulled this. Outside of the one time I had kneed him in a sensitive area by accident, I could never get out of it.

I attempted what I had been taught to break out, but Silver's strength and taller form allowed him to keep me in place. I firmly believed he had gone out of his way to learn how to counter the escape attempts.

"Get off of me," I ground out at him.

He shifted so his face was close to mine. "Do I get a kiss for winning?" He kept his voice low so only I could hear.

"What?" Where did that come from? The heat must have gotten to him.

He backed up a few inches, but still kept me pinned. His face instantly went from mischievous to worried.

Gritting my teeth, I reviewed my options. Pulling enough arcane energy for it, I glanced past his shoulder to get a reference for where I wanted to go before teleporting.

Dropping a few feet, I landed with both feet firmly on his back, making him fully collapse on the floor. I squatted down and asked, "Who said you won?" I stood up and stepped off of him, stopping only long enough to pick up my staff. "We need to get going if we want to get there on time."

The other three had finished their workout and just stared at me as I crossed the room. I fought the urge to shift nervously. I shrunk the staff to keep from fidgeting. I had forgotten we had an audience.

"About time someone figured out how to beat him," Mark commented. "Thanks for making him kiss the floor, boss."

I bit my lower lip and looked back at where Silver was still on the floor. He remained as I had left him, his shoulders shaking from laughter. Would I ever figure him out?

"I'm going to go clean up while I can have some peace. Don't forget the dinner tonight," I reminded the agents near me, and headed to the locker room. I was worried about Silver, but his strange behavior had me keeping my distance. I hoped it cleared up soon, I did not need something else to concern myself over.

16

———————

"I WISH they said you were lead," I muttered as I sank down into the truck's heated passenger seat. Silver insisted on driving again and I was more than content to let him - enough times being a passenger got me used to him behind the wheel. At least his behavior had evened out again.

"Hm?" Silver glanced over at me. "Lexi said for both of us to be early, so I don't think they're concerned about which one of us is listed as lead."

I sighed. "I know. I just don't like arriving with nothing to show."

"Oh, so you want to dump the responsibility on me then?" Silver smirked.

"It's not like that." I pinched the bridge of my nose again. When I had something to do I was fine, but stopping like this only served to remind me I was tired. My levels had made it back to full when we drove through a concentrated pocket of arcane energy en route, but it had not done anything to help the physical exhaustion. "Even if someone else was lead, I wouldn't want to report I have nothing."

"We actually have something to report," Silver said.

I shook my head. "Pieces of the puzzle, not the picture."

Silver made an odd noise. "We were going to need to come talk to them again anyway. I think you and I will need a guide and start hunting."

"Hunting? We have no idea who we're looking for. All traces of any of the wolves just vanished." What on Terra was he talking about? Had I missed something? Was that where he got the idea we would not be able to finish this investigation without a fight?

Silver glanced over at me. "You really are still tired. Ketayl, you and I are the only two who will be able to sense an arcane or divine presence. One of them will be able to sense when the other werewolf is close. I've been mapping out the trails and they're all originating west of the Alpha Prime's residence."

I felt worse that I had not only been unable to follow his train of thought, but I still had not considered looking more closely at the paths they took. I asked quietly, "What's in that direction?"

"Dense forest as far as I can tell," Silver said. "There's another small town about 50 miles away, but it seems like a long distance. All of the unidentified werewolves and their trails originated within about 25 miles."

Biting my lower lip, I thought about Silver's observations. "I still don't understand how these werewolves are teleporting. You'd think the necromancer would want to hold onto his or her people."

"Maybe not if they've broken through the spell. Lexi said once they've been turned they're resistant to outside forms of control." Mentally I grumbled at him.

"So just let one loose and the werewolf you're working with to hunt them down? Seems a bit extreme," I commented. There had to be an easier and cleaner way of dealing with rebels. Possibly use them for other experiments if I wanted to try and follow a twisted train of thought.

Silver gave me a sidelong glance. "You do remember the last necromancer we dealt with, right?"

I really did not want to, but Silver had a point. Brown created an elaborate scheme to get to what he wanted.

"Ketayl, just rest. We've got at least another 45 minutes before we arrive." Silver put his hand on my head. "I know you'll want to be going most of the night if you can."

Why did this man have to be so reasonable? I shifted into a more comfortable position before I asked, "What was that about earlier?"

"What?"

I could feel my face heat up thinking about it. "When you thought you had won." I refused to speak of the action he requested at the time.

"I, uh... I mean... It was just... Sorry. I'm not sure what I was thinking."

I waved him off. "It was hot in there. Neither of us is used to it."

"Yeah, I guess it was the heat."

Glancing over at him, I wondered if there was something else. He would speak when he was ready. For now I decided to simply enjoy the warmth where I sat.

"THANK YOU, Lexi. Can you go see how dinner is coming along?" Sasha said as we entered her office.

Lexi bowed and closed the door.

Then Sasha turned to me. "Recruiting mine now, huh?"

I looked up at Silver with wide eyes and then back to Sasha. I shifted from one foot to the other, trying to come up with a way to explain.

"Easy, Ketayl." Sasha sat back in her chair. "I'm actually glad in a way, though I'm going to miss having her around. It'll be hard breaking in a new assistant. She told me of her visit with you earlier. She's been needing to find a path for herself. I'll work directly with Lockonis so you can focus on your task."

I took a calming breath.

"If I may?" Silver asked, stepping up to stand alongside me. Once Sasha nodded, he continued, "I'm not sure how much she told you about the questions we asked her."

Sasha tilted her head at us as if considering what she wanted to say. "Enough that I have a fairly decent idea of what you're working toward, but it seems you're focused on what I would not consider a priority."

Silver answered, "Unfortunately Lexi only saw what Ketayl and I were working on. The team as a whole is working on different angles given each of our strengths. I've also been working on a map of the locations and the trails your people have been able to follow."

"And they're all coming from points west. We've gotten that much." I knew she would not be happy that we were coming with more questions than answers.

"What's out there?" I asked, stepping into the conversation.

Sasha looked at me for a moment. "There's an abandoned mine that is part of our territory. Sometimes a few of the pups go looking for treasure." She reached to the side of her computer out of my line of sight before holding out a large gem before us. "These were heavily sought-after for a few years and I don't know why that particular mine closed. Sometimes the pups come back with something. Usually just tales of mischief."

"May I?" I asked, pointing at the gem. Sasha handed it to me and I held it up to the light in her office.

"It changes color depending on the light - both source and direction," Sasha informed.

I looked up at Silver. Something spells could be stored in and the unique type of gem might make it more powerful, though it was not something I could confirm right now. The reaction could be the complete opposite.

"We've checked the mine - there's nothing there," Sasha said. I could hear annoyance laced in her voice.

Silver took the gem from me. "You're thinking otherwise, aren't you?"

"Wouldn't be the first mage to store spells or information in gems. I'd still like to check it out if that's okay with you." I directed the last part at Sasha.

Sasha crossed her arms and sat back, her eyes going back and forth between the two of us. "Okay. I'll have Lexi go with you. There's a path through the forest where you can drive up to the mine. I keep forgetting the two of you can sense things we can't. Can you at least explain to me why you two are going this route?"

I glanced at Silver before speaking. "It gives us an idea of the caster we're dealing with. The intricacy of the spells used so far points at someone roughly the level of an Archmage. And if we do find other werewolves like the last one, we need to figure out a way to separate them from the spells. Otherwise we could have a larger problem on our hands."

Sasha raised an eyebrow at me. "How so?"

Silver took over. "Not only are the spells draining the life out of these werewolves, but Ketayl has found it's also controlling them."

"You think this necromancer is creating an army?"

"It's possible," I said. "The motive for this individual is still unknown, but…"

"But…" Sasha prompted.

I bit my lower lip for a moment, debating if I wanted to get into too much detail, but I was already this far. "I'm still waiting for them to finish with the lab results. There's a chance someone is altering the means to turn someone."

Sasha paled - my comment struck a chord. "We've had more than a few requests to study our biology. Some are more adamant about it than others, but we continue to turn them away. They want to dissect us and treat us like animals." She spat the last part. "We maintain our own lab for the purposes of dealing with our people, but what you're suggesting is far beyond what anyone here would be even remotely familiar with."

"A werewolf with no arcane or divine on him who may be working with a necromancer and a scientist?" The combination spelled something strange and dangerous. Provided they were all separate individuals. And provided we were not reading too heavily into the situation. "It's all still speculation though."

"We know for certain about the werewolf at least," Silver said.

There was that. "Any ideas on who that could be?" I asked Sasha.

She shook her head. "No. There were a number of wolves opposed to the government regulations, but most of them came around when they realized it was for the good of our people. We forced a lot of lone wolves into packs and it took them a while to adjust, but eventually they adapted. And the ones who refused were terminated. We could have missed someone, but our records from back then are nonexistent. Please understand, we could not survive as a fractured people fighting over territory with each other when there were others who would happily hunt us down. The only reason we survive even now is due to Nikolai's ability to lead the leaders. We only force control when it is absolutely necessary."

I had gotten uneasy when she mentioned terminating people, but I understood they did what they felt necessary. I simply nodded.

A knock on the door stopped any further speculation. Sasha got up and answered it. Lexi stood on the other side. She said, "Our other guests have arrived. I've already escorted them to the dining hall. I told the others to behave, but…" She fidgeted with her hands.

Sasha laughed. "I think the little one has already proven his place. Let's get these two settled with them though to emphasize it." She held the door open for us.

"I don't understand," I said. I tried to remember what I read in the primer, but nothing equaled what she spoke of.

"When Sparky drank one of the werewolves under the table I think," Silver commented.

"As I said before, very few can do that," Sasha commented. "Between what the two of you displayed and your friend's more playful nature with mine, the others don't have anything to worry about. They'll behave, though what little mischief they do cause will be light. Since you've come on board to help, they've been able to relax. They know they're safe."

What did dining with werewolves involve?

"So then Faring tells me to turn the machine on and I'm like 'this is a bad idea' but I did it anyway because she's supposed to know what she's doing, right? Sparks fly everywhere. Then I get blamed," Sparky said.

The group around him erupted in laughter.

Once the laughter died down he continued, "But I guess being called Sparky forever beats everyone tripping over how to say my name."

Silver laughed softly while he ate. He glanced across the table at me and paused. "You okay?" he asked quietly.

I looked down at my plate, not giving an answer. This was awkward. Silver and I sat near Nikolai and Sasha. I had remained quiet through the meal thus far. A few times Sasha apologized for the childish behavior of the other werewolves. I did not have the nerve to tell her I thought the same of my crew.

"Ketayl," Nikolai said, drawing my attention. "You are our guests here. Something tells me you rarely have a down moment."

Silver commented, "I'm fairly certain she's mentally working on something right now."

"Your mate knows you too well," one of the male werewolves said. I remembered him being the one who delivered the box.

"Shut up, he's not her mate."

"Uh, sorry, I thought…"

One of the other werewolves smacked the one who spoke about Silver being my mate in the back of the head. "You need to get your nose checked, Zack."

"I can't help it - I'm allergic to cats and that damn stray has been hanging around the shop again," Zack whined.

They laughed at the exchange and I fought back the embarrassment.

"I'm thinking I should send this lot with them just to get them out of the house," Nikolai commented.

"Where are we going?" one of the girls asked.

Nikolai told them, "They need to take a look at the mines to the west. See if they can sense something we can't."

"Can we go tonight? I haven't been there in a long time."

"If you go wolf, you won't be able to dig up anything."

"I don't care about rocks. That place is just cool."

I looked up in time to see Sasha shake her head. "You started this," she said to Nikolai.

The Alpha Prime simply shrugged. "It would be up to our guests if they want to go tonight or not. Some of you will have to stay in your native form so you can communicate."

"I can do that," Lexi said quietly.

"Me too. I want to see if I can find some gems."

The others began planning the trip - figuring out what they needed and who would go wolf and who would stay in their native form. I turned to Silver. He asked, "I guess we're going tonight. Do we want to take anyone else of ours?"

I bit my lower lip and looked over at our team. They had taken interest in the conversation. "Um…"

Sparky spoke first, "I'm not going. I've got samples running in the lab."

"Awe, you're no fun," one of the werewolves said.

The Halfling shrugged. "I'd rather catch this bastard before going exploring." The other three agreed.

Holly said, "I can stay here and see what I can learn that may be of use to us."

I nodded. They did not need direction or coaxing to get work done.

Silver said, "Looks like it's just you and me then from our team."

I would have rather waited until daylight, but time was not on our side and there were enough volunteers with the werewolves we should be safe.

1 7

CHATTER FILLED the cab of the truck. I sat in the front stuck between Lexi, who was driving, and Silver. I shifted uncomfortably and shivered. I turned to see the middle section of the back window was open so they could talk to the people loaded in the bed. I had not realized how many people planned on going while they discussed it over dinner.

Lexi spoke softly, "It's rare we're allowed out on a trip like this. Well, at least since the issues started. And I'm glad most of them decided to stay in their native form. I'm not sure the truck could handle that much weight if they decided to go wolf."

"Lexi, we can't collect gems if we're wolf," someone in the backseat said.

"The ones who went wolf are all horror movie addicts."

"Shut up, we don't need to scare people."

"Except that they went wolf because they're scared! The rest of us know there's nothing there."

Voices kept drifting in from behind me - some shouting to be heard through the window. Part of me did not want to know what the horror movie reference was, but I found some comfort in their banter. I think I needed a little normalcy even if they sounded like children.

Lexi rolled the truck to a stop as soon as the headlights showed the large pile of rocks covering the road. "I don't remember this much debris before."

"No big deal. We can go on foot," one of the werewolves behind me said. "I can take the cutie up if it's too much for her."

"Hey, leave her alone. She's not going to want your furry ass. I swear I've never seen another wolf shed so much."

"That's because he's mixed with... what was that dog breed again? The big white fluffy ones with the curled tails."

They laughed and continued to pick on each other as they got out of the truck.

I sighed. This was going to be a long night, but hopefully a fruitful one.

"Come on," Silver said softly holding out his hand to me. He already stood outside of the truck. "It doesn't look too rough."

I declined the offered help and slid myself out. I took the handlight Silver held out and turned it on, examining the rocks Lexi thought were odd. It could not have been a rock slide from the rest of the mine - the entrance was too far away and the outside did not look to have been disturbed.

The wolves already began climbing over the rock pile, racing each other to the top. A few slipped as rocks shifted. The debris blocked any chance of being able to drive the truck over it.

The road did go between two rock formations. I bit my lower lip and moved my attention to one side, shining my handlight against the rock face, studying the destruction. The outer edges appeared to have been blasted with an explosive, but the deeper center caught my attention.

Silver came up behind me. "What is it?"

I touched the rock gently with my fingers. "It looks like the rock was hit with magic to break it apart."

Lexi came back toward us. "Is everything okay?"

"I'm not sure. It could be nothing. I can't tell how old these marks are and there's no arcane remnant so it wasn't recent," I said and then stood up fully. There was little left for me to look at.

"Do you think we should head back?" Lexi asked nervously and turned in the direction the others had headed.

I shook my head. If they could not remember if this much debris was here or not, this could have been from something completely unrelated to the case. "Depending on how hard the rock is, they could have employed a caster to break it. And either magic or explosives could have weakened the surrounding rock."

Silver insisted on helping me over the debris after I slipped a couple of times. We walked up to the mine and I hugged myself against the cold. I hoped it would be a little warmer in there without the wind.

Laughter rolled out of the mine. At least the others were having fun. The moment we passed the wooden support marking the entrance, I could make out a faint arcane presence. I swung my hand-light around, trying to figure out a direction, but it emanated from everywhere.

"You sense something too?" Silver asked quietly.

"Yeah, but I can't make out a direction," I said quietly.

"Me either. Maybe further in?" Silver pressed a warm hand against my back and I moved away from him. Lexi stayed near us.

Going further in could not hurt. It bothered me I could not discern a direction, but if this mine had gems in it, then they could simply be reflecting the presence. I made a mental note to ask Sasha what the gems in here were so I could study them in my free time later.

Granted, that would be one of many side projects I wanted to get to at some point. They were pretty gems though, if the one in her office was any indication.

Something shiny caught my attention. Dusting it off with my fingers, I thought I found what the others were searching for. "Lexi," I called, since she was closest, though her attention was directed toward the others. "Do you want to let one of the others know I think there's a gem here?" I might as well indulge them in their game. They were acting as guides and security for us after all.

She nodded and trotted down the tunnel, grabbing the nearest person, directing them back toward us. "Yep, that's a gem," the male werewolf said, "Bet it's a big one too. Damn, how'd we all miss this one?"

I moved away while the werewolf dug into the wall with his tools to get the gem out. Slowly as Silver and I walked I began narrowing down the direction as the arcane presence became stronger. Then it became fragmented and I stopped. What happened?

I closed my eyes to focus. More than one presence?

"What is it?" Silver asked.

I reached out with my hand and used my power to get a better idea of what I was sensing, but came back with the same thing. "I don't know. I think there may be more than one, but it's still pretty distorted."

Lexi sniffed the air and then shook her head, blowing a sharp breath of air out her nose. "It's hard to get anything in here. The air gets staler the further in we go. It's worse if you go down to a lower level."

I shined my handlight ahead, trying to make out how far it went. It looked like there were tunnels off to the sides and I could not see the end of this one.

"Ketayl, this way," Silver said quietly, shining his handlight down a side passage. I hoped it meant he was having an easier time pinpointing a location.

I followed him down the passage a ways. We moved slowly in the dark - our handlights not providing enough illumination to progress faster. Lexi still trailed behind us. I wondered if she had not wanted to come.

Silver stopped and looked around, his light scanning from the floor to the ceiling. "It feels like I'm right in the middle of it. Are there floors above?"

"No," Lexi said. "Only down."

I sensed something stronger in the arcane and moved further. We were almost to the end of this passage. Reaching out, I touched the wall in front of me. It felt solid underneath my fingers. I was still getting a sense of the arcane all around us, but the strongest point felt like it came from further inside and below. I knew I had decent range, but the gems must be reflecting it through all of this rock for me to sense it at all.

"How deep is this place?" I asked.

"Only a couple more levels. There's about 10 to 20 feet between each floor. The lower levels are really short in comparison to this one. My guess is they shut down the mine before they could get far." Lexi sounded nervous and while I did not know the exact reason for it, I could not blame her. This place made me uneasy.

The floor beneath me shifted oddly as I turned and Silver stepped toward the wall with me, but assumed I stepped on debris. "Do you think...?" I started to ask Silver before he jumped backward as the floor gave out.

Both Silver and Lexi called, "Ketayl!"

I coughed from the dust stirred up in my fall. "Ow..." I said rubbing my left hip and thigh. Cool, fresh air blew through the tunnel I was now in. Shining my handlight up, I saw I fell roughly seven feet - it was definitely higher than Silver's height.

"I smell more wolves," Lexi said quietly after making the huffing sound again. "Not ours. And a lot of them." She and Silver looked down at me. A wolf head appeared over the opening as well.

"Are you hurt?" Silver asked. He leaned on the edge of the hole and slipped, knocking more dirt down on me. I counted myself lucky he did not fall as well - that would have hurt.

"Only my pride," I muttered. I would probably have some bruises, but nothing I would speak of. I shined my light in both directions. "There's a tunnel down here, but I can't see the ends."

"That's not one of the tunnels the miners used," Lexi said. I could hear the panic in her voice. "We need to get you out of there."

But finally the distortion had faded. I swung my handlight in the direction the multiple arcane sources were coming from. "Whatever is arcane is down this way."

"No, Ketayl, if there are other werewolf scents, we need to get out of here now and get reinforcements," Silver said. I could barely make out the concern on his face in the odd lighting.

Someone jumped down next to me. "I've got you, ma'am." It was bad enough I could not remember their names when I could see who I spoke with, but in this lighting I had no idea who it was and shifted away as much as I could in the small tunnel. The man simply wrapped an arm around my waist and jumped back up to the level we had been on. He set me down in front of Silver. "Yours I believe."

I shifted to get my weight off of my left leg - standing on it hurt.

Growling echoed up from the tunnel below us. That would be why they wanted to leave. Part of me felt stupid for not thinking those arcane sources belonged to the affected werewolves.

"We've got to go. Now!" Lexi pushed us ahead. I chanced a glance back. The wolf who joined our group remained behind for a moment, growling at the hole before following. I ignored the pain in my leg for the more immediate threat.

As we reached the junction to the main tunnel, I saw the others running for the exit. I paid little attention to the cold bite of the wind as we ran from the mine and slid to a stop in front of the pile of debris. Before I could figure out how to cross the treacherous terrain, someone grabbed me around the waist and jumped.

Once we landed Lexi said, "Forgive me for being rude, but we need to move."

Silver arrived a moment later with another.

Lexi blew out another sharp breath of air through her nose. "Oh no."

I turned to see what was wrong - the tires were flat. It was about 20 miles to get back. I could not teleport all of us that far.

The others made the same huffing sound to try and clear their noses.

"We can drive on the rims," a female voice said, "but they'll overtake us quickly if they decide we aren't far enough away. Sasha can be mad at us later."

Growling came from the mine.

"I think we're going to need to stand and fight," one of the male werewolves said. "We need to get our guests to safety. Lexi, take them and go. The rest of us can hold them back."

Lexi nodded, rushing toward the driver's seat before skidding to a halt. "Shit. I couldn't smell it before with everything else - the fuel lines are cut."

Silver had his weapons out a moment later. "Then we stand and fight too. Can we get a call back for help?"

"We already sent for help. They just need time to shift first," someone said.

I brought this fight to their doorstep. How far could I teleport this group? I mentally calculated the energy needed and the distance I could conceivably travel. It would have to be somewhere on the road, but it all looked the same in the dark. I would never be able to remember a spot to teleport to.

"I can't teleport all of us back to the estate. It's too far for how many are here," I said quietly to Silver.

"Then grab your buddy and go. We've been cooped up too long anyway," one of the male werewolves called back.

"No, we'll stay and fight also," Silver argued.

"Just get out of here. We can't have you two getting hurt. Nikolai and Sasha will have our hides."

Should I argue to remain? What if I hurt an ally by accident? Retreating was the best option, but even taking just Silver might be too much. "I'm not sure I can teleport both of us all the way back. I've never gone that far before and it's going to take too long to cast."

"Ketayl," Silver said. "You can do it. I'll cover you."

One of the werewolves said, "Unless you want to watch the old man fight - he's on his way."

"I can't just leave..." I started.

"Just do it," Silver commanded, cutting me off. He shoved me so I was between him and the truck. I stared at his back for a moment - he stood at the ready, flipping his sword around once.

The werewolves accompanying us fanned out and I heard bones breaking as the others with us started shifting. I cringed at the sound, but I did not have time to keep doubting myself.

I knew my calculated range, but never attempted to go that far. I stopped and took a deep breath - I would get us back to the residence or at least as close as possible. I started the spell, pulling on everything I had. When I got closer to completion, I would grab Silver.

Affected werewolves started bounding over the debris pile and the surrounding rock formations. They were met with both full wolves and hybrids. I faltered in building the bridge for the teleport as teeth and claws clashed.

"Ketayl, focus!" Silver ordered again.

I closed my eyes to push out the fight around me. Another minute and I would be done. The sounds kept breaking through my concentration and part of me thought I should help them fight. But I had never really fought with others before. I could end up unintentionally hurting my allies.

I opened my eyes when I heard Silver's shield hit something. A couple of affected werewolves had broken through the line. The one I assumed he hit staggered as it tried to get up. Silver's sword came down on the other as it tried to take advantage of his open stance.

I had to get Silver out of here - we were far more vulnerable than our guides. I clenched my jaw - just a little more. I needed to stretch my teleport bridge just a little farther. I was at the end of my reach, but tried to bring it closer to the ground anyway. Only a little farther to go. If I could pull just a little more power...

Silver cried out in pain as I pushed to finish building the bridge. A werewolf had clamped its jaws around his left leg. My partner brought his shield down on the werewolf's head causing a loud snap. His attacker fell limp.

I grabbed the back of Silver's armored jacket and teleported us. I had not been able to reach any farther than just inside the tree line near the estate and we both fell several feet. I landed hard on my left hip and thigh - I would definitely have a bruise now.

Silver did not get up. He laid there, clutching his chest. His weapons were gone.

Then I sensed a faint arcane scent on him. No. No, no, no. I looked in panic toward the house where Sasha, Holly, and a couple of other werewolves in their native form ran toward us. I pulled Silver's head onto my lap, brushing loose strands out of his face and trying to get a better idea of what lurked inside.

Sasha reached us before I could begin my analysis. "We've got to get him inside now," she said, pulling Silver away from me. I saw a large werewolf take off in the direction we had come.

I let the others take Silver. There would be no way I could carry him.

Holly hung back while I struggled to my feet. She said angrily, "What in the Hells? He's your partner - you're supposed to watch his back!"

I stood shakily and glared up at her, my hands on my knees for support. Bringing myself up to my full height, I took a step and fell. My head still swam from the teleport. I had not teleported more than just myself in tests since I got the children off of the slave trader's boat. This was also much farther than I had ever teleported just myself.

Holly was right though. I should have stood my ground and fought instead of trying to retreat. I did this to Silver. He got hurt because I hesitated. Because I had not been strong enough or fast enough.

My body refused to move and I remained on my hands and knees on the cold ground, taking deep breaths. Holly yelled something and tried to pull me off the ground.

"Just leave me," I finally said. The world still spun even from the ground. The intensity of the teleport had not yet worn off and I expended close to all of my arcane energy. How I still remained conscious, I did not know. I needed to get moving and deal with the current situation.

Someone picked me up and got under my shoulder. "No can do.

Nikolai and Sasha will *really* have our hides if something happens to you too," a male werewolf said.

I stared at the ground. How could I fix this? "Call Sparks. Get blood samples," I said, directing it at Holly.

She muttered something I could not make out, but made the call. I had to fix this, and I would pull on all the resources at my disposal to do so.

WHEN I REACHED the room they had taken Silver to, they had already removed his jacket and shirt, the left leg of his pants from the knee down where he had been bitten was now torn away and bandaged. He was covered in sweat.

Sasha prepared an injection. "We've already taken the blood sample you wanted," she said calmly, never stopping what she was doing. "This will slow down the progress of the change, but only until tomorrow night. Another dose would kill him if the change doesn't do it first. Elves have the lowest survival rate of all the races."

What lurked in Silver's mind could kill him even before those two scenarios. I struggled to stand next to the examination bed he lay on. This room looked similar to the one the affected werewolf had been in. "Is there a way to reverse it?"

Sasha remained silent for a moment. "No."

That one word caused my heart to sink.

"I already know what happened, so you don't need to tell me. If there was a time for a miracle, now would be it," Sasha said.

I wheeled a stool over and sat at his head, placing my hands on either side to examine the small spell lurking there.

"Oh, don't tell me. No, I should have realized it from the look on your face earlier," Sasha said, putting what was in her hands down on the cart and then paced. "Dammit."

Holly stood in the doorway with her arms crossed.

"Just say it," I told her. "I don't have time for games."

"This is your fault," Holly said after a few moments.

I focused on studying what lurked inside of him. The spell had nestled itself deep in his mind already. I managed a moment to mutter, "Tell me something I don't know."

"And you're being downright cold. He's your partner! Don't you care about him?!" Holly was yelling now. Sasha stopped to glare at her.

My voice was quiet when I replied, "If I didn't care, I wouldn't be trying to use all of the resources at my disposal. I don't have the luxury of time right now to act the way you think I should."

I had to tune her out and get to work. My arcane energy levels were still abysmally low, but I regained just enough to analyze the spell. It was like a seed. With the outer layer of the spell I encountered in the affected werewolf not present, I could begin to see the connection to the divine side, but it gave me little more in the way of information.

Closing my eyes to keep from being distracted by the shallow rise and fall of Silver's chest, I tried to think on how to deal with the spell. At nearly full energy, I could not destroy the full spell, but there must be something I could do to contain it while it was small. At least until I recovered more of my arcane energy. Modify the spell itself?

It would be worth a shot if I could alter it slightly to feed my shield spell to keep it contained. That meant Silver would be powering it. The thought caused me to hesitate and I bit my lower lip while I debated if it would be worth hurting him further.

"Whatever it is, do it. I'll manage." Silver sounded so weak.

"But..." I would hurt him. Though Silver would waste more energy arguing with me than my spell would drain. "I'm so sorry," I whispered. I brought this on him.

"No apologies," Silver said quietly, his breathing becoming ragged.

"I..." He was right, we did not have time right now. I began forming a miniature version of my shield spell to keep it contained. Connecting it to the source of power for the spell so I would not have to continually maintain it took longer and Silver shifted uncomfortably, grunting in pain. I was doing this to him, but the other option was to let the spell take over whenever it decided to activate.

When I finally finished, I rested my head next to Silver's. How on Terra was I going to have enough energy to destroy it before it activated? My modified shield spell would only hold for so long. When it failed, Silver would get taken over by it if I could not figure out how to destroy it first.

"Hey, boss," Sparky said quietly. I sat up with a start. How long had I been sitting there like that? I checked my watch - several hours if I read it right.

I pushed my bangs out of my face. "I'm sorry, what?"

Sparky looked at me in an inquisitive manner before shifting uncomfortably. "I've run the sample. You're not going to like it."

I got up, quickly checking to make sure that the seed of a spell still sat nestled in my modified shield spell, and then signaled for Sparky to follow me out the door and to the opposite side of the hall. Silver needed to rest.

I glanced back in for a moment before I asked, "What have you found?"

The Halfling ran a hand through his hair. "I expected a difference in the genetic code since it wasn't the rogue, but it's also another variation. The lab here is a lot better equipped, so I was able to see what looks like crystalline structures in the virus itself."

I crossed my arms and turned my attention back to Silver. "That would explain how the spell was delivered."

"Holly said you were doing some magic thing. She's pretty upset. Mark and Danny have been trying to comfort her," Sparky commented, his attention also turning into the room.

I closed my eyes and pinched the bridge of my nose. "I probably didn't handle her well."

"You handled her the way you needed to," Nikolai said from behind me. "I would not have been so gentle."

I stiffened up at the sudden addition.

Nikolai came around so he blocked my view of the room. "What do you need from us?"

"I..." I looked down at Sparky for a moment. "I don't know. I know Sasha said there was no way to reverse it, but has there ever been anything even close? A way to halt it or put the virus into some state of hibernation? Something to give me more time?" I knew I sounded desperate.

Nikolai shook his head. "If there was anything we knew, we would have shared it by now. I fear until more recent decades, we were not good record keepers. There are many factors which go into attempting to calculate the survival rate of a particular individual: race, age, health..." he trailed off. "Being full Elf, we're looking at a five percent base and that's being generous because of his previous health that I observed. How old is he?"

"61," I answered absently. Numbers were good. Numbers I could work with as much as I did not like where I started.

Nikolai raised an eyebrow and looked back into the room for a moment. "Still a child by Elven standards. That helps and between that and what I've seen of him being able to adapt, I'd say we're up to somewhere between 10 and 15 percent, but I don't know if being a sworn paladin will lower that. The divine complicates things as much as the arcane does."

I rubbed the bridge of my nose. We were back to having too many variables, but I had a rough base to work with. I wanted to ask about what Silver would need to do if he survived the change, but my mind kept focusing on the small spell nestled in his mind. I could not let him be turned into a puppet for some necromancer to control.

"Ketayl," I heard Silver's weak voice come from the room.

I quickly went around Nikolai to my partner's side. "You need to rest." It bothered me how weak he looked.

"First light." I barely made out what he said.

"What? I don't..." My gaze bounced between him and the other two who followed me into the room.

"Cleanses." Silver touched my arm and trailed down until he found my hand. He squeezed it before pulling it up to his collar. Then he dropped his hand and groaned in pain.

"Hey, you shouldn't be..." I trailed off sensing a tiny thrum of power beneath my hand. I rolled my hand to see why he placed it there. The small sun pendant on his necklace lay beneath. The connection hit me. "First light. I forgot." I turned to Nikolai. "How long until sunrise?"

The Alpha Prime looked at me in confusion. "A couple of hours. Why? What does 'first light' have to do with anything?"

"He's a paladin of The God of the Sun. I'm guessing he means to say he thinks he can cleanse the virus," Sparky said. Then he looked up at us. "What? You have him for a roommate sometime. Jackass is always up before dawn."

I bit the tip of my thumb. "The hard part is going to be the spell. Can we move him to where he can see the sun rise?" I doubted my ablity to deal with the spell and keep it from interfering with his attempts to heal.

"The lounge faces east," Nikolai said as he got my partner into a sitting position. "Silver, how much can you walk?"

"Not sure," Silver managed to say before slowly swinging his legs over the edge of the bed. It looked to take everything he had. I did not think he could even move.

I came around his other side, intending to help him walk.

Nikolai shot a look at me. "You're a little too short to be of help."

Someone much taller rushed in and took my spot. "Damn buddy, you're heavier than you look."

"He's a lot of compact muscle," Nikolai commented. "Let's move."

I silently watched them leave, unsure of where to go - there was still time until sunrise. Sitting around watching Silver would do him no good. I had to figure out how to fix this.

Sparky shifted next to me. "Aren't you going with them?"

I shook my head. "I should help you and the others out. Maybe there's another..."

"Hells no," Sparky said sharply, cutting me off. "We can handle stuff just fine. Just tell us what to do. You're the only one who can do the magic stuff. And Silver needs you right now."

I took a deep breath before I said to him, "Okay. Figure out what you can. We may still need a scientific solution. And see if the others can get a list of scientists who were interested in studying werewolf physiology. Look at the ones who didn't want to take no for an answer first. I want to know who we're dealing with."

"Got it, boss," Sparky saluted me and rushed out the door. I hurried to catch up with Silver and his escorts.

My legs felt as if they moved on their own and each step sent waves of exhaustion through my body. I managed to recover some arcane energy from my short rest, but nowhere near the levels I would need to deal with the spell.

I managed to find my way to the lounge and saw Silver resting in a chair facing the windows. I sat down on the arm and shifted for a moment to get off the tender area on my left thigh, forcing me to balance awkwardly. My discomfort mattered little - I had never seen my partner looking so weak or in so much pain. His left leg was up and Lexi worked to replace the bandages.

"Hey," Silver said softly. "You don't look so good."

I forced a small smile for him. "You're one to talk."

"Feel better sitting up."

I moved his right shoulder so I could gently pull his long braid out and put it over him. "Now you can occupy yourself."

Not seeing it there bothered me more than I wanted to admit. The only time I had not seen his braid over his right shoulder was either when he was fighting or depressed.

Silver forced a grin. Lexi finished and excused herself. Silence fell between us for a while and I found myself staring out the windows wishing for dawn to hurry. If I could do what I did with my modified shield spell, I might be able to turn the power of the spell on itself and perhaps eradicate it completely. Well, the arcane portion anyway.

I bit my lower lip. The theory seemed sound in my head, but in practice it would be far more complicated and would heavily depend on how much arcane energy I managed to recover by then. Not to mention how much Silver had to keep going. I could kill him with the attempt.

Never before had I felt so completely powerless.

"Name?"

"Huh?" I had not been expecting to hear anything from my partner.

"What your name would have been. Tell me in case this doesn't work?" At least Silver sounded stronger than he had, but his words worried me. Usually he was more optimistic.

I raised an eyebrow at him. He wanted to talk about this now? "No, you're going to have to pull through to have any sort of chance of finding that out."

"Motivation then," Silver said smiling weakly.

"How about who you're interested in?" I needed him to talk. I had started to become too scared I was going to lose him. As much as he might act like an overgrown child, I needed this person in my life.

And that thought scared me more - I had gotten too close.

I rationalized that the least I could do was contact this woman and let her know if the worst happened.

"Name."

"No."

"Then you have your answer." Silver smirked with as much mischief as he could manage.

I rolled my eyes. Even near death or at least a large, unexpected life change, he still could not stop being obnoxious.

I sighed, thinking about his reaction when I shielded the spell. "It's probably going to hurt."

"Shoulder."

Immediately I rubbed my right shoulder, remembering the pain of his restoration spell. "Well, at least I'm warning you."

"Ketayl," Holly said softly, pulling my attention up to her. I had not even noticed her enter the lounge.

I sat up straight. "Holly, I'm..."

She held up her hand. "It's not the time to be thinking about that right now. I brought both of your gear bags. Sparky told us you came to do magic stuff and I was here the last time you did that. Do you need me to take images again?"

I closed my eyes at the thought of needing the evidence post-mortem. No, we needed it to help the others. I absolutely could not fail this time. "Yes. The spell is small this time. I may be able to use it to help the others affected."

Holly gave me a strained smile.

"I'll help you set one of them up for video recording." I started to stand up and Silver grabbed my arm. What was he doing? His grip was strong given how weak he appeared.

"No, stay there. I've got it," Holly said quickly.

I sat back down. Silence hung awkwardly and I returned to staring out the window, letting Silver hold onto my arm.

As the sky began to lighten, he said, "You're not sure you can do it."

I hung my head. I could not lie to him.

"You will."

How on Terra could he be so confident? He was not the one who could calculate the amount of arcane energy needed for a particular spell. I knew my chances given my limited reserves.

"Ketayl." I looked down at Silver. Rarely had I seen such intensity in those blue eyes. "You will."

The only thing I could do now was sit and absorb as much arcane energy as possible and pray to whichever god was willing it would be enough.

After a few minutes, Silver announced softly, "First light approaches."

Standing up, I mentally prepared myself for what I needed to do. "Tell me when."

Others began gathering just inside the door to the lounge. Nikolai and Sasha stood side-by-side. A few more of the werewolves filtered in and stood or squatted along the walls. Sparky and the others also came up. Many folded their hands in prayer. Their words to their chosen deity would probably be more effective than my abilities.

"Now."

I used my power to contain and lift the spell from Silver, hoping it would be enough to start the healing process for him. I clenched my teeth and dug as deep into my reserves as I could manage, my arcane energy running out quickly - I might not have enough to hold the spell never mind try to turn its power against itself at this rate.

I could not fail here.

Silver cried out in pain, but I could not spare a moment to look down and see what was going on. I knew someone came over to hold him still. A few short orders were shouted.

It took everything I had to hold this seed - it was not even a full spell, but it drew harder on Silver's energy. Small tendrils began creeping out from the seed, making it harder to hold. My shield spell dissipated the instant they touched it making my attempt to hold this now growing seed of a spell that much harder.

More power - I needed just a little more. I would never forgive myself if I failed.

"Oh, Gods. Move!" a very familiar voice shouted.

Digging deeper for any scraps of energy I could gather, I pulled whatever I found to maintain my hold. My levels be damned - I refused to fail here.

Something snapped.

My hand went to my chest and I stared at the white sparkles surrounding me, drifting lazily to the floor. The world slowed as I tried to make sense of the sensation - something had broken, but it was as if I had been struggling for air and could once again breathe.

I managed to keep hold of the seed with my other hand while I recovered from whatever just happened. The spell seemed haphazardly put together, but I knew I could only comprehend what was going on with it on the arcane side.

It took me a moment to realize I also gained more arcane energy. Then the world slammed back to its normal speed.

Gritting my teeth, I brought my right hand back up and started channeling the newfound energy into destroying the spell. Iridescent tendrils of pure arcane energy sped out of my hand, impacting hard with the seed and breaking it apart one piece at a time. Sickly green chunks flew off, dissipating before they could reach the floor. The spell regenerated itself, but not as fast as I was breaking it apart.

My reserves were draining quickly so I would not be able to keep this up much longer.

I could still hear Silver in pain before me and shifted from breaking it apart into a straight assault at the core of the seed. It was weak enough I should be able to destroy it completely. My power hit and it shattered. The effect continued through sections of the spell I could not previously see.

Then there was nothing. No more seed. I staggered back a couple of steps from the sudden lack of a spell to dissipate. I looked down and Silver laid still, his eyes closed. Golden-white light and iridescent tendrils trailed just beneath his skin. I failed?

Sasha had been the one holding Silver still. She put two fingers to his neck. I was uncertain of how long I held my breath until she said, "His pulse is strong and steady. I don't smell the virus in him, but we'll do a blood test to be certain."

I just stared at her. She said I did not fail, but he was not moving. Then I noticed his chest rose and fell at regular intervals.

People started talking excitedly and my brain could not process the words. I saw someone standing across from me I did not expect.

Lockonis grinned broadly. "Ket, you look like Hell. I'm ordering your team to get some rest. That includes you." Stoney stood behind her.

I swayed lightly on my feet. Rest? For as exhausted as I had been, I felt like a live-wire now.

"Oh no," Lockonis quickly came around and pulled me back to a seat. "Ketayl, look at me."

I did as she told me to. I still did not understand what was going on. Why was Lockonis here? Was she where the additional arcane energy came from? She sounded concerned and had used my full name. She never used my full name.

Sapphire blue eyes searched my face for something. "Silver is fine. They're going to move him somewhere to rest. Understand?"

I nodded. Then I blinked and shook my head. The world spun too quickly. I leaned forward on my knees to try and get the dizziness to pass.

"That's it, Ket. Sorry, I should have realized using that much power would have put you into some type of shock. Especially with the sudden stop," Lockonis said and I assumed it was her rubbing my back.

"One Hell of a display for certain," Stoney commented quietly.

"Let's get your coat off at least," Lockonis said. "Then you're going to get some rest. I'm sending your team to get rest also."

"Okay," I whispered.

Lockonis was already unzipping my coat. I had not realized in my haste to deal with the immediate situation last night I had not taken it off. She pushed it off of my shoulders and somehow got my arms out. Then she began tugging the half-gloves off. "These are nice."

"Silver," I managed.

I received a broad grin from Lockonis.

"I forgot mine," I said.

Lockonis held up a finger to her mouth to signal for silence. "Hey, normally I try to get you to talk, but not right now. Once you're rested up, we'll talk, okay?"

I nodded and sank back in the chair. Here was good.

1 8

The warm spot I had been curled up against moved away. I made a
whining noise and searched for it. Someone brushed my hair out of
my face and I did not care to find out who. I wanted back whatever
was warm. The warm spot near my feet shifted, but remained.

Curling down more into the pillows and blankets, I created my
own little bubble of warmth if the other one was not coming back.
The draw of sleep was strong.

I had no idea how long I bordered between awake and sleep
before someone said, "You see her like this and you don't think she's
capable of wielding the power she does. Or the sheer determination."

Someone else snorted. "Thanks for bringing me a change of
clothes, Sparky." It sounded like Silver.

"No problem. Well, you won't be turning into a furball once a
month now. Too bad, it would have been an improvement," Sparky
said sarcastically.

I cracked open my eyes and peeked over the fluffy blankets to see
what was going on. Sparky stood there with his arms crossed looking
toward my feet. Silver pulled a dress shirt on, but left it open. The
warm spot by my feet shifted again and a large wolf head turned itself
in my direction.

Perhaps this was simply a weird dream. I curled back under the
blankets.

"Good job, metal head, you woke the boss," Sparky said sharply. "I was exhausted watching her - can you imagine being the one doing that?"

A weight landed softly next to me and the covers were pulled away from my head. "How are you feeling?" Silver asked, brushing my bangs out of my face.

I pulled the blankets back over my head.

"Wow, she's really tired if she's not pushing herself to be up and moving," Sparky commented. "Why don't you leave her alone?"

Silence was the only answer for a moment. "Because this isn't over yet."

Sparky started, "But the blood tests came back..."

"I'm talking about dealing with the rogue and his pack. Then there's whoever has been tinkering with the virus and the spells being cast," Silver said, cutting him off.

"What?" I asked, coming out from under the blankets. This was not my bed at the hotel. Where was I?

I tried to recall what happened. I thought I curled up in a chair in the lounge at the Alpha Prime's residence. My boots and the holster, which seemed to have been permanently attached to my thigh this trip, were also missing.

Lockonis popped her head in. "Hey, Sash said Lexi said Ket was awake. Is she...?"

I just looked in Lockonis' direction, confused.

She put her hands on her hips. "Well, you look slightly better at least. Would the three of you mind giving us a few minutes? I'm sure you all need something to eat."

Silver grabbed his boots and exited the room after Sparky. The werewolf jumped off of the bed and followed. Lockonis closed the door behind them. Her expression changed from her usual cheerful one to something much more serious.

I sat up further, brushing my bangs out of my face. I looked around, still unfamiliar with my surroundings. "Where are we?" Honestly, I wondered if I was still dreaming.

Lockonis paused in her walk over to the large bed. "This is one of the guest rooms at the Alpha Prime's residence. The biggest one I think. I thought it best to keep you and Silver together."

I felt my face heat up when I figured out *who* the warm spot was I had been curled up against.

"You're adorable when you're embarrassed. But that aside, do you recall what happened while you were holding the spell?" Lockonis sat on the edge of the bed.

I closed my eyes to try and remember. "It felt like something snapped and then I had a supply of arcane energy." I opened my eyes and looked at my hands now folded on my lap. "Thank you for transferring it to me - I might not have..."

"I didn't transfer you energy," Lockonis cut me off.

I tilted my head to the side as if the world would make sense. "Then where did the extra arcane energy come from?" I needed to move and began sliding my way out of the overly large bed.

"As far as I can tell it was yours."

I wished Lockonis would stop playing games like this. I looked at her once my feet hit the cool floor. She appeared serious.

My boss sighed. "None of us said anything because it was all theory. Remember I told you about how you couldn't maintain your arcane levels for a while when you were in the hospital in Ocean's Edge?"

I nodded, wondering what kind of theories had been tossed about and why no one included me.

"We started barely being able to see some sort of spell on your reserves. It made no sense and none of us could get a clear enough picture to even guess what it was. I think you started weakening the spell when you pulled off that teleport - like stretching open a bag. Now, well, it obviously shattered."

I clenched my teeth and stared at the floor. Why keep this from me? "Why does no one ever trust me with things about me?"

Lockonis took a deep breath before she said, "As I've told you before, it's not a lack of trust. You've backed off on how many hours you're putting in, but I didn't want to give you one more thing to worry about that might not have even been true. I think I know you well enough to know when you're not going to let a puzzle go."

I hated it when she was right when it came to something like this. "Why are you here?" It came out more demanding than I planned, but my anger had yet to subside.

The fiery redheaded Elven woman held up three fingers. "Three reasons and none of them to do with you. Mostly. You did shine some light on issues I need to address. The first is the outdated technology this branch is using. I'm here to run a full evaluation of what they have so we can bring them up-to-date."

Lockonis did tend to prefer to be hands-on with things like that.

"Might want to check the air flow in the training area," I muttered.

Lockonis smirked. "I'll put it on the list."

I fidgeted with my hands. Why was I being so testy?

"Second, Stoney is planning to retire. I need to know what I'm looking for in a replacement."

I cringed. I knew that one had to have been because of me. "I didn't want to..."

"Ket," Lockonis said softly. "He's been toying with the idea for a few years now. It's been a combination of him not ready to fully commit and me continuing to push off starting the process of finding a suitable replacement."

I took a moment to breathe out the last of my anger. "And the third?"

"Lexi. She's a unique case so I may have to make adjustments to her training if she's serious. Figure it's best to work out the details in person with Niki and Sash."

Silence fell between us and I thought about what she said and the reasons she was here. I still could not wrap my head around the theory of what happened. But Silver was alive and not going to turn into a werewolf. Not that it seemed like a bad thing - these were good people.

"What does this mean now?" I asked. Lockonis had to know. She could see the big picture from random pieces whereas I still struggled with it.

Lockonis shrugged. "You're guess is as good as mine. It would explain why your capacity had been so low, but who knows if this was the only tie. And it was tied to your heart which probably meant when your heart rate went up with a strong emotional response, your power became harder to control. Just a theory anyway."

I had paid little attention to my power once I woke. It was low, though it did not push at me when I started becoming angry at Lockonis. "You may be right."

"Actually, that was one Engelil came up with. She's been concerned about how you're so drastically different from every other Arcanist she's ever encountered. We'll just have to keep track and see."

I nodded. At least now I could be active about this, but now I was also more afraid. If my capacity increased, then my destructive capabilities also did. I was more of a danger to those around me.

"So you and Silver, huh?"

I sat straight up and looked at her with wide eyes, feeling my face heat up again. "No, we're not... It's not... I wouldn't..." I gave up and hid my face in my hands.

Lockonis laughed and I felt her weight shift off of the bed. "I'm going to head out shortly. You'll want to talk to Niki - he has his wolves scouting and they probably have come back with something by now."

I followed her, still trying to force my embarrassment down. Damn me and easily being cold.

"Ket, go clean up and then go down to the dining hall when you're ready. I have a feeling we're going to have a fight on our hands."

I could not take too long, but I was not ready to face Silver yet either. How was I going to explain myself?

I HAD MANAGED to stamp down my embarrassment until I saw Silver and turned away to hide the heat I could feel in my face. I had been such an idiot. Why could I not have paid attention? And I should have been working, not resting. Kicking myself seemed the better option at the moment.

Silver pulled me aside. He spoke as softly as he could, "Ketayl, don't worry, I understand. We've been through this before - you were simply searching for warmth."

I nodded, not finding any words to respond with.

"And thank you. Though I didn't expect you to break barriers for me." Silver put his hand on the back of my head. I had not expected to be pulled forward and to feel him kiss my hair. "And don't you dare blame yourself for me getting into that situation. I'm just glad you had been there."

I kept my eyes toward the floor. Silver was too forgiving. I doubted he understood how close I had come to failing.

"Though you really need to work on your landings. How far did you drop us with that teleport?" Silver's voice turned to a teasing tone.

My hands went to my hips and I glared up at him. "That was as far as I could manage to get. If you think..."

Silver's laughter stopped me from continuing as well as every else's attention turned our way. He patted the top of my head in a patronizing manner and walked back to the others. I clenched my jaw - he infuriated me sometimes.

I noticed Holly off to the side, her attention on the pad of paper in front of her. Pencil constantly moving. I made my way over to her and sat down. "Hey."

The woman jumped, her pencil thankfully away from what she had been drawing. I glanced at the page. She was working on a more recent event, but a quieter moment when I had been talking to Silver before first light. Holly quickly covered the page.

"I'm sorry," I said softly.

Holly shook her head, looking down at her arms over the page. "No. I should be the one apologizing. If I had remembered my training, I would have realized what you were doing."

"Everyone handles things differently," I said. "That's not a reaction you can simply change in a training class. And thank you for helping me despite what was said."

Holly smiled, still looking down. "You're a lot more forgiving of mistakes than the others."

I glanced up at the other TIO members in the room. Stoney seemed to have much of his team here, though they appeared to be simply socializing at this point. "Sometimes people forget how to listen. Perhaps I'm a little closer to where you are than the others."

"What do you mean?" Holly asked.

I should not have said anything, but I had already come this far so I elaborated. "I didn't go into the field for the first time until almost a year ago. I had no training for it - I was a lab tech. Had been since I got transferred to the TIO."

"I thought you said you were an Arcanist," Holly said, confusion in her voice.

I bit my lower lip - I really should think through conversations before I started them. "That's a genetic thing, not something in the TIO."

"Oh."

"It's... complicated. And seems to be getting more so," I said and sighed. It was times like this I truly started to believe I was cursed.

Holly remained quiet for a moment before she asked, "How long have you been with the TIO?"

"Hm?" I had begun retreating to my own thoughts. "Three years."

"Really? I would have thought a lot longer than that."

Silence fell between us and I watched the others milling about. Holly returned to her drawing, but she tried to hide what she was working on from me.

"Why did you join the TIO?" It was the piece to this woman's puzzle I still needed.

Holly looked up at me.

I brushed my bangs out of my face to hide my embarrassment at the blurted-out question. "I'm just curious. You have amazing talents and could have taken them in many different directions."

"It's a little sad, actually. I should have realized this probably wasn't meant to be," Holly said quietly.

I waited for her to continue.

She shifted for a moment and turned her pad over to hide what she was working on. "When I was little, I lived in this port town on the eastern side of Human Territory so we saw a lot of trade with other races. I'm still not sure exactly what happened to this day. All I know is I was on my way home from school and this Dwarven guy ran into me. The next thing I know I'm being held as a meat shield, but I couldn't see who he was hiding from. Not until he dropped me and these people wearing TIO insignia came out. Some took care of him and the others made sure I was okay. Had someone look at me to see if I was hurt. Talked with me for a while." She stopped and laughed. "One even came back with ice cream and another helped me with my homework while we waited for my parents to get there. I decided that day I wanted to be like them - able to stop the bad guys and still care for the people they were protecting."

I smiled. "It's a good reason. And there's more than just being a field agent. Trust me, I liked the inside of my lab just fine."

Holly hid her quiet laugh behind her hand.

A plate appeared in front of me on the table.

"I'm not hungry," I said.

"You need to eat," Silver stated firmly and sat down across from me.

I rolled my eyes and ignored the food despite what my stomach told me. I knew I should not be here - I should be keeping myself separated from the others. I was more dangerous now than I had been. It was the only reason I could think of why someone would limit my arcane capacity, but the need to connect with someone had been too strong to ignore.

"Ketayl, you haven't eaten anything since dinner last night," Silver said softly. "I'm not leaving until you start eating."

Why could Silver not act more like he just came back from the brink of death rather than as if nothing happened?

"It's actually quite good," Holly commented.

Now I was being ganged up on. Fine, I would eat. Once I took a bite, Silver got up and left.

"He just worries about you," Holly said softly. She sounded a little sad.

"Too much," I grumbled.

She gave a short laugh. "Sometimes I wish I had special abilities like you. It's a little hard to compete."

I stopped and looked at her, finishing the food in my mouth. Then I turned back and looked at the others in the room. "I've often wished to just be normal."

"Why?"

I closed my eyes and debated if I should say anything. I needed to be better about checking what I said. "I can't get too close to anyone. I don't want to accidentally hurt or kill someone I care about."

"I never thought about that - it sounds so lonely. Does Silver know?"

I nodded. "Nothing seems to deter him. He's like that annoying overprotective big brother."

Holly laughed quietly.

I sighed. I needed to get back out to the mine and do my own investigation, but I doubted Silver would let me leave without clearing my plate.

STANDING out in the cold was not what I had in mind for continuing the investigation. I rubbed my arms - my hands the only things kept warm by Silver's enchantment on the gloves.

The Alpha Prime's werewolves had been at this for hours trying to find where the rogue and his pack had been hiding. Now all of the affected werewolves seemed to be out and running erratically. At least I hoped it was all of them.

They discovered the tunnels between the floors of the mine led out to various points with heavily shielded doors that blended in with the scenery enough to fool a werewolf's sight. The ends of the tunnels sealed tightly to fool their sense of smell. Some of the doors matched up where the trails disappeared which ruled out a mage using teleport to get them in and out. Heading inward though, many of the tunnels had collapsed.

I was short for an Elf, but the tunnels were barely big enough for the smaller werewolves to traverse through. If Silver or I went, we would not be able to move fast if we got in trouble.

Sasha came up over the debris pile. "Well, that rogue certainly did a number on the truck. I'll have to get one of my pups to bring a tow truck up here."

"I'm sorry about the truck," I said softly.

Sasha waved me off. "Some of my pups have rebuilt that truck a couple of times already. This will be no different. Besides, it's just a thing. They keep telling me I should invest in a new one, but it does the job."

Silver came over to us. "I'd like to go into the mine and take a closer look at the hole we created. I might be able to give you a better sense of direction."

Sasha made an agreeing noise.

The hole I created. I was fairly certain I bruised something during the fall since my upper leg and hip still hurt. Well, between that and the poor landing from teleporting myself and Silver. When I had a quiet private moment, I would take a look. Until then, I figured I was better off not knowing.

"Ketayl, would you come with me? At least with the two of us, we might be able to narrow the search down." Something in his expression was off, but I could not figure out what.

I stuck my hands in my pockets, bringing my arms close to my sides, and silently followed Silver who wielded a handlight.

"The enchantment on those gloves not work?" Silver asked softly.

"Hm? Oh no, it works great. The rest of me is cold," I admitted.

Silver smiled softly. "Maybe once this is over, I can try it on your coat. Unfortunately I'm a little worn out on the divine side of things still."

I had not even thought he might run low on his capacity. He always seemed to have enough to handle whatever he deemed necessary. "Sorry."

I bit my lower lip as I watched him. Silver was sluggish in his normal movements. I should have ordered him to stay back and rest.

"Don't be. I'm still trying to figure out how you managed to destroy the divine side of the spell as well."

"I..." He was right. Even with my focus being on the arcane side of the spell, I recognized the parts I could not see before had been destroyed. "Chain reaction maybe?"

Silver toyed with the end of his braid for a moment. "It's possible. But your power also mixed with mine to help eradicate the virus."

"What?" Now he spoke nonsense.

"Perhaps we should leave the analyzing of what happened to another time. It's difficult for me to describe, but I knew the power came from you somehow - it basically gave a boost to mine," Silver said.

I shook my head and followed him slowly through the mine. I think he might have been too delusional at the time. It should be impossible for me to combine my power with his.

The arcane presence was much duller than it had been. It still echoed around me, but I had a feeling whoever had been here was gone.

"Ketayl?" Silver sounded concerned.

I knelt down next to the hole and shook my head. "I can't be certain, but I think they might be gone." Maybe if I dropped down into the tunnel I could tell better? How would I get out again?

Silver tugged on my shoulder. I hoped he had not learned to read minds. "I was starting to think the same thing. Retreated to someplace else?"

I shrugged. "You're better with battlefield tactics than I am. I would assume any mage with some sense of self-preservation would have a backup plan."

Silver snorted. "They are toying with werewolves. I don't know how much self-preservation they have."

"I could tell you if I could see their work space. It would depend on the precautions they had in place," I commented.

Silver paused for a moment. "You scare me sometimes with your insight."

I cringed. "Sorry."

Silence fell between us and I tried stretching my power out to make heads or tails of what I could still sense.

Finally I stood up and said, "There's still too much being bounced around. It's like this whole place is echoing what I can sense. We're probably too far for me to try to get anything distinctive."

Silver stroked the small patch of hair on his chin. "Maybe from all the werewolves affected by the necromancer's spell?"

I shrugged. "Possibly, but I'm thinking the gems in this mine might have something to do with it also. I don't know enough about them to be certain."

"Why don't we get out of here and get you warmed back up? I'm curious as to what Nikolai's patrols have found." Silver's attention was already directed away from the hole. It was as good of a plan as any.

I nodded and silently followed my partner back to our truck. I curled down as the passenger's seat quickly warmed up and closed my eyes. I needed to figure out what their next step was. Accidentally breaking into their tunnel sent them scurrying. I did not know how to predict their next move - it could be completely irrational.

"Ketayl?" Silver's voice sounded off.

"Hm?" Part of me was simply enjoying the warmth as Silver drove, but he had my full attention even though I remained curled up.

"I was thinking, when this is over and we get back to the main office, do you want to go into town with me and have dinner or something? No work - just us," Silver said, sounding nervous.

I glanced at him from out of the corner of my eye, but he faced forward and looked to be concentrating on driving. I was about to tell him no, but part of me craved the simple interaction he suggested.

"I guess."

It could not hurt to indulge him a little as long as I kept my distance. I wondered if he knew about the change with my arcane capacity.

I also worried his recent experience had shaken him more than he let on.

19

"Reports are coming in of upwards of 20 wolves per group and we've gotten confirmation on five separate groups," Sasha said. "Likely more since there are a number of loose wolves. They keep moving. I'm not sure if they know they're being followed or not. Young ones like this usually have a difficult time understanding all their senses are telling them."

"That's assuming they haven't given into their feral side," Nikolai commented as he stared at the map they put up on the screen to track the movements of the affected werewolves.

The sheer numbers worried me. There were quite a few of Nikolai's pack here at the estate and I knew more lived in town, but would it be enough to fend the affected werewolves off? And where would they attack? There must be some target in mind. The question now was of where and when.

If only I could have figured out a motive for this. Even the werewolves seemed confused by the movements.

There might be more than one motivation. If we were talking about three separate individuals in control of all of these werewolves, then they could each have their own objectives in mind. The necromancer and the scientist could easily overlap, provided they were separate individuals. That one still was out of my grasp, but the rogue seemed a little easier - vengeance, dominance. If he killed and left werewolves in the Alpha Prime's territory it had to be some sort of sign.

And yet the rogue was not attacking any members of the Alpha Prime's pack. It was as if he was after the Alpha Prime, but not wanting to act on it. Perhaps under the direction of the others? He could also be making a mockery of the current government regulations for werewolves and vampires.

Apparently a motive for the rogue was not as easy, but it did point at the Alpha Prime mostly.

"I know that look," Silver said, handing me a steaming mug. "You're working on a puzzle. Might as well come out with it so I can try to help."

I took a sip of the warm drink and looked up in surprise at Silver. "Where did this come from?" I had not expected lavender tea with honey.

"I packed some in my bag. Lockonis and Sparky brought our suitcases when they came back. Figured you might need it."

I smiled at his thoughtfulness. "Thank you." I wrapped both of my hands around the mug and breathed in the aroma - I needed calm.

Silver gave me a moment to enjoy my beverage before he asked, "Alright, so what are you thinking?"

"Motivation. I'm not sure just one person is in control here, which is why we're seeing such contradicting movements in the groups." I looked at the map, not wanting to see Silver's disapproval of my thoughts.

Nikolai and Sasha turned to look my way. I had forgotten how sensitive werewolf hearing was.

I took a sip of my tea before elaborating, "All of them are still basic ideas. Why the necromancer and the scientist, provided they are separate people, want to experiment on the werewolves, I don't know. But I suppose you could go broad with them and say their motivation is knowledge."

"Which equals power to most mages," Silver interjected.

I shrugged in response. He was more-or-less right depending on the mage.

"What about the rogue?" Nikolai asked. He stared at me with genuine curiosity.

I moved away from the wall and looked at the map. "What we

know so far is he's not in RIGs and he's old. He's also leaving the dead werewolves in this pack's territory. Some kind of message? I think the only reason he hasn't attacked any of your pack until now is because of the orders of the others."

"But how do you hide over a hundred wolves? Surely someone would have noticed. And where do you get your subjects?" Sasha asked.

Taking a deep breath, I stepped closer to the map. "No need to hide them all in the same place and they would be foolish to pull their subjects from the same source. You suspected rejected petitions. We came across missing travelers. I had an encounter with slave traders a few months ago. And then there's homeless or transient people. I could keep going."

Sasha shook her head. "I'm glad you're drinking that. I think I'd be getting very riled up if it wasn't for the calming effect of your tea."

I looked down at my mug - I had not even thought of the effect it would have on others with a more sensitive sense of smell.

"We're going to have a fight on our hands," Nikolai said. "Probably sooner rather than later. While the territory may rightfully belong to us, I doubt they see it that way. They'll come to us once the rogue manages to round them up."

What was the Alpha Prime seeing that I was not? Apparently this is where my knowledge fell short. He lived and breathed werewolf customs.

Nikolai turned to me. "I would like your continued assistance after this is over - we'll need to figure out how to handle them if any survive the fight."

"I'm not staying out of the fight," I said firmly. I had come this far and I was not about to run to some safe place. I was just as dangerous as they were if not more so.

Nikolai turned to look back where I left Silver. "No chance you can convince her otherwise, is there?"

"No," Silver said. Good, I did not have to argue with him as well. "And since we're dealing with a necromancer, you'll need both of us."

I turned to look at Silver. He admitted earlier to be running low on divine energy, but he never said how much this morning's ordeal affected him. Physically he seemed better, but I had no way of knowing what he might be hiding.

"Don't you even think about trying to sit me out either," Silver said, directing it at me. "You know as well as I do that necromancers are both arcane and divine casters."

I shook my head and returned to the map. "At least don't push yourself too hard."

"I should be telling you that. You're notorious for it," Silver tossed back at me.

I rolled my eyes and ignored the amused expressions on the faces of Nikolai and Sasha. We needed to get back to work. I stared at the map, hoping an answer would form somehow. "Did we ever narrow down a name of potential scientists?"

"No," Silver said. "Mark figured whoever it was would either be in the area or considered missing at this point. Anyone who was aggressive about wanting to study the werewolves has been located and cleared."

I pursed my lips and thought about it. "Have they checked the others?"

"Still working on it," Silver said.

Damn. There had to be something. "Are there any other mines in the area?"

"No," Nikolai said. "And nowhere else we can think of to hold even a group of those wolves unless the mine is far more extensive than we figured, but we smelled no others nearby prior to scattering the pack."

I looked at the trails they marked. Some were within a few miles of the mine still. Others up north by the shore. Some further south. All points west. "There's a small town about 50 miles away, right?"

"Hilldale, yes," Sasha said. "It's a tiny community - the people there would know if something was out of the ordinary." She pulled out her phone. "I've got a friend there I can check in with." Then she walked away to make the call.

I pointed at the map up north. "Is there any chance they could have been hiding in the port?"

"It's possible, but this isn't a very busy port," Nikolai said. "It would be a lot harder to hide werewolves there."

"Could have been on a boat or in a warehouse," Silver commented. He was thinking about a few months ago. Though Mystic Port sounded far easier to hide activities than here.

Nikolai added a few more lines to the map. He commented, "We tend to avoid the water - we don't float well."

"They're circling," I noted. It seemed chaotic, but I could start to see the picture.

Nikolai stared at the map. "I've honestly never seen this many wolves move before. Most packs tend to only get as large as one of these groups. Mine is the largest, but we have nowhere near this many members."

"I think I can see it," Silver said. "Preparing for an attack from multiple directions?"

Suddenly there was a weight on my head. Silver rested his chin on me again. I ducked out from under him and turned a glare his way, straightening my hair.

Nikolai smirked, but kept his attention on the map. He said, "I'm assuming the only reason the rogue is able to maintain control of this many wolves is due to the necromancer's spells. They struck me as feral when I got over to the fight last night, but they were also retreating with their tails between their legs and those we were unable to strike down disappeared. Either way, my pack is capable of defending itself."

"But you have to admit these odds might be too much even for us," Sasha said coming back. She had her phone in her hand still. "Nothing. Hilldale has gotten some reports of minor poaching going on, but it's common enough. She suggested checking some of the hunting cabins in the area. There have been reports of break-ins and vandalism, but she didn't think anything more than some bored kids."

"I think we might be a bit late in trying to find their hiding places," Nikolai said. "I'd like to assume they're all out and showing their numbers. We're not exactly known for our subtlety."

"We're going to need more people to handle this," Silver noted.

"This is our fight - we'll handle it," Nikolai said sharply. "Though I'll admit I wish we had more time so I could pull in other packs."

I shook my head. "No, it isn't just your fight. I won't order people to come, but I'm going to ask for volunteers. If we want to try and save as many of these werewolves as possible, then we're going to need help."

"Ketayl, it may be too late to save them. These people likely were not only turned under very stressful circumstances, and many against their will, but I doubt anyone stayed with them and helped keep their sanity in-check during the process. I'm not sure any of them even know how to shift back to their native form," Sasha said.

"Then death would be a mercy," Silver said flatly. I looked up at his face and his expression was blank.

"Yes," Nikolai confirmed.

Silver closed his eyes and his lips barely moved. A small prayer perhaps.

I still held out hope there was a chance to reach someone. "Silver, talk to our team and call Old Stoney - see if he has anyone who might want to volunteer to help. We're going to need more than just fighters for this. Even if there's only a one percent chance, I'm taking it."

Now I also needed to step up and accept the abilities I had if I wanted to be useful. I just had no idea how to use this power without having it triggered by fear or anger.

"Lockonis likely won't sit this out either. She's been itching for a fight for a while and I won't deny a warmage's aid," Sasha said.

I had forgotten Lockonis was in the area.

"Gather your people. We'll need to coordinate quickly. If they're preparing to strike, it will likely be after dark and daylight fades quickly this time of year," Nikolai said.

I nodded to Silver who left. "If you'll excuse me, I have preparations of my own." I followed not far behind my partner, but headed for the dining hall where I hoped it would be quiet. If Lockonis was right and I had telekinetic capabilities, I needed to learn how to use them and fast.

***

I GLARED at my long empty mug. It would not budge. I picked up my tablet again and read through the information I could find. Everything was either theory or wild speculation. I doubted anyone writing this information was actually telekinetic. Or perhaps Lockonis was wrong.

Silver sat down and slid a full mug of tea in front of me, taking the empty one. "What are you working on? Other than staring at an empty mug."

I held my tablet to my chest. Suddenly this seemed like a complete waste of time. "A dead end," I replied. "Did we manage to get any volunteers?"

"All of them," Silver said as he toyed with his braid.

My grip loosened at the news. "I didn't expect... Hey!" Silver pilfered my tablet.

He glanced at the information on the screen. I should have locked it. "You're giving this serious consideration?"

I picked up the mug and breathed deep the aroma. "I don't know. I want to use anything at my disposal, but this is a waste of time. If it's true, then I have no idea how to use it."

Silver stroked the small patch of hair on his chin before he asked, "You didn't exactly have a manual for wielding the arcane, did you?"

I looked at Silver as if he lost it. "There are entire schools dedicated to the study of the arcane."

"Early on," he clarified. "Lindale and Kitteren heavily implied you were using the arcane untrained and I remember you admitting to running on instinct during the fight with the slave traders. At least by my observations your encounter with the slave trader captain was probably the most consciously you controlled this ability."

I shook my head and took my tablet back, clearing the search. "I can't devolve to that again. It's too dangerous. It would be worse now."

Silver shifted to try to look me in the eye which put him in an odd position given our height difference and the table in front of me. "How?"

So, no one had informed him. My hands around the warm mug suddenly seemed far more interesting. "I'm not sure how much you were aware of what was going on around you this morning."

He sat back and crossed his arms, staring at me. "Aside from feeling like I was being burned alive and torn apart, not much, but I did have Holly show me the recording you ordered. Something shattered. Your arcane levels shot back up again after that and it was a pretty spectacular display overall."

Taking a sip of my tea to stall, I ran what I needed to tell him through my head a few times before I said, "Something was restricting my arcane capacity. It's gone now and I can only assume it was put in place because I am a danger to those around me with my power. And now it seems like I'm able to absorb arcane energy around me faster as well."

Silver's hand snaked under my hair to rub the back of my neck. "Let's leave the speculation for another time. Right now we've got agents and equipment on the way and I need you to breath and relax."

"I still don't like being touched," I said softly. I did not even want to admit to myself I had grown accustomed to him doing things like this in the short period of time we had been working together.

Silver grinned broadly. "You keep telling me that."

2 0

ANOTHER GROUP of Nikolai's werewolves returned. He called them back slowly over the course of the day as to not tip his hand. Those who lived in the city drove in as their schedules allowed. His pack appeared to be double the size of what he had described as a normal pack.

I rubbed my arms against the cold and the wind. Clouds started rolling in before it got dark and the sky was now fully overcast, hiding the moon. The only illumination came from the estate. Lockonis and Stoney organized the others. Silver was with them, giving what input he could. I idly listened to the conversations going on over my earpiece.

This was insane. What had I been thinking saying I wanted to take part in the fight? I was far from competent in battle.

I closed my eyes and leaned back against the wall next to the large front doors. The affected werewolves were barely at the edge of my ability to sense. They seemed to be disorganized - sometimes coming a little closer while others moved out too far for me to track.

Silver was right - they were planning to attack from multiple directions. I wondered if they could sense the number of people here.

Many of Nikolai's people decided to shift in preparation and many sat or paced in the yard. Sasha had the vehicles moved so we would have more room to fight. There must be a way to thin the numbers we faced now.

A flash of light caught my attention and I looked up at the sky. Lightning?

"Looks like there's a warm front moving through," Lexi commented. She elected to remain in her native form for the moment. "It won't rain or snow if that's what you're concerned about. Just the lightning - maybe some thunder."

At least we would stay dry. I pursed my lips in consideration. My arcane levels were fairly close to full even with the increased capacity, but I should conserve as much as I could during the fight. I had no idea how long this would last. If they could be rounded up somehow...

I stood up fully when I felt the rush of arcane sources heading toward us. "They're starting their attack."

"Ketayl," Silver said approaching. "You should take a more defensible position."

I shook my head and walked down the stairs. "I have half an idea on how to thin the numbers."

"I'm not going to like it, am I?" Silver sounded resigned.

I glanced back over my shoulder at him. "Probably not. I need to round them up and get them packed closely together. I'll need you to cover me when I get back. Just tell the others to stay back and hold until I'm done."

Nikolai, Sasha, Lockonis, and Stoney had come out with Silver. The werewolves in the yard were on their feet growling.

"How will they know?" Silver asked following me.

"You won't be able to miss it," I said, drawing my staff from its holster and extending it. My other hand already raised with gathered arcane energy.

"Is she mad?" Stoney asked.

"Aren't we all?" Lockonis replied. "Switch to active communications and go get 'em, kid. I'll try to track you from here, but remember I don't have the range you do."

I flicked the switch on my ear-piece and then released the gathered arcane energy into a brief flight spell to head toward the northern most group. I broke the tree line so fast that the white bark of the trees flew by me in a blur. After a couple of close calls colliding with the trees, I put up my shield spell.

The first group came into view. My staff hit home hard on a couple of the affected werewolves as I had not slowed down. It was enough to get their attention to start chasing me instead. I began my swing southward to entice the other groups to come after me as bait. I doubted the rogue had as good of control over his pack as everyone continued to assume, magic or not, and the ease of getting their attention only proved it.

Dodging through the trees with quick bursts of a flight spell was difficult. I kept my shield spell up just in case I miscalculated. I heard growling behind me as I raced through the forest. I kept my speed down both to avoid hitting trees and to keep the wolves close. A few got closer than I liked, the hexagonal pattern of my shield spell flashing brightly as they bit at it.

I picked up one group at a time, often having to double-back to tighten the pack. Reaching the southern most of the groups, I held my staff with both hands, plowing into a couple, knocking them down before backtracking to the others I had gathered. Now I needed to bring them around to where Nikolai's people and the others waited.

I broke the tree line with a burst of full speed before dropping into a run. Silver stood alone in the middle of the large yard. As I got close to him, I threw my staff up in the air, using a small burst of magic to knock it higher. I came to a stop in front of Silver who brought his sword up behind his shield. A golden bubble surrounded us.

My hand reached up toward the staff in the air, causing it to slowly spin. Using my power, I pulled at the electricity the weather created as the affected werewolves came up and began snapping at Silver's shield spell.

My own power flared up - iridescent colors wove first around my raised hand and wrapped down around me the harder I pulled. This needed to work.

"Come on," I said to no one as I reached up with my other hand. Faint violet tendrils of lightning began to reach for the staff. I clenched my jaw and pulled harder, directing more of the electrical energy toward the staff. I needed to use the lightning if I wanted to try and thin out the numbers. I would not have enough to do it on my own.

"Hurry, Ketayl," Silver said. "I can't hold this much longer."

A loud boom rocked the area as the lightning struck the staff, which locked into a straight-up position. I clenched my hands into fists and brought my arms down quickly. I expanded the bolts first toward the affected werewolves closest to us before chaining the electricity out to the others. I heard a chorus of sharp yelps right before the affected werewolves that were hit dropped.

The outer part of the group remained standing, but I had brought the numbers down by a third to a half.

The staff fell, bouncing off of the golden dome surrounding us and buried one end into the dirt. An affected wolf bit the staff and then fell to the ground with a yelp from the remaining charge left on it.

I heard yelling and growling from the estate. A wave of werewolves came running down the stairs with a few TIO agents not far behind.

It took a few deep breaths to get rid of the dizziness caused from the exertion. I looked up at Silver who grinned madly. "Shall we?" he asked, flipping his sword around in his hand.

I nodded and moved under Silver's shield arm so I stood back-to-back with him. This time I would cover him.

Another wave closed in on us quickly and I created a strong gust of wind around us to knock them back. I saw a series of fireballs explode in the area of the outermost affected werewolves. Lockonis had wanted to get in on the fight.

Sounds of shield and sword striking home on flesh came from behind me while I continued to knock back my opponents. Gunshots rang out - the affected werewolves who decided to run to attack the estate staggered and dropped.

I continued to knock back any affected werewolf who came close. I felt uneasy using most of the destructive spells Lockonis insisted I learn - I did not want to accidentally hurt an ally. As the fight turned in our favor, a familiar wolf, much larger than the others, appeared. He looked to be about the size of Nikolai and began charging in my direction. This one had no arcane on him - this was the rogue.

I launched a ball of flames at him, but he merely jumped over it in his run. Bullets and tranquilizers pierced his side, but nothing seemed to slow him. I tried a wind-based spell to knock him back, but he simply ran through it as if I had done nothing.

Gunshots rang out from close by and a Dwarf wielding a warhammer finally knocked the rogue off course. Holly, with her sidearm in hand, stood not far behind Stoney who grinned madly and stood ready to take a swing at more than just the werewolf's flank.

"You can't be afraid to hurt them, girl!" Stoney yelled at me. "Because sure as Hells they ain't afraid to hurt you!" He bared his teeth and slammed a fist to his chest.

I nodded and refocused. The rogue got back on his feet and turned his attention to Stoney. He charged the Dwarf. I tried knocking him off course first with a fireball and then tried to gain his attention with an electrical spell. The rogue acted as if he was unaffected by the fire and lightning searing his flank. He dodged the warhammer before head-butting Stoney. He swung around to hit Holly with his tail.

They both hit the stonework in front of the estate. Stoney fell straight down against the pillar he had been knocked back into. Holly bounced like a doll over the railing, landing out of sight.

I took a step in their direction, but stopped because I needed to watch Silver's back. I could not leave my partner exposed, not again.

The rogue stared me down again baring his teeth and growling. He slowly stalked in my direction. Silver cursed behind me. I noticed a sickly green-colored pendant hanging around the rogue's neck almost buried by his fur. Was that how he kept control of the affected werewolves? How had I not sensed it?

Torn between anger at what just happened to Stoney and Holly and the fear of the rogue before me, I began backing up, mentally running through my options. Nothing I had done so far affected this werewolf. In the blink of an eye, the large mass of teeth, claws, and fur bounded at me.

I threw my hands up in reflex. My power flared again, easily breaking my control on it. When I did not feel a hit, bite, or claws, I looked up to see the rogue frozen in place. His sharp teeth were bared only inches from my face - his hot, rank-smelling breath threatened to suffocate me. I let out a strangled cry as he snapped his jaws at me.

I remained frozen in place. I had no idea how I held him. A couple of darts hit the side of the large werewolf before me and he began twisting and contorting in mid-air - bones audibly breaking.

Sasha stood at the bottom of the stairs with a rifle in hand, still aimed at the rogue.

Another werewolf, in hybrid form, charged in, hitting the rogue. I jumped, dropping the power holding him. The two fell in a tangle of limbs and fur. Their fight continued heading in the direction of the forest.

I looked around in a panic - the affected werewolves still fighting were on the outskirts. Others were caring for the injured. There was no immediate threat or situation I needed to take action for.

My attention immediately shifted to the arrival of a stronger arcane presence. A Human man in what looked like formal Arcane College mage's robes from this distance appeared at the edge of the battlefield.

"Silver!" I shouted before I took off running, grabbing my staff on the way. Lockonis was also in a dead run, she began forming a spell in her hands. I followed her lead and drew arcane energy to mine.

An affected werewolf broke off his fight to chase after me, it's teeth snapping at my legs and I heard my coat tear. Suddenly it went flying before Silver came running up alongside me. "Keep going - I'll cover you."

I struggled to keep up with his long strides.

The necromancer finished his cast and began collecting a glowing, blood-red essence in his hands. Affected werewolves dropped around us in waves starting with the ones closest to the necromancer. I began feeling the echo effects of the spell - the same we had run into in the forest and when the affected werewolf had died. I strained to forcibly hold my power in check as I ran through the effects.

"No," I whispered. I had no idea how to stop the slaughter. The necromancer was simply too far away to disrupt and I had no idea if interrupting him would return the life to the affected werewolves he had already drained.

Silver's long strides took him ahead of me. He drew back his left arm and threw his shield once we got closer. It bounced off a barrier around the necromancer. He jumped to catch it and kept running, sword drawn.

My partner's attempt was followed by a fireball from Lockonis. It enveloped the barrier. The smoke quickly cleared showing the necromancer unaffected.

Mentally I tripped, unsure of what to use to break it.

"Oh, now you I've heard of," the necromancer said, turning to me. Suddenly I was flying in the wrong direction. I hit the ground, shoulder first, rolling.

Once I stopped, I saw the necromancer with a smug expression on his face, staring at me. "If you'll excuse me, I need to see what I can salvage from this mistake and restart my research." He rubbed a ring on his hand and teleported away.

I slammed my fists into the ground and rested my forehead on the cold grass, resisting the urge to scream. I heard people calling my name and others running around taking care of the wounded. I remained where I was, fighting with my rising anger. The pain in my left shoulder where I had hit the ground first was the only thing keeping me grounded at the moment.

* * *

"You have no idea who that guy was?" Lockonis asked for what seemed like the thousandth time.

I shook my head, now sitting where I had been thrown. I had landed in a spot where the echo of the necromancer's spell was absent. Not having to fight to control my power was about the only positive thing at this point.

The cold ground felt good against my left thigh and I toyed with a tear in my coat at the hem. The opening torn in the shoulder area on my left side let unwelcomed cold air in. "No, and I didn't see anything that would connect him with the Arcane College besides the robes." Granted, it was dark and trying to make out a pin from as far away as I had been would have been difficult at best with the amount of the jewelry he wore.

I pushed the button on my staff, but again it would not budge. I must have fried the inner workings. Coburn would not be happy when I brought it back.

Silver had also been trying to figure out if I had any injuries, but I kept brushing him off. In the time I sat here, I went from seething to tired. I propped up a knee and leaned against it.

The teleport line sat there glowing brightly in the dark. Its golden arc pointing where the necromancer went, but Lockonis would not let me follow it. I was stuck sitting on the cold ground not doing anything except answering the same question over and over.

Nikolai, in wolf form, and Sasha, still in her native form, came over to us. "He wants to know why we're waiting," the Beta asked. "And frankly so do I."

Lockonis stood up to address them. "This necromancer, whoever he is, thinks he has the upper hand and I'd like to not show all of my cards. Ket can follow the teleport line, but despite recent events, teleporting all of us is going to expend too much of her arcane energy. Assuming she could even make the teleport without having previously been where she was headed."

I could teleport just myself and put an end to this madness. In truth though, what would I do? Could I even stand against an Archmage-level caster? I started to wish I had a rank assigned so I knew where I stood.

But she was right - I had no idea if I could make the trip myself having only seen through the teleport line.

Sasha raised an eyebrow at Nikolai. "If you say so. We'll gather whoever is strong enough to bear someone on their back and follow her directions. These wolves may not have been part of our pack, but we will not let their deaths be in vain."

Lockonis sighed and looked down at me. "Go follow the teleport line. Silver you're with her. I'll go with the next group."

Silver got his hand under my arm and helped me up despite not needing it. I walked briskly over to the end of the teleport line and knelt down, using my power to feel through it and see to the other end. I rushed over the forest to a house along the shore. It appeared to be by itself with a small dock in the water.

I pointed northwest in the direction of the building. "There's a house along the shore. Docks. I think it's the only one in the area. I'm not sure how far away. I didn't see any vehicles." The last part worried me as they might be long gone.

"Could be one of the hunting cabins. Some have docks for fishing," Sasha said. "Greg will be here in a minute to take Silver. You go with Nikolai. We'll keep the first party small. They'll be able to send back information and we'll get another team ready to go behind you."

I nodded and looked down at Nikolai. This was still horribly awkward. Silver picked me up and put me on the Alpha Prime's back.

"I'm familiar with horses so this should prove interesting," he said. I guessed my partner was trying to lighten the mood. He picked the oddest times to do it.

As soon as Silver seated himself on the much larger werewolf's back, Nikolai took off in the direction I previously stated. I wrapped my arms around his neck, clutching my staff with one hand, and held on for dear life.

AFTER A FEW MINUTES I got the hang of being on wolf-back and sat up more, paying attention to where we were headed, giving Nikolai corrections when he drifted too far. My eyes stayed directed primarily overhead even as the trees passed by us in a blur. Why was it so rare to be able to see teleport lines?

I shook my head - I needed to focus. These people were relying on me to stop this necromancer. The robes he wore bothered me. His attire appeared as if he had been trying to mimic the style of robes the Arcane College wore. Perhaps I had hit my head too hard when he knocked me back if I was considering choice of fabric and the way it fit him as good reasons.

I sensed the necromancer's arcane presence well before we saw the cabin.

As we got closer to the building, the werewolves slowed, circling around to be able to see the docks as well. I slid off of Nikolai's back and crept up alongside the large cabin.

"Please, you've got to see this is foolish," a female voice pleaded from the side facing the water. I peaked around the corner. A Gnomish woman stood there with her hands bound. "I've done all I can. Please let me go back to my family. I won't tell anyone."

Silver came up behind me and the werewolves stood next to us. How the necromancer had not noticed our presence yet, I remained unsure. He stood where the dirt met the dock, looking out over the water - a couple of boxes by his side along with a container holding the blood-red essence he had gathered from the affected werewolves.

"We're done when I say we're done. Werewolves are classified as immortal for a reason. They live and breathe forever and you will help me find out how. We'll come back when I find another rogue who wants a shot at the Alpha Prime. The life essence should be enough to start the next phase of my research."

Nikolai blew a sharp breath out his nose in a huff. Immortality research? I started to think perhaps the necromancer had already gone insane.

Silver knelt down next to the werewolves with us. "Can you both go around and make sure he doesn't run when I confront him?" he asked, his voice hushed.

They both left silently, going around the other side of the cabin.

A light tap on my shoulder made me turn and look up at Silver. He tapped his chest and pointed in the direction of the docks. I assumed he meant he wanted to be the one to initially confront them.

Fine by me. I stepped out of his way and silently followed as he moved to initiate the arrest. I had never actually done one before and I could not say I remembered the wording correctly. Perhaps I really did need to go through the same training.

I heard the sound of the motor before I saw the small boat, big enough for only a handful of passengers. I grabbed Silver's arm, pointing at it as it came into view. We still stood along the side of the house in the shadows so with any luck, they had not seen us.

Silver stood still as the boat came closer and docked. The pilot picked up a box while he talked with the necromancer.

My partner moved, starting the arrest. The words spoken escaped my attention as the necromancer and the pilot ran. The necromancer grabbed the container with the life essences he stole. The Gnome looked around in a panic as they left her behind.

They jumped into the boat and hurried to disconnect from the dock. The two werewolves bore down on them, skidding to a halt at the edge of the water. Silver also ran and I kept close behind him.

As the boat pulled away from the dock, I came up with an idea. "Everyone get back!" I shouted.

Quickly gathering the energy I needed, I slammed one end of my staff into the ground. A light shockwave was felt along the ground before a wave noticeably larger than the boat rose out of the water.

I brought my hand up, directing the wave higher before pulling it back toward the shore. The wave threw the boat onto the dirt. The motor sputtered and died. The werewolves shook the water off of themselves and the Gnome, soaked, sat looking dazed about what just happened.

"That works," Silver said, grinning broadly at me before he continued his approach to the necromancer and his pilot.

Blood-red tendrils began rising from the boat, dissipating before they reached the top of the tree line. I took a shuddering breath at the sight. The affected werewolves were now truly dead.

Silver spared a moment to look at me. "The responsibility was never yours. If nothing else they'll know peace now."

I nodded, but could not shake the feeling it was my fault.

The werewolves bore down on them once more, teeth bared and growling. More people showed up - Lockonis leading the group. "Well, looks like I missed the fun," she said. "Thanks, Lexi." She briefly petted the werewolf's head she had been riding.

The other two agents with her went over to help Silver with the arrest. Lockonis crossed her arms and came over to me. "Well, looks like things are under control here. Though I wonder if there are any more people involved in this..."

"I call for a duel!" the necromancer yelled. I felt the blood drain from my face at those words. That was not something used these days. I only knew of the old rule from spending so much time as a Researcher at the Arcane College.

Lockonis rolled her eyes. "Who is he kidding? I can't believe anyone still uses this," she commented quietly and then sighed. "Alright, let's go see what this guy wants. And remind me to complain about this loophole when we get back. Damn archaic rules."

As we approached, the necromancer held one of his pendants out toward the agents around him. He wore a lot of jewelry, which probably meant stored spells with the way he acted so far. The necromancer said, "I demand a duel for my freedom."

Lockonis wove her fingers together and stretched out her arms, palms away from her. "Sure, but you're going to lose."

"Not you. The Researcher," he said and pointed at me. I did not think it possible to feel the blood drain from my face again.

"Can he do this?" Mark asked - he had arrived with Lockonis.

"Unfortunately, yes," Lockonis said, pinching the bridge of her nose. "As stupid and downright archaic as this is. He can only challenge another mage and there are two of us here. You accept, Ket?"

Requesting a duel was highly uncommon and potentially deadly. The rules ended there with the request. Once the fight began, there would be no holding back unless limitations were previously agreed upon.

I nodded, knowing what turning down the request meant: I forfeit. I had come this far and I was not about to let the necromancer go. I would need to ride the wave of anger toward this man to have a chance. I truly did not want to return to instinct, but I may have no choice.

The necromancer grinned madly at me while Lockonis organized everyone away from the fight. He kept his pendant out and pointed in my direction. Perhaps if I ran him out of stored spells? I did not know what he had and what else he was capable of.

"Ketayl, I don't like this," Silver said quietly. He had walked over to me instead of heading up to the cabin with the others. "You can't take on a necromancer by yourself."

I bit my lower lip before I said, "I don't like it either, but we don't have a choice. Can you make sure the others stay safe?"

"Yeah, but..." Silver started.

I cut him off. "No, you can't interfere. He'll call it unfair and be allowed to escape. Go."

Silver opened his mouth to say something more, but closed it and went over to the others.

"You're awfully confident for a Researcher," the necromancer said. "What two spells can you cast? Had to rely on all those others when my former associate attacked, didn't you? I'm betting you only got in the way." He glanced over to where Silver stood, his sword and shield still out. "And fraternizing with a paladin. How scandalous. Such a shame the spell didn't take hold on him. He would have made a fine addition to my collection."

I clenched my jaw. I was not about to get into an insult war with this man. I refused to let what happened go. My power thrummed in anticipation as my anger rose. That he thought so little of the lives he ruined, or in Silver's case, almost ruined.

I thought about the pain I had to put the man who had become my closest friend through in order to eliminate the spell. What he had made me do to Silver bothered me as much as I tried to ignore it.

Lockonis called out, "Begin!"

The necromancer used one of his pendants and I put up a shield in time to deflect the fireball aimed at me. The force of the impact slid me back a few feet in the dirt.

I noticed, even in the low light from the cabin, the pendant turned black once it had been used. The necromancer already wore a few blackened pieces, but I had no idea what he could do without them.

A flash of a memory from long ago came to mind - another staff wielding Arcanist. I had tried to keep thoughts of my biological mother locked up tight, but right about now I needed the inspiration.

Spinning my staff, I slammed the end into the ground once more, creating long cracks in the dirt - the shockwave knocked the necromancer off his feet.

As I slowly walked toward him, I heard Lockonis say, "She's been holding back on me."

The necromancer scrambled to his feet, grabbing another pendant. "I guess I have my answer on how limited your abilities are. Not much of anything, are you? And you need something to help you cast."

He rubbed the next pendant and I managed to get my shield up in time to block the ice shards hurtling in my direction. Each sounded like glass shattering as they struck the shield.

I threw my staff aside. I would prove I used nothing to amplify my spells.

"Ketayl, don't listen to him!" Silver called.

Fine, if the necromancer wanted to play with fire and ice, I could do the same. I brought both of my hands up, palms down, concentrating my arcane energy.

Two serpent-like creatures, one of fire and the other of ice, rose out of the ground, circling around me. A few curses came from where the others stood. I trusted whatever it was, Silver would handle it. Lockonis had to focus on the duel.

I heard a low whistle come from the area of the cabin. "She's really been holding back on me."

The necromancer backed up slowly as I approached. "Those are illusions. You're just a Researcher."

"This one broke your spell," I said, my voice sounding strange to my ears, but I ignored it. I could hear the fear in his voice and wanted to make him more afraid of me.

As the fire serpent attacked, the necromancer tripped and fell. I set part of his robe on fire and the serpent disappeared. While he patted himself out, I sent the ice serpent into the ground between his legs. A sheet of ice formed, causing him to jump backwards, slipping on the frozen ground.

For all the harm he brought to not only all of the affected werewolves and the others, but also for what he had done to Silver, I wanted him to pay and he gave me this opportunity.

The necromancer stared at me with wide-eyes, his face appearing a few shades lighter. He scrambled to his feet, slipping a couple of times, but eventually found his footing. He searched his pendants and rings as if he could not decide which one to use.

I tilted my head, trying to understand my opponent. Where was his personal display of power? Why all the stored spells?

He picked something and I teleported myself behind him as he launched the fireball at where I previously stood. I kicked him in the back, sending him sprawling to the frozen dirt. Part of me wanted to do that or worse for each life he had harmed.

"We really need to talk about how much she's been holding back in training," Silver commented.

Once again the necromancer scampered to his feet, running to put some distance between us. When he stopped, he began casting instead relying on his stored spells.

While he went through the extensively elaborate movements and what seemed like an equally long incantation, though he muttered it so I could not hear what he spoke, I brought my hands together in front of me. Pulling them apart, one straight up and the other down, I rotated my arms out to complete the invisible circle. I pushed my hands forward and it made three soft thuds as the layers of the invisible spell separated, kicking up a small amount of dirt in the process. Done, I crossed my arms and waited for him to finish.

Foolish, yes, but interrupting him would be rude and part of me hoped for some insight into my enemy.

Finally the necromancer finished and launched a small, familiar, sickly green orb in my direction. I heard a few gasps from those who recognized the necromatic spell that had been used on the affected werewolf and Silver. It stopped short in front of me, caught in the arcane trap I set, which now glowed brightly.

He had given me the idea of letting something else power the trap spell.

Reaching out, my hand covered with swirling colors of arcane energy, I plucked his spell from the trap, which quickly dissipated. I held the spell up in front of me, examining it for a moment. The seed was little more than a set of instructions. It was designed to attach to a life force and then activate during the change or when a high amount of energy was being used.

This small, barely held together spell had been the cause of so much suffering and death?! I growled at him and crushed the seed with my hand, sickly green flecks of light drifting and disappearing before they reached the ground. I flicked the remainder from my hand and glared at the necromancer.

"What in the Hells are you?!" the necromancer yelled, backing away.

Lockonis answered, "I'm thinking pissed off."

"Call it," I told the mage. I kept my voice even, trying to at least appear calm.

The necromancer sneered at me. "No! I refuse to be brought down by the likes of you!"

Snarling at him, I cast a wind spell while he scrambled for another piece of jewelry, sending him rolling through the dirt.

I hoped he hurt as much as I had from getting thrown back.

He stopped when he hit a tree. The lightning bolt I sent next missed when he ducked, squealing. He was accompanied by a large crack as my spell split the tree behind him.

"Call it," I said again, attempting to maintain my calm. I walked toward him slowly to give him time to surrender. Part of me hoped he chose to keep going. I enjoyed this too much.

The necromancer got up and started running. I opened my hand, using my power to call my staff to me before I teleported myself a few yards ahead of his projected path. Grabbing it with both hands, I swung at the upper part of his chest, connecting and dropping him to the ground.

Stepping on his chest, I already had an electrical spell charged on my staff and it pointed at his throat just waiting for him to move.

He groaned and rolled his head to the side, but otherwise did not move.

"Enough, Ket, you won," Lockonis called as she ran toward me.

I breathed deep a few times before stepping back.

My anger faded and I felt empty. Doing this had not changed what already happened. All of those people were dead, others hurt.

Silver still had to deal with what he had gone through. And I still did not know the status of most of the others.

Silver and Nikolai approached, not far behind Lockonis who looked down at him. "He should have listened to me when I told him he'd lose. And something tells me Ket still held back."

I wanted to feel something at her words, but numbness had taken over.

21

"A PRIEST PRETENDING to be an Arcane College mage. Who would have thought?" Lockonis said, her eyes on the necromancer in question as he was hauled away.

His jewelry had been removed and he hung heavily between the two agents as they escorted him out. It explained why he focused so heavily on stored arcane spells at least, though I made a mental note to inquire later what offensive spells he might have been able to cast.

Nikolai stood to the side in a loose shirt and athletic pants someone brought him so he could shift back. "I think you forget the Arcane College is still held in high regard here in Human Territory. Personally, I have taken a liking to Magus Rivers' efforts, though I wish she would keep a tighter leash on her Archmages. Donovan will soon be barred from the Council floor."

I took an interest in their conversation. I did not even know the name of the Magus of the Arcane College. I had also forgotten Nikolai sat on the Terran Council.

"And if he even mentions Ketayl's name again, I may rip his throat out myself," Nikolai growled. "I would have thought transferring her to you fully would end his incessant whining. Though I'm starting to see why he didn't want to let her go."

"First of all," Lockonis commented, "Ket has come a long way since she came to us so don't give them credit. Second, Donovan tried not to say her name and you know it. Not to mention he's never been graceful about anything that doesn't go his way. And as for Magus Rivers, I think she's getting push-back from the Circle of Magi for her efforts - they're scared of change." She looked over at me. "Sorry, Ket, it's all stuff we've talked about."

I turned my attention away. Was the only reason Nikolai would work with me because I had previously been part of the Arcane College? It would certainly be opposite the disdain I normally received.

"How are Old Stoney and Holly?" I asked, trying to change the subject.

The silence in response got me to look up at the two.

Lockonis fidgeted for a moment before she said, "Holly's not doing so good. She hit pretty hard and they aren't sure the extent of the damage yet. Last I knew they were planning to rush her into surgery as soon as she arrived."

Silence fell once more, and I understood without anyone having to say anything.

"He didn't make it, did he?" Silver asked.

"No," Lockonis confirmed.

I turned my face toward the ground and closed my eyes. He died because I could not stop the rogue.

"I should have known better than to let him go into battle," Lockonis continued. "He would have survived the throw, but his heart couldn't take another fight. And to think he transferred here all those years ago because of his condition to ride out until retirement."

Now I was confused. I shook my head and shoved it aside to focus on the work still needed to be done, but my mind kept wandering back to my failures. I followed the others when they told me to go with them and sat quietly in the passenger seat while Lockonis drove. She insisted on it being just the two of us. Even the heat she had turned up to high could not break through the chill I felt.

"You even think about resigning and I will kick your ass all over the testing bay when we get back," Lockonis said.

I glanced over at her. The thought had not crossed my mind.

Lockonis blew a sharp breath through her bangs. "Trust me, I know what it's like to lose someone. It's not easy and it never gets easier. The only thing you can do is keep moving forward. You stopped one madman bent on finding the secret to immortality. Don't forget to count the good."

I nodded - my thoughts blank. Though I did note he did not seem to be of the same group Silver and I were tasked with tracking. Not once did he mention the Ancient Gods.

Lockonis sighed loudly. Then the Elven woman laughed. "All that power at your disposal and you take him down with a stick."

It was a little ironic. "Coburn isn't going to be happy I damaged his weapon."

"He'll get over it pretty quick and then delve into figuring out how to get it to withstand what you can dish out. Though I doubt you'll be calling down lightning all that often." Lockonis grinned. "Sometimes I wish I had your creativity with the arcane. The trap was nice - even I didn't see that coming. I look forward to reading your report on the spell."

People needed to stop wishing to be anything like me - I only proved tonight how dangerous I truly was.

I listened to the sound of the heater blowing for a while, my mind blank. Eventually Lockonis said, "They captured the rogue alive. They're going to keep him in his native form for as long as they can. It's the same stuff they gave Silver to stall the transformation, but werewolves can take multiple doses of it."

But all the others died - the ones who had become slaves to both the rogue and the necromancer. I did not know how many of Nikolai's pack got hurt or worse. I stared out the window and watched the trees pass by as we slowly wound our way back to the estate. I had become numb to the events of the evening.

"Dammit, Ket, I need you to snap out of it - we may have the people responsible in custody, but the job isn't done yet." I jumped at Lockonis' sharp words.

"I know. I just..." I took a deep breath. "I can finish."

"I need all of you here, Ket. Not you running on auto-pilot. I'll deal with the interrogations and all of that stuff, but I still need you to analyze the evidence and keep your team going," Lockonis said, sounding tired.

What would the difference be?

"I think I'm going to take Niki up on his offer for you to stay at the estate for the night. Besides, I'd rather have a bed than sleep on a couch. Haven't had time to get my own room yet so I'm crashing in yours. I grabbed your bag as well when I ran Sparky back to the hotel to get stuff while you and Silver recovered."

I nodded. It really did not matter where I rested. I just did not think I would be able to.

"Get your head back where it belongs because we're going to be having a long talk about how much you've been holding back in training. There's a lot you've shown that won't hurt someone else and Silver needs to learn how to deal with fighting a mage," Lockonis said firmly. "Granted, I doubt he's going to have to face-off against someone who can cast as fast as either of us."

I nodded. Likely the truth was Silver needed to learn to keep himself safe from me and what I was capable of.

AFTER A LONG, hot shower, I looked at myself in the large mirror to take stock of how I was physically. My eye color seemed a shade or two lighter, but figured it was a trick of the lighting. Moreover, I appeared as if I had not gotten a decent rest in a week. It certainly started to feel like it.

I wore only my underwear and the mint green tank top from my night clothes - I could not stand to look at myself without being somewhat covered.

I twisted to examine the bruise that had started to form on the back of my left shoulder and arm where I hit the ground first after getting knocked back by the necromancer. I had a few smaller ones along my arms and legs likely from the same event.

The back of my left thigh bore another large bruise covering much of it and reaching up under my clothes. Must have been from when I fell down the hole or the rough landing from the teleport. Probably both.

I guess I got off easy this time.

The door opened. Both Silver and I stared at each other for a moment. "I'm sorry. I didn't realize you were... Where did those bruises come from?" Silver started backing out of the room, but changed his mind and came in. He put the bundle of clothes he carried down on the counter and gently pushed my shoulder forward, lifting my left arm before I reacted and pulled away from him.

"Nothing. Please leave." I knew my face was turning red - there was a mirror in view after all. Embarrassment was the first thing to break through the numbness.

"No," Silver said firmly. "Why didn't you tell me about this?"

"I've been a little preoccupied. I didn't know I had them until now. Go, please." Granted all I had left to put on were the pants to the set, but I would feel less exposed.

Silver looked at me in the mirror, his face firm. "Tell me when these happened." His healing power washed over my shoulder.

I squirmed, but he held me still with one hand, never stopping in his tending. "I thought you were running low. You should conserve your energy."

"When?" He ground the word out at me.

I sighed and gave up - making him angry would not help anyone. "That one was from when the necromancer knocked me back and the other one from when I fell down the hole and the rough landing from the teleport." So I bruised easily. It was no big deal and could heal well enough on its own.

Silence filled the room as Silver worked and I wanted to disappear. Unfortunately, if I was close enough, he could sense roughly where I was even if I was invisible. Provided there was nothing to distract him.

I hissed when he touched a particularly tender spot on my thigh. "Sorry," Silver said. "I guess we're roommates for the remainder of the evening."

His statement caught me off-guard. "What?" I twisted to look down at him.

I swore his face reddened. "I came in here thinking I was the only person in the room. I didn't mean to barge in on you."

Nikolai sent me to the guest room I had been in before shortly after we arrived back at the estate. Neither he nor Sasha said anything about me sharing the space. I knew others from the team elected to remain at the estate for the evening instead of making the long drive back, but they said little about the arrangements.

"Anything else I should know about?" Silver asked, standing back up and handing me my pants.

I had never jumped into them faster. "Nothing I know about. Excuse me." I hurried around him and out of the bathroom. Though

I knew my privacy was only temporary since we were both assigned to this room.

The room was sparsely decorated with the large bed in the center facing a wall of windows. A couple of the windows were doors which would open onto a narrow balcony. The room seemed fairly elaborate for a guest room. A dresser sat to one side and a desk adorned the other. A small couch had been set along the windows and I ventured over there. It would be far to small for Silver to rest comfortably. I could figure out something to use for a blanket once he got settled.

I picked up my tablet off my bag en route. I needed to start drafting up a report. How do I write up a report for this? Delving into the guidelines first would be more prudent.

The thought of brushing my hair crossed my mind, but in my haste I left my brush in the bathroom.

Tucking my feet underneath me, I started searching for the document I needed to reference. I was still trying to figure out which guide I needed, bouncing back and forth between a few, when my tablet disappeared from my hands. "I'm really not in the mood for this."

Silver stood over me in his night clothes, his hair down and damp. "I don't care. You're done working for the night." He held my brush.

I sighed. He would pick now to be in overprotective mode. "Look, I'm not going to be able to rest anyway, so I might as well get something accomplished. Do you need me to dry your hair?"

Silver looked at me as if I had lost all sanity. He put my tablet on the small table to the side. "No, it's fine as it is. Why won't you be able to rest?"

I reached for the device and Silver put his hand on it. He narrowed his eyes as if daring me to do something about it.

"I'm just not. You can take the bed. I'll be fine here."

Silver sat back on his heels and stared at me. I reached for my tablet again, but his hand remained on it. Fine. I turned my attention out the windows. Lightning still flashed occasionally. I thought I saw the clouds beginning to part, but it was probably just me searching for something else to focus on.

And I still felt Silver's gaze on me. I could not keep contained the emotional turmoil hidden beneath the apathy. "What do you want?! This was my fault! People got hurt and died because of me. I almost got you killed or worse." I brought my knees to my chest and buried my face. If only he would stop looking at me.

Silver gently tugged my hair out from between me and the couch and started brushing it. This was easier to deal with when I was the one taking the risks. My shoulders shook as I tried to keep everything contained.

Eventually he moved away and I heard the covers on the bed shift. Silver needed the rest given what he had been through. Neither of us managed to get much in the past two days. I doubted I would ever do anything other than pass out from exhaustion again.

Part of me wondered why Silver stayed silent. I jumped when I felt hands snake under my legs and behind my back. It did not deter him from picking me up. I tried to get out, but both of us knew he was physically far stronger.

"Put me down," I demanded.

"No, you need rest. You're so tired you can't even think straight to see how wrong you are," Silver said sharply.

"I can stay on the couch." Something, anything to get me away from him. I continued to try to escape him. I still had not figured out how he could get past my barriers.

Silver deposited me on the bed. "What kind of man sleeps in a bed when there is a lady sleeping on the couch? It's more than big enough for both of us."

"I don't think..." A finger pressed against my lips and I shifted away, glaring at him.

"Well, that's a little better." Silver sat down next to me. "You need to let it out. You can't keep holding onto everything. I promise I won't tell anyone." He smiled softly.

His words broke the last floodgate and I looked away, my vision blurring from the tears starting to form. Why did Silver have to do this?

When he pulled me to him, I just stayed there, quietly crying at the loss of life and the pain everyone had gone through. Silver stroked my hair. I wanted to stay here where I felt warm and safe, but I knew, despite my calmed power, he was not safe from me.

Something caused me to wake and I sat up, not sure what time it was. The sky had lightened to predawn. I looked around trying to get my bearings. What I would not give right now to be back in my quarters and in my own bed.

Then I noticed Silver kneeling in front of the windows - his hair loose, creating a wavy waterfall. I hoped he had not spent his rest there.

Moving quietly, I got out of bed and went around, seeing his eyes closed and hands folded in prayer. First light - I had forgotten again. I never before witnessed his rituals for the day. Quietly I sat down facing him, hoping to gain some insight.

Silver remained still and silent, only opening his eyes as the sun broke the horizon. His gaze fixed out the window. A golden-white light washed over him as the rays came into the room. For some reason with the way Sparky spoke of it, I expected it to be noisier. This was calm, quiet, peaceful.

Something I wished I could attain.

We sat there until the sun fully cleared the horizon. Then Silver turned to look at me. He straightened up. Likely he was confused by my presence. "I'm sorry, I didn't mean to wake you."

I shook my head and shuddered as a chill went through me. Somehow I had ignored the cold floor until now.

"Go back to bed. You still need rest," Silver said softly.

"So do you," I shot back.

"Is that an invitation?" A mischievous grin graced his face.

I rolled my eyes. "No."

"You know, this is the second time I've shared a bed with someone," Silver said, grinning broadly.

I felt the heat rise to my face. "Knock it off. What about the person you're interested in?"

Silver cocked his head to the side, the smirk on his face told me he was amused by my statement. "What about her? She has nothing to be jealous of."

I shook my head and got up, moving away from him. Then something struck me from a previous conversation we had. "Wait, you told me you didn't have anyone in Ocean's Edge." He had lived and spent time training there. Having found someone there made the most logical sense.

"And I don't. She doesn't live there." Silver stood too close - his hair brushed my bare shoulders.

Silver would not lie. Continue to skirt a straight answer, yes, which was infuriating. Why was I fixating on this? It was a puzzle I had no business having my nose in.

I said, "Why don't you get more rest? I'm going to get ready for the day - there's a lot I need to get done."

"We, Ketayl, we," Silver corrected. "Though I'd like to let the others rest as long as they need."

I nodded. If he was not going to take a longer rest then I would not argue with him. "I also want to see if I can get an update on Holly's condition."

Silence fell between us as I dug for clothes. I managed to duck into the bathroom first to get dressed and ready. I opened the door as I brushed my hair.

Silver stuck his head in, fully dressed and his hair braided.

I wielded my brush at him. "No. I can do my own hair, thank you."

He raised his hands in defense and then leaned his shoulder on the door frame, watching. I knew his behavior should bother me, but I had started getting used to his oddities.

I scrunched up my face at my bangs not cooperating. I gave in and used some of my power to get my bangs to behave. "What?" His silence started getting to me.

"You seem to be in a better frame of mind today," Silver said.

I sighed, staring at the brush in my hands. "Doesn't change what's true."

"How?" Silver sounded genuinely confused. What was there to be confused about?

Taking a moment to organize my thoughts, I said, "I saw the pattern and I'm ultimately responsible for what happened. I fell down the hole and sent the affected werewolves running. I rounded up the groups and literally brought them to Nikolai's front yard."

"And if you didn't see it, someone else would have," Silver said, cutting off anything else I had to say. "We would likely still be here or worse, we wouldn't and they'd still be chasing their tails. More people would be getting abducted and forcibly turned. You had no idea there was a tunnel beneath the one we were in and that the floor was weak there. Besides, it didn't break until I put my weight on it. You're so damn light you could stand on it. You thinned the numbers and did what you thought was best in terms of strategy. And before you start in about the necromancer, who was actually the one to kill the affected werewolves, the draining spell was divine. Not to mention he was a priest who was pledged to the God of Family."

I glared at him for a moment in the mirror before I sighed and said, "Sometimes I hate your logic."

Silver smirked. "And sometimes you're irrational. It's good to change things up."

I shook my head, securing the end of my hair with an elastic.

"I'm curious, why this?" Silver asked picking up the end of my hair where it was bound.

I shrugged. "It felt like a reasonable compromise. Fully down felt wrong and I didn't want to cut it shorter. Got tired of the bun."

Silver grinned broadly. "I think it suits you."

I was not sure why, but I needed that right now. Just some small approval given everything else.

"Actually," Silver said quietly, "There is one thing I'd like you to do before we get started for the day."

I raised an eyebrow at him.

"Just..." Silver paused and tugged on his braid nervously. "Just head down to the lounge. I'll meet you there in a few minutes. I'll pack up everything."

"Okay." His words worried me, but I had gotten to know Silver well enough that his request would be reasonable. I grabbed my boots and headed out.

I STOOD at the windows in the lounge watching the sun continue on its path through the sky. Part of me wondered what drew people to one God over another. And especially what would drive someone who pledged their service to the God of Family to research immortality. I supposed in time that answer would reveal itself.

So many had today stolen from them. I tried to tell myself it was better this way - they were no longer suffering. Even if they saw today and I managed to eradicate the spell from them, how many would live to see tomorrow? Nikolai said the ones he ran into seemed feral. There would be no return to an even remotely normal life for any of them.

But the fact of the matter was no one knew what today would have brought for them if they had lived.

"Ketayl," Silver said softly.

I turned and he stood far closer than I expected. I had not even heard him enter the lounge. I looked down at what he carried - it was my violin case. It had been in my suitcase when Lockonis and Sparky brought them to us.

"Can you play for those who have fallen? Please?" He held up the case to me.

I hesitated before I reached out slowly and took it from him. "I'm really out of practice." As much as I wanted to outright refuse on principle, I found I could not. I needed the time playing to bring back balance. Why not ask me in the room?

"That's fine. I don't think anyone will mind," Silver said and found a seat facing the windows.

I took a deep breath. I could do this. It was just us and my electric violin was quiet - I should not draw the attention of the werewolves. I had not crossed paths with anyone on my way down here and figured no one else at the estate was awake. Certainly my crew would not be up and going yet.

I paused as I opened the case. When had I started considering them my crew? I shook my head and got the instrument out, checking the tune and tightening up the bow.

"Something wrong?" Silver asked.

I stopped and looked over at him for a moment before returning to my tasks. "No, just a passing thought."

"Oh?"

"It's nothing," I said quickly. I did not need Silver's curiosity. I dug out the rosin to give myself something to do. I should have turned him down instead of delaying the inevitable, but I remembered playing for those lost in Ocean's Edge and the peace I found. I needed that here as well.

Finally I gave up fiddling with things and stood facing the windows. It would be easier if I could not see Silver - I still disliked having an audience. Searching through my memory, I found something simple but fitting to play and worked my way up from there. At least he was quieter than Kitteren when she insisted I play for her. She liked to make sure I knew she was there.

After a few songs, I forgot Silver sat behind me and just stared out the window playing.

The remnants of the fight were visible in the early morning light. I had come around the estate with the affected werewolves to try and get the group more tightly packed together, but I had not realize I had gone so far around to the other side. I could see scorch marks from where Lockonis had thrown her fireballs. The arcane remnants had already begun breaking down and I could not make out the spells in the daylight from this distance.

There were also black marks on the lawn from the lightning. Dark patches of blood seemed to be everywhere. Large black tarps were laid out on the far side of the yard near the drive in neat rows.

Eventually I came to a stop and my hands hung at my sides with the violin in one and the bow in the other. I did not know how long I played, but the sun seemed to have traveled a fair distance in the sky and my fingers ached.

I stared at the lumpy black tarps. The bodies of the affected wolves must be under there. Where would they go? How would we ever identify all of them? Or any of them for that matter?

"Don't stop," a soft female voice came from behind me.

I turned to find a much larger crowd gathered in the lounge. How had I not heard anyone? It looked like everyone, both werewolves and the TIO agents who remained at the estate, had come down here.

"I... uh..." I could feel the heat rising to my face and I glanced over at where Silver had been, but he had moved at some point. It took me a moment to find him again. This had been his idea.

He shrugged. Some help he was. He probably set me up for this.

"Alright, let's get breakfast going. There's still work to do," Nikolai ordered and pointed at the main exit for the room. Silently they filed out.

Sparky stayed and stared at me openly. Sasha also remained. My eyes bounced between them and Silver, waiting for someone to speak.

Finally I caved and turned to Sasha. "I'm sorry, I didn't mean to wake everyone. I thought it would be quiet enough."

She shook her head. "You didn't. One person heard in passing and the word spread. They needed that - mourning is for the living. The weight needed to be lifted before returning to the remaining tasks. And you do continue to surprise me." She pointed at the violin still in my grasp. "I'd swear you were trained by a bard because that was more than just music."

Following her gaze, I felt the heat rising to my face and hurried to clean the violin and put it away. "My adopted mother taught me."

"What's her name?" Sasha asked, her tone conversational.

I busied myself with my tasks and sank a little in the chair. Suddenly I did not want to admit my association to the Elven songstress.

"Lindale Erulastiel," Silver said while I fiddled with items in the case.

"Liar," Sparky shot at him. "You're talking about a legend."

I closed my eyes for a moment, debating my next words. "Silver doesn't lie, Sparks."

Sasha laughed. "Okay, I think I've had my fill of surprises for the morning. At least I wasn't wrong thinking you were trained by a bard." Then she got up and left.

I fought with the zipper on the case. It started getting stuck every so often. I might have to cave eventually and invest in a new one. I better not mention it to Mother - she would have far too much fun "helping" me shop for a new one.

While I did that, Silver said, "Sounds like the months of not being able to play didn't hurt your ability. And thank you for indulging my request. I know you don't like having an audience."

I simply shook my head. Silver must have known this was going to happen when he cornered me in the lounge with my violin. I could not decide what to think of his actions. No harm was done. The opposite really.

"Hey boss," Sparky said quietly. I looked over at the Halfling. "Thanks. And I totally didn't know you could play. And Lindale of all people, damn." Then he left shaking his head.

I picked up my now closed case, partially worried of what would come with the admission.

"Ketayl?"

I shook my head again, curling my legs up under me, holding onto my case and staring out the window at the black tarps again. Nikolai was right - there was work to be done. I unfolded myself and walked out of the lounge. First I needed to put the case away and then I could get to work.

22

I STARED at my schedule - it had been almost a week since we fought the rogue, the necromancer, and their affected werewolves. Most everyone else returned to a state of relative normalcy. Holly remained in the hospital.

The small memorial service here at the branch office for Stoney concluded a few hours ago and Lockonis sent the others home. I let Silver and Sparky go also since we obtained a second vehicle to use. They were all planning on heading out for drinks.

While I turned down the offer to join them based on work needing to get done and that I cannot drink, the truth was I still felt guilty over Stoney's death.

Lockonis poked her head into the room where Silver and I still primarily worked. "Hey, kid, can you come to the office for a minute?"

I nodded, locking the computer before I followed her out the door. Stoney's warhammer hung outside of what had been his office. I stiffened up when she closed the door behind me.

"Take a seat," Lockonis said flatly.

Those three words set me further on edge. Slowly I did as Lockonis told me. She leaned back against the desk.

"Geez, take it easy. I was about to tell you that you're not in trouble, but you might feel that way once I tell you what I have planned," Lockonis said.

Should I tell her she was not helping?

Lockonis took a deep breath before she spoke. "The short version is I can't hang around here forever. There's a team coming with equipment in a few days to upgrade the place and I need someone to take charge for a while until I can find a replacement. Nikolai was right in you showed you were capable of working with both rookies and werewolves - especially in dealing with him and his pack. So I'm leaving you here to take charge. Silver's staying also to keep you grounded. I'm taking Sparky though."

I blinked, trying to process what she said before a question came to mind. "What about the other senior agents here?"

"Joe and Talon requested transfers before I even came to a decision of what to do," Lockonis said. She sounded tired suddenly. "Both of them cited they also lost sight of what made good agents and needed to get back out with other teams. It's something I'll have to look into with the other training branches, but that's neither here nor there."

"Why isn't Silver here?" She said he was staying, right? Would it not make sense to be telling this to both of us?

Lockonis raised an eyebrow at me. "Because you're going to be the one occupying this office and as much as this whole ordeal has pointed out how pointless this is, you have seniority. Divide up the work however you like, but your name is going on as temporary head of this branch. I may be cycling through a number of people so you two will be here for a few months at most. Which means I also need to find a more permanent place for the two of you. You don't mind sharing an apartment, do you?"

I shook my head slowly. As long as I had my own room, I was sure I could deal with Silver for a few months.

"Good. I'm going to contact Savanas and have her start working with you. She knows you enough that I'm more comfortable having her talk you through than anyone else. Honestly, it's a lot of boring paperwork. The stuff you like." Lockonis smiled broadly. "I'll go over pay adjustments and other stuff later after I fight with Personnel."

That did not sound quite so bad, though I cared little about the pay adjustments - I never spent much.

Lockonis continued, "And I'll be having similar technology installed to what you've been using back in the main office so you'll be able to keep working on your own stuff. That room you've been working out of will be the one receiving it. I'll check in with you regularly to see if you've come up with anything."

What else could I say? The decision had already been made and the only thing I could do was the work assigned to me. I briefly entertained the idea of reminding her I was not cut out for this, but I knew it would be a losing battle.

One thing did come to mind. "How do I handle the rest of the semester?" I could keep up with the written work from a distance, but the practicals would be impossible.

"I'll have to contact a few people. Since I'm the one sticking you out here I'll see what I can arrange. And if there's anything you need or want from your quarters, let me know."

I sighed and directed my gaze at my lap. So much for that idea.

"Anything else?"

"How's Holly?" I asked after a short silence.

Lockonis blew out a breath. "That depends on your definitions of good and bad. She's awake and alert - no trauma to her head, but she's not likely ever going to walk again. Last I heard she was not really responding to anyone. You might want to head down there and see for yourself."

I sighed and looked at my hands on my lap. I had mostly been avoiding going to the hospital or doing anything to interfere with the others who knew her better. "She's not going to have to leave the TIO, is she?"

There was silence and I feared the answer to come. "No," Lockonis said and I looked up not expecting her response. "It'll take some time to find her a new position, but by the time she's recovered enough to return to work, I'll have something arranged. Provided she wants it. I'll leave you the task of telling her. I was already planning on evaluating her skill set myself to see where she would better fit. I'm not going to lie, she might get bounced around for a while until I find her the perfect spot, but I don't want to lose her if I can help it."

I nodded. "If you don't mind me leaving shortly, I'd like to head over there."

Lockonis made an odd face. "You know, I kind of wanted you to leave with the others. A heavy weight is hanging on everyone."

Why had she not said so earlier? "I just need to gather a few things and clean up."

She made a shooing motion at me. "Let me know when you're

heading out. I'll be here trying to get things straightened up and prepared for the transfer."

I bowed and left, stopping by Holly's desk first to pick up her art supplies. I had brought them back and stored them here. Perhaps being able to draw would help her mood.

***

FOLLOWING THE NURSE'S DIRECTIONS, I found Holly's room. She sat up in the reclined bed, staring out the window. I knocked lightly.

"I'm not in the mood for visitors," Holly said quietly, not turning to look.

Hesitantly I took a step in. "Then mind if I drop something off?"

Holly's head whipped around. "I'm sorry, I didn't mean to be rude, ma'am. I..."

I held up my hand for her to stop and entered. "I understand. I'm horrible as a patient - just ask Silver."

A small smile graced her face for only a moment. "Did you know he was looking to see if he could try and fix me? Unfortunately the surgeries made it impossible."

I sat down on the edge of her bed. "What he probably didn't tell you is that his restoration spell hurts. A lot. But they tell me there's a small chance you could walk again."

Holly's attention went down to her hands. "Too small."

"It's not zero." I paused. The sad stare told me my words were unhelpful. "Sorry, I guess I've been working with small percentages of things going in my favor lately." I took one of the bags off of my shoulder and handed it to her. "Thought you might like something else to focus on."

Holly opened the bag and noticeably forced a smile. "Thank you. I'm not sure I'm much in the mood for this either."

I tilted my head to the side, waiting for her to elaborate.

She took a deep breath before she said, "I haven't seen you here until now. I'm expecting bad news so you might as well just say it."

"What bad news?" What had the others told her? "I've been... I didn't know if you wanted me to drop by. I don't know you as well as the others do and I know how awkward it is when my superiors dropped by while I was injured."

Holly stared at me for a moment. "You're not here to tell me that the TIO doesn't want me anymore?"

I shook my head. "I already talked to Lockonis. She said by the time you've recovered enough to return to work, she'll have a new position figured out for you if you want it. I'm not sure what..."

Suddenly arms wrapped tightly around my neck and Holly buried her face in my shoulder, crying. Was I wrong in how I handled it? The only thing I could do was hold her and figure out what I did.

"Thank you," Holly managed after a couple of minutes. "I mean..." She backed up. "Sorry, I just thought with what the doctors are saying..." She trailed off.

I waved off her apology. "It's okay."

Holly refused to look up at me and focused on the bag on her lap. "Well, you're probably going to be leaving soon so..."

"I'm not," I said, cutting her off. "I'll be here for a few more months until Lockonis finds someone to head the branch or at least another temporary replacement."

"Really?" She sounded surprised. Well, I had been also. On the drive here I think it finally sunk in.

I fidgeted, uncomfortable. "Yeah, I'm not really meant for the role, but Talon and Joe already requested transfers before the decision was made."

Holly's face looked hopeful. "Is it just you staying?"

I shook my head. "Silver is also. Lockonis and Sparky will be leaving. Come to think of it, I'm not sure if Silver knows yet."

Holly laughed quietly behind her hand. "You should probably tell him."

"Tell me what?" Silver asked as he entered the room.

Well, it was as good of a time as any. "Lockonis is leaving us here for a few months until she can find someone else to be the head of the branch. They're also going to be upgrading the facility."

"Should be interesting." Silver took a seat on the one chair in the room.

I stood up quickly, the situation suddenly feeling awkward. "Well, I should let you two talk. I probably need to start finding out what this temporary position entails. Call me if you need anything, okay?"

Holly nodded. "Thank you."

I waved and left. I knew Silver had been spending quite a bit of time with her and who was I to get in the way if something was to develop between them.

Part of me wished I had the chance to explore that aspect of life, but I was too dangerous. There was a saying about it being lonely at the top and perhaps that's where I needed to be to keep the others safe.

EPILOGUE

I sighed, staring at the screen but not seeing it. While I toyed with the large, now polished, gem the werewolves insisted I keep because I found it, my mind wandered toward what Kitteren and our adopted parents would be doing for the upcoming Winter Solstice. I would even put up with a shopping trip or two if only to see them.

Ghost Forest was nice and I spoke with Kitteren and our parents regularly, but when this all started a couple of months ago, I had not expected to be heading a branch, even if only temporarily.

I forced myself to focus and clicked through the inventory report, mentally noting what needed to be refilled. How did we go through so many pens?

Silver had taken the agents not working a case down for physical training. While I got out of this session, I knew he wanted me to train with him later today. I refused to think further about what he might have planned.

Holly came into the office frequently - mostly I thought she was lonely. Everyone always greeted her with smiles and stopped to talk. Some even got her input on their open cases. She also started working on drawing people from description only, which helped out on a few cases. Technically she had not been cleared for work yet, but I refused to turn her away. As soon as she was medically cleared, she would head for the main office for evaluation. Lockonis had said nothing so far about her new position.

A knock at the open door to the office perked my head up. Sasha stood there with Nikolai beside her in wolf form. He padded over and dropped his head on my lap.

She said, "You look positively bored."

Absently I started petting him and signaled for Sasha to enter. "I could have come to you."

Sasha dropped a bag on one of the chairs before leaning over and glanced at my screen. "With what you're working on, I wouldn't blame you for wanting an escape, but our presence was requested here."

I looked at her confused. "I don't remember..."

"It was set up by Lockonis. That woman works in strange ways." Sasha said, taking a seat.

That would be putting it mildly. I clicked over to my calendar, but it told me nothing. "I don't even know why you're here."

Sasha shrugged. "I don't know either. I have a feeling he knows, but he won't tell me." She gestured at Nikolai. "And he insisted on coming like that."

Nikolai betrayed nothing, keeping his eyes closed while his head rested on my lap.

"I never asked how things have been going with the rogue." The werewolves had taken him under their jurisdiction and I had no desire to argue with them. They knew how to handle their people and were willing to work with us.

She shook her head. "He's still either ranting about how we are killing our own people by complying with the government regulations or screaming about how he was betrayed and his pack was murdered. We hoped for something more given the amount of time we allowed before passing judgment, but I think he might have gone insane a long time ago. Though losing his pack likely pushed him even further. Due to the severity and nature of his crimes, he'll be executed during the next hunt."

I closed my eyes. We all knew it would eventually come to this. I buried my fingers deeper into the soft fur.

"On a lighter note, you should come up to the estate for the Winter Solstice after the festivities in town." Sasha smirked. "Some of my pups have quite the evening planned."

After having accidentally played for them a couple months ago, a few of them cornered me into helping them out with their Winter Solstice show they were putting on in town. I still felt uneasy taking part.

I kept secret from Silver that I practiced with them regularly for it. Granted, it became easier after the music shop owner heard me play my violin and insisted I use a more professional level one in its place. Then mine remained at the house we were living in.

I opened my mouth to politely decline citing work that needed to be done, but another voice stopped me. "Hey, is this...? Ket!" Kitteren said, then walked in. She came around and gave me an awkward hug. "Sorry for the interruption. Wow, that's a big wolf. Beautiful though." She rubbed his head.

After blinking for a moment and looking to Sasha to make sure I was not imagining things, I finally asked, "What are you doing here?"

Kitteren grinned at me. "Oh, I'm your replacement - thought it would be more fun to surprise you. Rathal and I will be here until it's time to head back for the next training session. He went down to talk to Silver."

"Gods help us," Sasha said quietly, putting her hand over her face.

"What?" Kitteren asked, standing up. Her body was rigid, telling me she was ready to be confrontational.

What if she had not read the primer? I opened my mouth to tell her to settle, but I was beaten by another.

"Not you," Sasha explained and pointed at Nikolai, "Him."

Nikolai picked up his head and looked as if he was trying to laugh with his jaw open.

"Kitteren, I should introduce you to Sasha Orel, the Beta for the area pack." I paused as she gave her a short bow. "And this is Nikolai Orel, the Alpha Prime."

"Wait, this is...? Well, this just got awkward quickly." Kitteren slowly removed her hand from his fur.

Sasha held up the bag she brought in. "Would you go shift already? I swear you're insufferable."

Nikolai took the bag Sasha held out and left. He flicked his mate with his tail.

"So, I'm fairly certain I just did something horribly insensitive toward your people," Kitteren said.

Sasha shook her head. "No, actually you made a quick friend."

She paused looking at the two of us. "Half-sisters, am I right? It's hard to tell sometimes."

"Yes," Kitteren answered, pulling up a chair. "I'll get the run down from Ket about what's going on here, but what can I do for you?"

The meeting continued from there. Eventually Nikolai came back on two legs, fully dressed. I mostly remained quiet, not sure why Kitteren thought it was a good idea to surprise me about her and Rathal's arrival.

***

I WRAPPED my arms around myself as I walked. I hated the cold and it was snowing. Would I ever get an assignment somewhere warm?

I adjusted the fleece wrap over my ears - my long hair made it hard to pull the hood up on the purple and black ski coat. Outside of my other coat would not have been warm enough, it had taken damage during the fight against the affected werewolves and I wanted to see if I could get it repaired back in Great Tree before Silver tried to put the same enchantment on it as my gloves.

I thought about trying to repair it myself, but I had only done simple fixes before.

The house Lockonis found for Silver and me to stay in was in a quiet neighborhood. It had beautiful walking paths when it was not covered in snow.

Many of the houses in the area decorated for the upcoming holiday though some people went a little overboard. The neighborhood even decorated some of the trees like the one I quickly approached.

Between the cold and the Winter Solstice decorations, I could find no peace as I walked. Normally I loved taking in the light displays, but this year everything seemed off.

It had certainly been an interesting year. So much had changed. I still did not know what to make of it all.

I slipped a little as I continued on my trek. I grimaced at having found another small patch of ice.

And yet I was out here walking in the cold, practically surrounded by Winter Solstice decorations. I needed to think, and that was hard with Silver around. He grew excited for the Winter Solstice and wanted to decorate the house and plan celebrations.

I wanted none of it, but stayed silent on the matter.

It was times like this I thought him childish, but he just wanted to take part. I tried not to ruin his mood as he browsed the catalogs the stores sent out at this time of year. He had even gotten a pencil and paper out to start sketching his ideas.

Kitteren and Rathal's unexpected arrival earlier today also still bothered me. There was absolutely no warning a replacement was on the way or when I should be expected to return to the main office.

Part of me wanted to stay. I had gotten into a comfortable routine and while I wanted for more privacy at times, sharing the house with Silver had not given me the problems I had expected.

Kitteren arrived with my change of orders as well as news that our adopted parents would be arriving in a few days so we could spend the holiday together. Though she seemed reluctant to tell me of their plans.

There was plenty of time to take care of packing and transfer the branch over to her, but I still hated surprises. I would have thought after what happened several months ago, they all would have realized this by now. I was torn on how I felt about them coming. Maybe if I had some warning I would be less conflicted.

"Ketayl!" Silver called. I turned to see him jogging up to me. His boots must provide better traction than mine - I had slipped a few times. "What are you doing out here?"

"Walking."

Silver gave me an exasperated look. "I can see that. You hate the cold. Why are you out here?"

"I needed to think. I didn't want to bother you." I turned and walked away.

"Ketayl, stop," Silver said quickly and moved to stand in front of me. "What's wrong? Please tell me if it's something I did."

"No, it's..." I trailed off and looked up at the lights in the tree above me. How do I explain it was easier to deal with all of this when I kept it at a distance? When I was merely an observer?

Silver followed my gaze. "My wanting to decorate bothers you, doesn't it?"

"Yes... no... it's hard to explain." I sighed and turned my gaze to the side. "Look, I don't want to ruin this for you. Whatever you want to do is fine. Just remember we're leaving a few days after the first of the year."

Silver's hand touched my face, his glove-covered palm warm on my cheek. He gently turned my head to face him. I should move away, remind him I do not like being touched - something, but he was warm. I often wished he had a better sense of self-preservation. "I'm sorry I didn't notice I was making you uncomfortable. I guess I got caught up in the excitement of being in a house and it being kind of like a family."

I did not understand what he meant by the last part. We just happened to be living in the same house for the moment. Kitteren and Rathal would move in once we left. The arrangement was always known to be temporary. I guess without the notice of the coming change even I had forgotten that fact.

Then I realized Silver's focus was lower - normally he looked me in the eye as unsettling as it was. I froze, not sure what was going on. Did I have something on my face? My coat?

"Hey, Ket!" Kitteren called.

I thought I heard a low growl from Silver as I turned my attention in the direction of my sister's voice. She closed the car door and hurried over to us. Rathal got out of the driver's seat.

"What are you two doing out here?" Kitteren asked. "It's freezing."

"Just taking a walk," I said. Did everyone have to interrupt me?

Rathal walked up to Silver and said quietly, "It's what sisters do."

What was that supposed to mean?

"We were coming by to see if you two wanted to go get something to eat. You need to fill me in on the good places around town," Kitteren said cheerfully, grabbing my arm and tugging me along.

Stumbling, I got my footing better secured before I said, "I don't really know them. I could ask Holly to come with us and she would be able to tell you better."

Rathal made a pained look at the mention of Holly.

"She's not the same as you remember," Silver told him. "It'll be fine and I'm sure she'd appreciate being able to get out - it's been hard for her with the snow."

"Come on! Let's get you back so you can pick up your vehicle. I want to see the house anyway before we go." Kitteren tugged me along. "And then we can split up and you and I can go shopping for the Winter Solstice.

I rolled my eyes and suppressed a groan. I remembered idly wishing for it while I worked on the inventory earlier. As she crawled into the backseat with me, I asked her quietly, "Is there something on my face or coat?"

Kitteren looked at me like I had gone crazy. "No, why?"

I shook my head and pushed the thought away. Silver's recent strange actions were just one of many which had occurred in the several months of working with him on a regular basis. Though they seemed to have gotten more frequent while we were here. I doubted I would ever understand what went on in his head.

Kitteren patted my head mockingly. "You're so cute sometimes."

I batted her hand away and Rathal looked at the two of us in the rear-view mirror once he got in. "Should I ask?"

"I'll tell you later," Kitteren said. Silver glared at her as he got in and she smiled sweetly at him.

I shook my head again and turned my attention out the window. How had I managed to get mixed up in this? Despite all the times I had shown how dangerous I was, people still stayed near me and I could not figure out why.

ACKNOWLEDGMENTS

Joshua Jackson, Amy Stoll, and many others I've met over this past year who continue to encourage me and keep me going.

My local critique groups: Brandi Burns, Kenneth Jorgenson, Skip Knox, Loni Townsend, and many others. A few of them also were subjected to being beta readers as well.

And all of my friends and family who have been cheering me along.

ABOUT THE AUTHOR

J.C. Jackson is originally from New England and currently lives in southwestern Idaho with her husband and daughter.

On top of writing, she enjoys gaming whether that is picking up a controller or throwing down some dice in a tabletop RPG (as well as other board games). She has also been a fan of science fiction and fantasy since she was little.

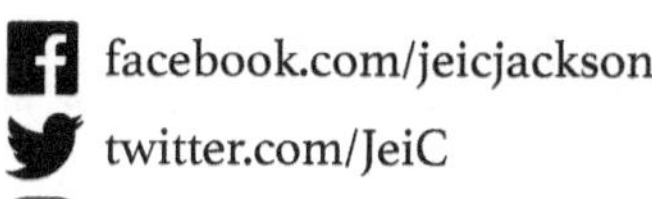

facebook.com/jeicjackson
twitter.com/JeiC
instagram.com/jeicjackson